More
Drama in the Church

More

Drama in the Church

A novel by
Dynah Zale

Q-Boro Books
WWW.QBOROBOOKS.COM

An Urban Entertainment Company

Published by Q-Boro Books

Copyright © 2008 by Dynah Zale

ISBN-13: 978-1-933967-52-3
ISBN-10: 1-933967-52-8
LCCN: 2007933866

First Printing August 2008
Printed in the United States of America

10   9   8   7   6   5   4   3   2

This is a work of fiction. It is not meant to depict, portray or represent any particular real persons. All the characters, incidents and dialogues are the products of the author's imagination and are not to be construed as real. Any references or similarities to actual events, entities, real people, living or dead, or to real locales are intended to give the novel a sense of reality. Any similarity in other names, characters, entities, places and incidents is entirely coincidental.

Cover Copyright © 2007 by Q-BORO BOOKS all rights reserved
Cover Layout & Design—Candace K. Cottrell
Cover Photo by Jose Guerra; Cover Model: Shauna Faith
Editors—Tee C. Royal, Candace K. Cottrell, Brian Sandy

Q-BORO BOOKS
Jamaica, Queens NY 11434
WWW.QBOROBOOKS.COM

Dedication

Dedicated in loving memory of
Alberta Stewart
May you dance among the stars forever.

Acknowledgments

This time around I don't have too many people to acknowledge. But I would like to express my gratitude to a few special people.

My stylist, Rau'berd at Studio Whisper. You are such a good friend; not just to me, but I've witnessed first hand your generosity to others. You are such a giving and caring person. Every customer who has the pleasure of sitting in your chair will leave with not only a fly do but also intoxicated with positive enthusiasm. Every life you come in contact with is encouraged. It's an honor to call you a friend . . . and FABULOUS HAIR STYLIST . . . Love ya

To my new family the EXTENDED FRIENDS BOOK CLUB. I look forward to spending time with you every time we meet. You ladies are not only fun, but also an answer to a lonely writer's prayer. I prayed for a book club, and as we know . . . God answers prayers. He not only sent me the best group of women to meet with, but also a hoard of new friends.

In Baltimore I made two new friends, Mondel and Tracy at Urban Knowledge Bookstore at Eastpoint Mall. I thoroughly enjoyed the time we spent together. Mondel, you are now a part of my inner circle. It's a pleasure conversing with you about different books. Please keep the suggestions coming. Thank you for being so real with me.

I'd like to shout out two special fans. First is Malika D. from Dayton, Ohio. Receiving your e-mails on the regular always makes me laugh. Secondly, I owe plenty of thanks to my MySpace friend Sharlean Frazier, you were always looking out for my best interest. Thanks for the support and encouragement.

Love,
Dynah
Dynah.Zale@comcast.net

Prologue–1961

"Albert, make sure you get back here before the sun goes down." Those were the last words Albert heard his momma say before he raced out his aunt's house and down the dirt road toward the church. It was his turn to pick up his family's monthly stipend of government milk, butter and cheese the church distributed every month.

Albert ran a few feet before losing momentum. He slowed down to a turtle's pace and dragged his feet along the dusty road while kicking up rocks along his path. It was hard being the oldest of three. At twelve years old, he was the man of the house. He chopped wood, washed clothes, cooked and even worked a part-time job with his uncle. Albert would do anything to help out his momma.

From across the field Albert could see the sky turn different shades of pink, a sure sign that the sun was beginning its descent to retire for the night.

Albert jogged the remaining distance to the church. The last to arrive, he pushed through the church doors and gathered the last package sitting on the table in his arms.

"I didn't think you were gonna make it here in time." The reverend's smile condemned him for being so tardy. "Your momma called and said you were on the way."

"Yes, sir. They need this stuff to prepare our Easter Sunday dinner tomorrow," Albert replied.

"Are you ready to star as Jesus in the Easter play?"

The reverend and Albert walked to the church doors together.

"Yes, sir." Albert regarded it an honor to portray Jesus and took his part seriously. He rehearsed his lines at least twice a day and prayed for a flawless performance.

"Good." The reverend patted Albert on the back and guided him out the door. "It's getting dark out, would you like for me to give you a ride home?"

Albert opened his mouth to accept the offer, but quickly changed his mind. The Reverend liked to talk, and he had bad breath. Albert couldn't fathom being locked in a car with him for any period of time.

"That's okay, Reverend. It won't take me long to walk home."

"Okay, son, but make sure you go straight home. It's unsafe for a young man to be out alone after dark."

Albert waved good-bye and pressed on toward his final destination. Suddenly, he stopped. Only a few hundred feet away from the church steps Albert heard the familiar call of crickets. Certain he could catch at least a dozen crickets for his fishing trip before nightfall, he disregarded the strict instructions from his elders to go directly home and stopped by the banks of the swamp that stretched out behind the church.

Albert pushed his way through the thick brush and knelt down close to the ground. He set the package by his feet and listened closely for the crickets' mating call.

He was on the verge of capturing his first prey, when out

of nowhere, the roar of the reverend's car engine frightened the crickets into silence. In a swift motion, the car's headlights swept over Albert. When he looked back, Albert saw the Reverend's car driving off into the distance.

Caught unexpectedly, Albert looked around at the darkness that surrounded him. Without him realizing it, the moon had crept into the sky and its light cast an uneasy feeling deep down in Albert's bones. Regret filled his mind. He should have obeyed his momma. As he prepared to gather his things and leave, Albert stood up straight to stretch his legs. Then, he heard a menacing voice holler, "Get 'em, boys."

Without warning, Albert's frail, thin eighty-pound body was lifted up off the ground. He kicked and screamed for his captors to let him go, but it was to no avail.

"Shut him up," another man commanded before Albert's mouth was gagged with a handkerchief.

His eyes frantically perused the white faces that surrounded him, searching for a look of empathy. Instead he found a slew of pale faces, all with beady black eyes that expelled hatred from within their soul.

While a pair of strong arms wrapped themselves around Albert's neck and held him in an unbearable chokehold, sharp fingernails pressed hard into his arms.

From behind the gag, Albert released muffled and distorted cries for help. The men shoved him against a nearby oak tree that sat in close proximity to the church's front door. Next, they pulled his hands around the tree and tied him to it.

Albert was terrified. At school, stories circulated the schoolyard about missing children who were rumored to have been torched alive. Their bodies were burned until there was nothing left but ashes.

"Is he tied to that pole tight?" Wet, sweaty, loose strands

of hair hung in the man's eyes as he chewed on a piece of hay. "Fellas, look at what we've caught. Didn't your momma tell you not to go anywhere by yourself?" The man's tart breath ripped through Albert's nostrils.

Tears gathered in the corners of Albert's eyes, but he wouldn't allow them to see him cry.

"What do you think we should do with him?" The man swallowed the remainder of his beer from the can, dropped it to the ground and crushed it with his boot.

"I think we should stone him."

While everyone laughed at the man's suggestion, the guy who asked the questioned held up his hand to quiet everybody. "A modern-day stoning is not a bad idea."

"I was just joking."

The two men talked as the others tortured Albert by pulling his hair and spitting in his face.

"I wasn't. Stone him like they did in biblical times." The burly white guy snatched up a huge rock from the ground and tossed it from one hand to the other.

Albert's vulnerability gave his oppressors power. Their ringleader felt like Goliath, and Albert was David. Through his eyes, Albert was a worthless nigger. His chapped lips, knotty hair and charred skin were enough reasons for him to rid the earth of his kind.

The white man stepped a few feet away from Albert, and with all the strength of a baseball player trying to strike out a batter, he threw the rock at Albert's face. It hit him an inch above his right eye. His skin split open, exposing a bloody wound. Again, the man picked up a few more rocks, and with even more force, he aimed each one at Albert's face. The other men mimicked their leader's actions, and within minutes they were simultaneously stoning Albert with rocks. Every rock was treated like a missile that was aimed at Albert's face and body. He was defenseless against their torture, and while they attacked him they jeered and taunted him by calling him names.

"Hold up!" Another man pushed his way to the front of the crowd. "We can't do this . . ." he said to the crowd.

Albert's swollen left eye prevented him from clearly seeing the man who was shielding him from their torture.

". . . Without a crown for his honor." He strutted up to Albert and placed a crown made of barbwire down on top of his head.

Everyone watching laughed heartily.

"Where'd you get that from?" someone asked.

"I used this to keep the sheep at Old Man Crother's place safe from those sly foxes that come around at night." He pressed the crown down hard on top of Albert's head so it fit securely.

The pressure of the crown felt like thorns being crushed into Albert's skull, and he cringed at the pain. A small stream of blood slid down the side of his face and onto his shirt.

"This is your lucky day, kid," the man teased. "You can pretend to be Jesus and ask God to forgive us for our sins."

The entire group of men screamed out in laughter.

The minute the man removed himself from the line of fire, the constant hammering of rocks being thrown against Albert's slim body continued. Ultimately, he endured the suffering until he finally passed out.

Albert's head dropped down in front of him, and his body slumped forward. The men noticed his body become limp and stopped their persecution against him. The man in charge tried to push the kid's head straight up, but it instantly dropped back down. The power he'd had ten minutes prior was gone. The kid was dead. The rocks in his hand fell to the ground, and he ordered everyone back in their pick up trucks. They left the scene as dark rain clouds moved in and rain poured down on the kid's head.

The rain revived Albert long enough for him to part his lips to speak with God, "Father, forgive them, for they know not what they do."

It rained all night, and the following day was Easter Sunday. The boy's body was discovered at sunrise service.

Chapter 1

December 2007

The serious look on Reverend Simms's face spoke volumes throughout the church.

" 'Why are you persecuting me?' That's what Jesus said to Saul," he screamed from the pulpit. "I want everyone here to recognize how some of our ways are displeasing to God." He slammed his fist down on the podium. "We gossip. Oh! Do we gossip?" The reverend exaggerated his words. "We gossip so much that we'll talk about anybody. We talk about our friends, our family, our co-workers, and we even talk about complete strangers. 'Look at him with that shirt on that's two sizes too small.' "

The congregation giggled.

"The things we say about others, whether it's said out loud or private thoughts we keep to ourselves, hurt God. Let me give you an example. Yesterday, the daily newspaper reported a story of a junior high student who died as a result of an eating disorder. When they laid her to rest she weighed a mere forty-six pounds. The reporter talked with family and friends, but the most frightening revelation came from the girl's best friend." Reverend Simms read directly from the news clipping. "The thirteen-year-old was apparently the victim of vicious name-calling by classmates. *Fatso*, *hippo*, and *wide load* are just a few of the insults that were hurled at her within the hallways at school. To lose weight she starved herself, purged her meals and allowed herself to only eat two meals a week."

Reverend Simms rubbed his chin, heavy in thought. "Those children who did the teasing did not set out to intentionally kill their classmate. They thought they were being funny. But the consequences of their words were slowly killing not only her spirit, but also the healing process of her loving herself. They were persecuting her through their speech. My final words—Beware of what you say to others."

The moment Reverend Simms sat, the women's choir rose to their feet. Clothed in matching button-down blouses and blue denim skirts, they waited for their cue. Danyelle, the soloist, climbed her way out of the cramped and crowded choir box over to the microphone. The piano keys spun a familiar melody that embraced her soul.

Danyelle closed her eyes and swayed her forty-four-inch hips from side to side. Without thinking, she pushed a single braid away from her eye before performing her rendition of "Oh Mary, Don't You Weep."

The passion Danyelle poured into the song was reflected in the tears she cried. Her strong soprano voice touched everyone. A few members dropped to their knees, while others waved their hands back and forth, thanking God for his goodness. Sister Gardner did her usual insanity act by grabbing the Christian flag, lifting it high in the air and sprinting through the church as if she had just lit the Olympic torch. Afterward, she always claimed Jesus had embodied her spirit.

Once the song concluded and Sister Gardner finished her marathon, Reverend Simms again approached the podium.

"I'm not going to hold you this morning, but I must mention two things. First, I would like to thank Reverend Baxter for joining us again for the second Sunday in a row." He turned around to give his colleague a firm handshake. Then the congregation rose to their feet and gave him a round of applause. Reverend Simms stepped to the side and encouraged him to speak to the crowd.

The strikingly handsome thirty-something man possessed a close resemblance to Matthew McConaughey. His blue eyes sparkled. Golden locks of hair swept away from his face. His smile was charming. Dressed in black from head to toe, he stepped up to the podium. A tarnished cross dangled from around his neck. "Thank you, First Nazareth and Reverend Simms. It's such a blessing to be in the house of the Lord. Now, I know when Reverend Simms told me to come back soon, he didn't think I'd be back the very next week." He laughed. "But my family and I"—he pointed to his wife and three young children who sat on the first pew—"enjoyed ourselves so much, we had to come back again."

Everyone applauded.

"Now I understand why Reverend Montgomery comes into work dancing on Monday mornings. He's filled with the Holy Ghost."

Reverend Colin Montgomery was First Nazareth's new associate pastor. One year ago the church began its hunt for Reverend Simms's successor. They prayed for a man of God who was not only a counselor, but also a teacher of the Word. Then they stumbled upon Colin at the Philadelphia Bible College. He was a professor there and happened to be looking for a church to call home. Colin was immediately interviewed and hired. His youthful spirit was refreshing, and that helped win the teenagers over to Christ.

"Church, Reverend Montgomery and Reverend Simms are both anointed. It's obvious how much they care about this church and their community."

The church gave Reverend Baxter a round of applause, and Colin stood to give him a manly hug.

The bond shared between Colin and Reverend Baxter went beyond the usual boss-employee relationship. Colin felt like he could talk to him about anything. Reverend Baxter was a shining example of the kind of preacher he strived to become.

Reverend Simms stepped back up to the podium. "Lastly, the time has come for anyone interested to register for our annual Singles Retreat. This year it will be held at Split Rock Resort in the mountains of Northern Pennsylvania, and before anyone asks, yes, Reverend Montgomery will be attending the retreat."

The single ladies blushed, the married women laughed, and the men in the church seemed upset over the amount of attention the new associate pastor received from the ladies. Reverend Montgomery's face turned red from embarrassment. He ran his fingers over his soft, curly hair. His thick eyebrows and heart-shaped lips made him the most sought-after man in the church. Women, young and old, flirted endlessly when in his presence.

"How old is Colin?"

Dean, Olivia's boyfriend, gave her a questioning look.

"I'm asking for my sister," she quickly cleared up.

"Twenty-seven," he whispered.

Satisfied with her man's answer, Olivia sat back in her seat with her four-year-old son Bryce sitting quietly on her lap. She nudged her cousin Val with her elbow to get her attention. "Cuz, are you going to sign up to go on the resort with me?"

Without hesitation, her fiancé, Julian answered for her, "Valencia will be a married woman soon, and she won't have any reason to attend a singles retreat." He wrapped one of his long, thin arms around her shoulders and hugged her closer to him.

Olivia giggled inside. It was amusing to watch how overprotective Julian was of Val. Their love for one another seemed stronger than ever. Three years ago, Olivia thought she would never see them this happy again. The rough time they endured when Julian was drafted into the NBA put a rift between them that seemed beyond repair. The lure of money, women and cars was too much for Julian to bear. He gave in to his lustful desires, and a disastrous affair destroyed all Val's trust in him. Eventually he came to his senses and realized his mistake. Humiliated, he begged Val for a second chance. It took her a while to forgive him, but once she did, Julian wasted no time. He proposed, again. Their wedding was less than a week away.

Julian reached over Olivia and tapped Dean on his knee. "Yo, man, keep your woman in check."

Dean turned his lips into a loving smile before planting a soft, gentle kiss on Olivia's cheek. She giggled like a teenager in love.

They'd been dating for close to two years, and it was apparent to any bystander that they were madly in love. A day wouldn't go by without someone asking, "When's the wedding?"

Dean West, a devoted Christian, also was raised at First Nazareth and lived on the same block as Olivia when they were kids. Growing up, Dean was quiet, kept to himself and didn't have many friends. Throughout high school he was often found in the library with his head buried in a book. Right after graduation he left Philadelphia to attend Tuskegee University on a full four-year academic scholarship.

Like Olivia's parents, Dean's parents died when he was young. When he was eight months old, Dean's mom and dad were killed in a car accident, leaving him in the custody of his paternal grandparents.

It wasn't until he'd finished school and returned home from Alabama that Olivia appreciated his less-than-average looks. The product of a white father and black mother, his blonde, curly hair and blue eyes were in stark contrast to his full lips, wide nose and chestnut brown complexion. He was nicknamed "Soul Man" after the movie, because of his close resemblance to the main character.

At the onset of their relationship, their love for one another blossomed. Dean treated Olivia like a precious jewel and would do anything to make her and Bryce happy. He loved them both and couldn't wait until they were a family.

Olivia felt blessed to have Dean in her life. He was not only a good man, but also a positive role model for her son, unlike his father. Bryce's biological father, Bryant, was currently doing time in a federal prison for trying to sell their son through an illegal adoption. Olivia would never forget the way he manipulated and used her. By being so naïve she almost lost her son forever.

That experience marked the beginning of a life makeover for her. Determined to make a drastic change, she cut twelve inches of her hair, leaving a short, classy, chic haircut tapered above her ears. Then she upgraded her outdated wardrobe by dressing more like a mom instead of a grandma.

Her final act of independence was noted by moving out of the apartment she shared with her sister. She no longer lived with Danyelle. Her need to be a responsible parent meant putting distance between her son and her sister's weed smoking.

Bryce bounced up and down on Olivia's lap and pointed excitedly. Olivia figured by her son's reaction that he'd spotted Tressie sneaking into church. Late as usual.

Tressie slid into the pew behind her friends. After taking off her coat and hat, she quietly acknowledged everyone before reaching out for Bryce to sit with her.

Olivia did a double take when she glanced back at Tressie. "You colored your hair?"

The entire pew turned around to get a good look at Tressie's honey blonde hair.

"Do you like it?" Her medium-length hair was full of bouncy, vibrant spiral curls.

"I love it," Val responded. She ran her fingers through her shoulder-length hair. "Maybe I should get something done to my hair."

"No." Julian loved everything about Val. Her smooth ebony skin, thick shoulder-length hair and wide hips were what he dreamed about every night.

Bryce flashed the picture he drew in Sunday School class in Tressie's face.

"This is beautiful," Tressie complimented him.

"It's for you." His cheeks turned beet red when Tressie expressed her gratitude by kissing him on the cheek.

Olivia was mindful of the fact that her son was a flirt. That was why she prayed daily that he wouldn't grow up to be like his father.

Olivia beckoned Tressie closer with her index finger. "It's nice of you to join us this morning."

"You know I was out of town on business. My plane arrived late, but I came straight here from the airport," Tressie replied.

"Every week she has a different excuse." Val eyed Tressie suspiciously. "Are you sure you're not meeting a man?"

Tressie gave her a ridiculous look. "It's not my fault my job requires extensive traveling."

"Aunt Tressie." Bryce tapped her shoulder. "Did you bring me anything?"

"I sure did."

"Whatever it is, I hope it doesn't make any noise."

Last Christmas Olivia had made all the girls promise to not buy Bryce any more toys that made any sound.

"I bought you back a drum set."

The entire pew turned around to see if she was telling the truth. Tressie excitedly nodded her head.

"She's not bringing those drums to my house," Olivia whispered to Dean before turning around. Then she summoned Tressie to her. "Tressie, will you go with me to the singles retreat? I don't want to go by myself."

"Julian must have told you that Val couldn't go, because that's the only reason you would invite me," Tressie sarcastically replied.

When Julian snickered, Tressie knew she was right.

Olivia pleaded her case. "That's not true. I always ask you to go."

"Only after you ask Val." Tressie shook her head. "It doesn't matter, because I'm not going. I don't like those singles retreats. The only thing there is saved men." Tressie held up her hand to stop Olivia before she said something smart. "I already know that we're supposed to associate with saved men, but you know what kind of man I'm looking for. I want a—"

"A thug that knows Jesus," Val, Julian and Olivia said in unison. The kind of man Tressie desired had been branded in their minds through the years, and everyone knew she would settle for nothing less.

Her infatuation with roughnecks who usually led a life of crime that eventually landed them behind bars was a mystery. Payce, Tressie's last boyfriend, cheated on her, conceived two children and jeopardized her freedom, but that wasn't a deterrent for her. Instead, she remained persistent, faithful and prayerful that God would send her the type of man she longed for.

Reverend Simms rambled on for another five minutes before praying over his congregation and bringing services to an end.

As Dean and Olivia gathered their things, Dean's grandpa

approached them. "Don't you two forget, I'm expecting the both of you over for dinner tonight."

Judge Ernie West, the only white member of First Nazareth's congregation and Dean's paternal grandfather, was a faithful member who demonstrated his love for Christ by helping his community. He took advantage of his power and position to put a stop to the injustices targeted toward minorities. Plus, he promoted programs that encouraged self-empowerment for the youth.

"Not to worry. We'll be there." Olivia reached out to give him a hug and quick peck on the cheek. "Bryce is looking forward to spending time with you."

"Bryce reminds me of Dean when he was his age. I enjoy the time we spend together, but if you two will excuse me, I see Reverend Simms calling me over." He quickly wobbled away on his cane.

"All right, Grandpa, we'll see you later." Dean turned toward Olivia. "What would you like to do before dinner?"

"I thought maybe we could surprise your grandpa and cook dinner for him this time. He always cooks us a delicious supper. I need to stop by the market and pick up a few things before we head to his house. By the time he gets home we'll have everything waiting for him."

Dean loved Olivia's thoughtfulness. "That sounds wonderful." He lifted her lips to meet his.

An hour later Judge West, followed by Reverend Montgomery, Reverend Baxter and his entire family entered his home, greeted by the tantalizing aroma of sweet cornbread.

"Thanks for inviting us over, Judge West," Colin said. "I was going to take Reverend Baxter and his family over to Mrs. Tootsies for some soul food."

"Boy, don't you know I can cook soul food? Just because I wasn't born with soul don't mean I can't get down in the kitchen."

"Judge West, don't look now, but I think somebody is already cooking in your kitchen," Colin kidded his elder.

"It smells as good as my cooking." He sniffed the air.

Dean came out of the den and met them in the dining room.

"Boy, what are you doing here? I thought you and Olivia were coming over later."

"She wanted to surprise you by having dinner ready for you by the time you came home from church."

"She is so sweet." He pushed by Dean. "Let me go give my future granddaughter-in-law a hug for always thinking of others."

Colin took off his suit jacket and draped it across the dining room chair.

"What are you doing here?" Dean held up his hands in a boxer stance and playfully swung a punch at Colin.

"Your grandpa invited me not only for dinner, but to also continue our discussion on the deteriorating school systems in the neighborhood." He pointed toward Reverend Baxter. "Reverend Baxter thought he might be able to assist us in some way, so were all here to put our heads together."

"Good. The more the merrier." Dean invited the adults to sit while Bryce and Reverend Baxter's children took off toward another part of the house to watch television. "Olivia made plenty of dinner for everybody."

Twenty minutes later the men talked amongst themselves and Mrs. Baxter helped Olivia in the kitchen.

"Fellas, I don't have to tell you the number of school officials who have been indicted on charges of embezzlement," Judge West said.

"It makes me sick to think how these men are stealing from the poorest schools in the city. Their gain is these children's loss." Colin popped a peppermint in his mouth from the candy dish that sat on the end table.

"I went to visit one of the elementary schools so I could

see for myself the damage lack of funding has done in the schools. It was horrible. I've never seen such conditions in a school. The first grade classes have huge rocks placed along the walls to block the rat holes. There are approximately thirty-seven to forty-seven students per class. I spoke to one of the teachers, and she complained that because there weren't enough desks or books to go around she moved all the desks out of the classroom and everyone sits on the floor."

"This is so unfair. They don't have these kinds of problems in the suburbs." Reverend Baxter shook his head in disgust.

"That's why I want the church to build its own school for the community," Judge West said.

"That's a great idea, Grandpa, but that is going to cost a lot of money," Dean said.

"Boy, I've already done my research. I do have a law degree," he reminded his grandson. "We can start off by getting grants from the government, and the rest of the money we need will have to be provided by the Lord. This school will have a huge impact on the community. I've already outlined a curriculum, and since I have two professors in the room I was hoping one of you could review the initial business plan I put together." Judge West pulled the papers out and handed them to Reverend Baxter.

"This sounds like you put a lot of thought into this." Reverend Baxter studied the plans a moment. "You want to extend the school day and place students in an environment that speaks primarily in a foreign language. Plus, it looks like you have an intense math and science program here."

"Yes, we are one of the richest countries in the world with the poorest educational systems."

"What about this negative two hundred and nineteen thousand in the budget section?" Reverend Baxter pointed out.

"That's the part I was talking about when I said we will need to rely on the Good Lord's help."

The men all laughed together.

"With God, anything's possible."

"Why don't we hold a fundraiser?" Dean suggested.

"I don't think a fundraiser will solve this problem." In Judge West's mind, he knew he had to think bigger than a fundraiser.

Olivia stuck her head into the den. "Dinner's ready," she hollered.

"Great! I'm hungry." Dean was the first one to run to his place at the dining room table. The other men rose from their seats and followed.

"Judge West"—Reverend Baxter patted the old man on his back—"I don't know why, but since the first time I met you at church last weekend I can't get rid of this feeling that I've met you somewhere before."

"It's possible we could have been on a committee at one point together. Your face isn't familiar to me, but I'm getting old. I can't remember every face I met. I hope you don't remember me from being in my courtroom."

"No. I know for sure I've never been in any trouble with the law," Reverend Baxter replied.

On their way to the dining room, the judge was stopped by a knock at the door. He told his guests to go ahead and he would join them once he answered the front door. It would only take him a moment, and then they could bless the food.

When the judge swung open his front door, uneasiness filled his soul. Standing before him was a deliveryman holding a huge dark-brown box in his arms.

"I have a package for Judge Ernie West."

Hesitant to answer, the judge gave the young delivery guy the once-over look. "It's Sunday. I thought you guys didn't make deliveries on Sundays."

"No, that's not true. We deliver packages seven days a week. Anything to satisfy the customer."

West doubted the man's story. He was ready to shut the door closed in his face when he pushed the clipboard out toward him.

"I need you to sign here." The deliveryman pointed to the dotted line.

Judge West could usually discern if strangers he met were friend or foe. For some reason, he felt this man was foe. Before taking the clipboard, he noticed the man's nicely manicured hands. He didn't look like a blue-collar worker. In fact, he looked like someone who rarely got his hands dirty.

The judge didn't want to cause a ruckus, with his family in the next room, so he decided to take the package and immediately discard it outside his home. He signed the form and took ownership of the box. "Have a blessed day, young man."

The judge's well-wishes were insincere. "I wonder what this is," he mumbled to himself. He turned around to walk back inside. As he attempted to close the door, it was suddenly thrust open and Ernie was forced against the wall.

"FBI," an agent screamed in his face and flashed a badge. The agent pulled out his handcuffs and slapped them around the judge's wrists. "You are under arrest for murder."

The commotion made everyone in the house run to the door.

"What's going on?" Reverend Baxter stepped toward them.

Another agent stepped in front of him and held out his arm. "I'm sorry, sir. Don't come any farther, or I'll be forced to arrest you."

The entire house watched as the police treated Judge West like a criminal. The last thing the judge remembered seeing before they hauled him away was the sad look in Bryce's eyes.

Chapter 2

"I don't understand." Olivia slammed a folded wedding program down on the table so hard, it disturbed her two sleeping shih tzus. "I'm sorry," she spoke to her puppies. "Mommy didn't mean to wake you."

"You act like you actually gave birth to those two mutts," Val said.

Olivia lightly punched her in the arm. "Don't call my babies mutts. They're sensitive. Anyway, back to what I was saying. Dean has been down to the justice building three times. Everyone he speaks to acts clueless. He can't get any information on his grandpa. The only thing we know for sure is that his grandpa is in their custody for the murder of a little black boy."

"That's hard to believe." Val listened closely to Olivia's every word.

"I said the same thing. Dean thinks he's being set up because Judge West is such a huge advocate for equality for minorities, but we can't say for sure because he hasn't talked to his grandpa."

Val threw her a look of shock.

"Every time he requests a visit they tell him that Judge West refuses to see him. Dean is so upset, he doesn't know what to do."

"Reverend Simms was furious when he got the call on Sunday. Julian and I were in his office for our very last counseling session when he politely kicked us out. I had never heard him in such an uproar."

Olivia took a deep breath to calm her nerves. When she looked across the table, Val's three-carat canary yellow diamond caught her eye. The brilliance of the diamonds dazzled under the light. "I remember the day Julian proposed and placed that on your finger." She pointed to the ring. "Time sure does fly." Olivia folded another wedding program in half before handing it to Val to place in the huge stack of programs already assembled. "I can't believe you're getting married in only a few more days."

Val's face glowed from happiness. Thoughts of her big day made her cheeks rosy and her heart skip a beat. She couldn't believe the day she had dreamt about her entire life was finally here. "I can't wait to walk down that aisle." She paused a moment to try and picture what the church was going to look like. "Livie," Val addressed Olivia by her childhood nickname, "did I tell you I ordered twelve thousand dollars worth of calla lilies for the church?"

Olivia sighed, smiled and nodded her head yes. Val had repeated every detail of the wedding to her several times already. There wasn't anything she didn't know.

"Last night my wedding planner told me that the church had approved the candles I wanted set throughout the church." She tapped Olivia's shoulder to make sure she was listening. "Picture this, the entire sanctuary lit with long white candles, the intoxicating fragrance from the flowers surrounding our friends and family. Then, at the stroke of midnight on the New Year, Julian and I will be joined together as husband and wife." A serene look spread over her face.

"You don't appear to be nervous at all," Olivia said.

"I've been ready to become Mrs. Julian Pennington." Val grabbed a handful of grapes from the bowl of fruit set in front of her. "The part I'm nervous about is the wedding night."

Bryce ran over to Val full speed and crashed into her lap. "Aunt Val, can I spend the night with you and Uncle Julian tonight?" he begged.

"Baby, I'm not going anywhere. I'm staying the night here with you and your mother. Besides, don't you want to wake up here? Tomorrow is Christmas." She kissed him on the cheek.

"I forgot tomorrow is Christmas," he replied. "Is Uncle Julian staying the night here, too?"

"Your uncle is out of town. He has a game tonight. So we're going to watch him on television later tonight."

Bryce cheered before running back toward his bedroom.

"I don't know how he forgot tomorrow is Christmas. He asks me every morning how many days until Santa comes back to our house. Now, back to you. You never let on that you were scared to share your bed with Julian." Olivia felt insulted that Val hadn't voiced her concerns sooner.

Val carelessly shrugged her shoulders. "It's funny, because I have every detail of my wedding planned out. In my mind I can picture how the church will look, the smell of the flowers and the taste of each entrée served at the reception, but I have no expectations for my honeymoon. Do you think that's weird?"

"I think you need to stop worrying and allow your love for Julian to lead you through the night."

Val got up from her chair and grabbed a shopping bag. "Let me show you what I bought." She pulled out a black-and-red teddy and dangled it in front of her bosom.

"Is your chest going to fit in those cups?"

Val's full-size breasts developed at the age of ten, and the rest of her body was still trying to catch up.

She playfully punched Olivia in the arm. "Yes, it's going to fit. I tried it on and I must say that it looks good on me."

"I'll take your word on that."

A hard and rapid knock at the front door interrupted their conversation.

"I bet that's Danyelle and Tressie."

When Olivia opened the door Danyelle rushed past her and down the hall to the bathroom. When the dogs saw her running they jumped up and started chasing her, biting at her pants legs.

"Clinton! Kennedy! Get off!" Danyelle yelled. "Livie, call your imitation guard dogs off me."

Olivia whistled and the dogs came running to her side.

Tressie knelt down and played with them a moment before giving Olivia a quick hug. "I didn't think we were going to make it here in time. Danyelle has been drinking herbal tea all day, trying to clean out her system for this drug test she has to take tomorrow."

Olivia closed the door behind Tressie. "When will my sister learn that all she has to do is quit smoking and she wouldn't have to do these things?"

When Tressie stepped into the dining room she sucked her teeth at the sight of numerous wedding materials scattered around. "Please don't tell me this is going to be another night of wedding planning," she wailed while pulling out a chair. "Why did you hire a wedding planner when we're doing all the work?"

"Stop complaining." Val placed a pile of unfolded programs down in front of her.

Olivia chuckled at their innocent bickering.

Danyelle finally joined them at the table. "If you can't keep those dogs under control I'm going to have them picked up by the animal shelter." Danyelle sneered at them from across the room. "Anyway, guess what I did today?" Danyelle expected the girls to fall out in surprise when she shared with them her news.

"You guys will never believe this. I still don't believe it." Tressie sat up straight in her chair so she wouldn't miss their reaction.

Danyelle cut her eyes at Tressie. "I applied to Bible College."

A hush fell over the table. Val and Olivia eyed one another before breaking out into a hearty laugh.

"Right, stop playing with us. What did you really do today?" Olivia couldn't stop laughing.

"I told you they weren't going to believe you." Tressie placed her first finished program in the pile.

Shock filled Olivia's face when she realized Danyelle was serious. At a loss for words, she looked to Val to rescue her.

"I've been thinking about it for a while," Danyelle said.

Olivia wasn't sure what to say and was glad when Val finally spoke up, "What brought on this decision?"

Danyelle's decision to enroll in college was so sudden she couldn't explain it herself. Recently, episodes of uneasiness nagged at her soul. She prayed, fasted and studied the scripture, looking for peace.

Suddenly, His plans for her life poured into her heart like the feel of a refreshing ice-cold glass of spring water on a hot, sweaty summer day.

Danyelle was considered an expert when it came to exploring facts, memorizing scripture and interpreting meanings within the Bible. She believed her intellect came from smoking at least one blunt a day, until it dawned on her that her wisdom was one of her God-given talents that was supposed to be used to glorify Him.

"Did you think I was going to work at the drugstore forever?"

The three of them slightly nodded their heads in agreement.

"Okay, I must admit, college has never been a part of my game plan, but I feel like I'm standing on the sidelines watching the three of you advance in your field while I'm stuck in a bottomless pit. Val's in law school. Tressie is a child counselor working toward her masters in psychology. When Reverend Baxter spoke at our church it was plain to see how close his relationship with God is. A part of that is because he understands the Bible. I want that relationship. I want that insight."

Olivia got up from her seat, walked around the table and wrapped her arms around her sister. "I'm so proud of you. I believe you can do anything you set your mind to, and that includes school."

Academically, Danyelle had been labeled the underachiever in the family. Mediocrity was acceptable for her, and she never strived for anything greater. Olivia saw her potential and realized the initiative it took for her to enroll in Bible College. This was not only a blessing, but a miracle only God could do.

"Did you choose a major?" Val asked.

"I've decided to take on a double major in biblical studies and children's ministries, and I've chosen to minor in church music."

"Big sister, don't take on too much," Olivia advised before taking her seat again.

"I won't. I'm fully prepared to battle this small hurdle." Danyelle was proud of herself, and she wasn't going to allow anything to hinder her calling from God.

Tressie's head was bowed down working on wedding favors, but she shifted her eyes up. "You know they don't allow drugs on college campuses."

"That's okay. Because I plan to smoke before I get there." Danyelle had decided that the day she received her acceptance letter. "Tressie, will you go to the school with me during registration? It's the second week of January. You know how hard it is for me to make a decision."

"Sorry. I'll be out of town. Right after the New Year my boss has me scheduled to fly to Milwaukee. An eleven-year-old cut his classmate's throat and killed her," Tressie said as if she were giving a weather report.

"Doesn't it bother you that your job is to get inside the minds of kids who have committed such violent crimes?" Val asked.

"Of course not. Tressie's used to it. She used to date them." Everyone looked at Danyelle because her joke wasn't funny.

"It gets a little disturbing sometimes," Tressie admitted. "Sometimes when I speak with these children, some have no remorse. It's like they have no value for life and I'm looking straight into the eyes of an empty soul. The others act like they have no idea of the seriousness of what they've done. They play head games, and sometimes they are so smart that I get confused. It's a hard job."

"We live in a horrible world," Olivia said out loud.

Everyone gathered around reflected on her words.

The girls talked and worked well into the early morning hours. They managed to finish folding the programs, assembling the wedding favors and even helped Val memorize her wedding vows. In the end everyone was tired and ready for bed.

In the process of everyone cleaning up their mess, Val's cell phone rang.

"Hey, baby!" The fatigue Val felt a moment ago disappeared at the sound of her fiancé's voice.

"Hey, baby!" The girls mocked her in unison and laughed at her. They knew it was Julian on the other end. It was customary for him to call her after every game.

Val rolled her eyes and fled to Olivia's room for privacy.

"Did you watch the game?" Julian screamed over his cel-ebrating teammates in the locker room.

"Yes, I did. I wish I could have come with you." Val missed him so much. She hated being away from him. "But there is no way I could leave with all the things that still need to be done before the wedding. I called the caterer and told him you wanted to have one last meeting with him to discuss a few minor details. At first he told me he wouldn't have any free time until the day before the wedding. You know the holidays are the busiest season for him, but I told him you had to get in there sooner than that. It took for me to be a little persistent, but he's going to go into work an hour early the day after Christmas. So we have to make sure we meet him at the restaurant no later than nine. So when does your flight leave?"

Julian kept trying to interrupt her, but she talked so fast.

"Valencia." Julian knew his future bride was not going to be happy with what he had to tell her. "Baby, the weather is so bad here that I don't think I'm going to make it."

"I heard it was snowing there, but I didn't think it was that bad. Did they close the airports?" Val's temperature rose. She hated it when things didn't go as planned.

"No, but my coach suggested I leave out tomorrow morning with the rest of the team." He loved Val, but there were times she could be spoiled and intolerant.

"Julian, I don't want to spend Christmas without you. You promised you would be here," she reminded him.

"I know, but I'll still get there in time for Christmas. I just won't get there until late in the afternoon."

"Late afternoon," she repeated.

"Yes. You have to account for travel time and we're in a different time zone." He tried to explain, but his argument wasn't very convincing. Julian was the kind of man who didn't like to go back on his word, especially to his woman. He broke the uncomfortable silence over the phone. "All right! I'll catch the next commercial flight out of here. Once we get married you're going to stop getting your way all the time."

Val giggled. "Do you need me to pick you up from the airport?"

The sound of happiness in Val's voice assured Julian that he had made the right decision. He couldn't wait to pledge his love and life to her in front of God, family and friends. Val was a priceless jewel, and nothing in this world was more valuable to him than her. He vowed to spend his life making her happy.

"You don't have to do that. I'll catch a cab to my mom's house and I'll pick you up from Olivia's. See you in the morning. I love you, Valencia."

"I love you, too." She disconnected the call and savored the moment. She couldn't believe how the sound of Julian pronouncing her full name still sent chills down her spine. He refused to call her by anything other than Valencia.

Val reentered the living room just in time to see Tressie and Danyelle gathering their things to leave.

"I thought you two were going to stay with us tonight?" Val settled into the fluffy couch pillows.

"I can't. My parents pressured me into staying the night at their house tonight. They miss having their only child." Tressie reached out to give the girls a goodnight hug. "I think my mother is experiencing the empty nest syndrome." She rubbed her temples and strolled out the door with Danyelle following close behind her.

Olivia put Bryce in the bed with her and told Val she could sleep in his room. Afterwards, Olivia checked to make sure all doors and windows were locked before heading to bed. As she passed by Bryce's bedroom, she saw Val pulling the blankets over herself.

"Hey." She walked into the room. "If I haven't already said this"—She paused a moment—"I am so proud of you."

Dimples formed in Val's cheeks. "Why?"

Olivia walked over and sat on the side of the bed. "When Julian came home from Seattle I was sure you were never going to be able to forgive him. You treated him like dirt."

They laughed together.

"But I'm glad to see that you finally found it in your heart to forget the past."

"Livie, his lies and infidelity blinded me from seeing that just because he made a mistake he didn't stop loving me. But it's him who deserves all the credit for us being together. He was the one who made the sacrifice. He loved me enough to forgo his multi-million-dollar contract in Seattle to play in New York for only a third of what he's worth."

"The trials we endure in life can do nothing but make us stronger," Olivia reminded her.

"I've learned that, although my last name will change, who I am on the inside will still remain the same. I'm going to be a wife and hopefully one day a mother, but I still want a life of my own. I will never put my life on hold like I did before. Don't get me wrong, you know I will support Julian, but not at the expense of me falling back ten steps to push him forward two. Am I making any sense?"

"I understand and I'm jealous of you."

Val gave her a puzzled look.

"God has blessed you because it's not too many women who can say they have it all. You have the degree, the man and pretty soon you'll be adding babies and a career to your resume. God has blessed you." She wrapped her arms around Val. "I love you."

"I love you, too." She pushed Olivia back away from her. "But I need to get some rest for tomorrow and so do you, miss maid of honor."

Olivia's insides tingled at her honorary roll in the wedding.

* * *

In the early morning hours, while the outside temperatures were still way below zero and the wind made the chill factor in Philadelphia feel like it was in the negative twenties, Olivia was awakened by the sound of someone pounding on her front door. She turned over to check on Bryce. He was sound asleep.

"My son could sleep through the second coming."

She crawled out of bed and threw her robe on. Olivia was going to kill Julian for waking her up so early in the morning. She knew it had to be no one but him. He was the only person who would be up at this time in the morning. Julian lacked patience, which would explain why he couldn't wait until later that morning to see Val. When she flipped on the living room lights the knocking became louder. She looked for Kennedy and Clinton, who were sleeping soundly under the dining room table. Then Olivia fixed her mouth to tell Julian to quiet down, but when she flung the door wide open it wasn't Julian on the other side. It was Julian's stepfather, Mr. McCormick.

The distraught look in his eyes made Olivia's body tense up. She sensed that he was there to deliver bad news. This man who usually stood tall and strong like a tower was now bent over. He leaned his muscular body against the doorjamb for support. The whites of his eyes were bloodshot, and Olivia could see his eyes full of tears. She was scared to ask what was wrong, because she knew it couldn't be good.

He finally parted his lips to say something, but choked on his words. He held out his arms for Olivia, and she helped him into her apartment.

When they sat down together on the sofa, Mr. McCormick's head fell down in front of him. He had cried the distance to Olivia's house, and it took him another twenty minutes before he found the strength to get out the car and to her door. Eventually he would have to tell her why he was there, and once he did, this nightmare would become a reality.

"Mr. McCormick, is Mrs. McCormick okay? She's not sick, is she?"

He lifted his head so fast that the look in his eyes startled her. "It's Julian," he sobbed. "His mother sent me over here to tell her in person before she heard it on the news."

"Heard what?" Olivia braced herself for the worst. Goose bumps broke out along her arms, and she prayed that Julian was all right.

"Julian's plane crashed last night right after takeoff. We received a call about an hour ago. There were no survivors."

Shaken to the core, Olivia fell back in her seat. Mr. McCormick hugged her numb body tight. She immediately assumed he must have been mistaken. Julian wasn't dead. Just a few hours ago they were watching him on television. He was alive and well, jumping, running and slamming the ball into the basket.

Across the room sat over two hundred wedding favors and programs for a wedding that was not going to take place. "No," she cried. The pain was too deep for her to contain, and she cried hysterically.

"How am I going to tell Val?" Olivia said more to herself than to Mr. McCormick.

"You don't have to."

They turned around and found Val watching them.

"I've known for hours."

Olivia rushed to comfort her. She expected Val to cry, kick, scream or get mad. Instead she stood frozen, emotionless like a statue. Olivia helped her to sit down, but Val remained unmoved. Olivia figured she was upset and in shock. She and Mr. McCormick sat with Val until her parents arrived later that morning.

Chapter 3

Dark gray rain clouds hung suspended over First Nazareth A.M.E. church. A long black hearse sat parked in front of the church, several black limousines lined up behind it. The police blocked off the street, and barricades held back fans holding up signs expressing their condolences. News vans filled every corner with correspondents trying to get a glimpse of the coffin that held Julian's last remains.

Inside, the church pews were full of Julian's friends, family, colleagues and teammates all gathered together to say good-bye. The entire New York Knicks team stood in attendance along the back wall along with people from the NBA organization, including Commissioner David Stern. Even Owen Torres and a few of Julian's old teammates from Seattle showed up. Flower wreaths surrounded Julian's coffin and a soft melody drifted from the organ.

On the first row, Julian's stepfather cradled his wife in his arms as she wept loudly.

The days following Julian's death were hard on everyone. Mrs. McCormick wouldn't leave the kitchen. She mourned her only child by baking cakes, pies, and loaves of bread all from scratch.

Mr. McCormick pulled out videotapes of Julian's high school basketball games. For hours he locked himself inside his bedroom and watched Julian turn his basketball skills from average to phenomenal.

Val fell into a deep depression. She wouldn't eat, sleep or talk to anyone. Her parents tried to convince her to get her mind off of things by getting her out the house, but she refused to go anywhere. Even when Mrs. McCormick went to visit her she wouldn't leave the confines of her bedroom.

When it came time for Val to attend the funeral her mental state hadn't changed, so her parents chose to stay at home with her.

From the choir box Danyelle stared down at the closed coffin that held her good friend. She wondered why bad things happened to good people. Val and Julian were on the verge of making a commitment to spend the rest of their lives together, and on the day they were supposed to be standing in this church saying their I do's, the groom was being buried.

"God's ways are not our ways," Danyelle softly recited to herself.

"You may not know how much it hurts my heart to stand before you this morning," Reverend Simms stuttered from behind the podium. "I've watched Julian grow from a little boy into a man and to have him taken away . . ." Reverend Simms paused. "I'm sorry." He wiped a single tear away from his eye.

Colin patted him on the back and told him to have a seat.

"I may not have known Julian as well as most here, but the few times that he and I did speak, I felt in my heart he was a man of God. He was a consistent figure in church, and it's rare to find young men his age so committed to the Lord. The last time Julian and I talked he asked me to pray for him. He told me that he would be on the road for a few weeks playing away, and it was important for him to stay close to God while he was on the road. It's a hard thing for a man not to be taken in by money, fame and power, and I commend him for that. I'm proud to say that now that he's been called home he doesn't ever have to worry about being separated from the Lord ever again."

Olivia tapped her foot on the floor, trying to hold back her tears. It was important for her to remain strong for her son. When the time came for Olivia to explain to Bryce that Uncle Julian had died, she was unsure of how he would react. Since Bryce's father wasn't in his life, Julian stepped up as a surrogate dad and he often did a lot of father-son things with Bryce. They were close, and she feared her son would act out in a negative way.

Christmas morning was when Olivia told him the news. She didn't plan to, but when he kept asking for Val and Julian she felt as though she had no choice. His reaction to the news was not what she expected.

"Honey, did you hear what Mommy just said?" Olivia sat in one of her son's miniature beanbags in his room.

Bryce walked around his room, picking up toys from off the carpet. Olivia had been trying to get him to clean his room for weeks, and she wondered why he had chosen that moment to start listening to her.

"Yes, Mommy. Uncle Julian is in heaven and I won't see him anymore because he's with God."

She watched him put his books back on the shelves and store board games away under his bed before suggesting they go out to dinner to talk some more.

Olivia felt Bryce had taken the news too well, and she kept a close eye on him for any unusual behavior.

It wasn't until they were getting ready for the funeral that Bryce started asking questions.

"If Uncle Julian is in heaven, how can he be at the church?" His innocent eyes waited for an answer from his mother.

Olivia knelt down in front of him and searched for the right words to say. She knew it was too confusing for a four-year-old child to understand.

Dean could see Olivia was nearing her breaking point. He intervened and brilliantly explained how important it was for them to say their final good-byes to Julian's memory. Olivia was thankful.

Now they sat in the church, surrounded by hundreds of flower wreaths, songs that serenaded the dead and enduring heartfelt words that made the funeral that much sadder. Several people spoke beautifully about Julian's short life, and afterward the choir sang one final song before the last viewing.

The choir stood, and just as Danyelle opened her mouth to lead the choir, the church doors abruptly swung open and Val entered the sanctuary. The entire church gasped loudly at the horror they witnessed.

Val marched slowly down the aisle in her white Jessica Zamir backless wedding gown. The form-fitting twenty-seven-thousand-dollar gown was badly wrinkled and looked slept in. A tattered train with small holes and dirt stains trailed behind her. Over one hundred man hours was needed to custom make the veil that hung haphazardly over her head. She held a bouquet of red roses directly in front of her belly.

She paraded down the aisle and stopped directly in front of Julian's casket.

Scared of what Val might do next, Olivia lifted Bryce up from off her lap and handed him to Tressie. She raced out into the middle aisle. "Val." Olivia walked up behind her and placed one hand on her shoulder. "Sweetie, let's go."

Olivia tried to steer her away from the casket, but Val refused to move.

From the back of the church Val's father raced in after her. He charged toward them, but Olivia put up her hand to stop him.

"I can't . . . I can't leave without . . ." Val whispered before pressing her hand against the top of the casket, searching for a piece of herself that was lost. She dropped her bridal bouquet to the floor and cried for the first time.

Olivia hugged her in front of the church for several minutes before again trying to get Val to leave with her.

"Are you ready?"

Val looked down at her engagement ring one last time. She pulled it off her finger and placed it on top of the casket. "I will always love you," she whispered before she allowed Olivia to lead her out the church.

When they walked outside, the photographers snapped pictures, and reporters asked for comments, but Val remained silent as Olivia led her to Val's Mercedes Benz, left running in front of the church.

Olivia took Val back to her parents' house and, once they were safely inside, Olivia helped Val out of her wedding gown and back into bed.

Val balled herself into a fetal position and cried into her pillow. Olivia lay next to her and rubbed her back for over an hour. She knew the girl was releasing grief she had been carrying around for over a week.

After Val's cries subsided, Olivia went into the bathroom to run her a bath. She lit a few of her aunt's aromatherapy candles and hoped it would help Val relax.

She was gone for less than ten minutes before she went back into Val's bedroom to find her missing. Olivia panicked. She searched Val's parents' room and then the guest bedroom before she smelled something burning.

Olivia rushed down the stairs and toward the living

room. When she walked in she saw Val standing in front of the fireplace with nothing on but her underwear.

"Val, what are you doing?" Olivia didn't realize until she stepped closer that Val had stuffed her wedding gown into the fireplace and set it ablaze. She rushed over and tried to pull the remains out the fire, but it was too late.

"Olivia!" Val cried. "Why? Why did Julian leave me? Again?"

Olivia pulled Val into her arms.

"It's not fair!" She fell into Olivia's arms. "It's just not fair.

Chapter 4

January 2008

From his cot, Judge West could see the sun sprouting rays of light across the sky. "Lord, thank You for allowing me to see another day." The judge never missed an opportunity to give God praise for the things he took for granted.

He stood to his feet and stretched his limbs. Against the far wall, right beneath the window West had started keeping track of how many days he had been locked away. He picked up a piece of drywall that he used as a pencil and drew another mark down on the wall. Today was the twenty-first day of his incarceration. Twenty-one days, and he hadn't seen anyone. No visits. No letters. No lawyers.

After his arrest he was shoved into an unmarked car and brought here. No newspaper. No books. No radio. He did nothing but stare at the four walls. He had no idea what was going on, but he had a funny feeling that his past had come back to haunt him.

The first few nights he spent in that cell he racked his

brain, trying to figure out what was going on. He wondered if he had done something wrong. Then he thought back to when he was a confidential informant for the agency. They had worked on numerous cases together, and he had helped them convict a lot of heartless murderers, but it had been over twenty years since he'd last heard from the bureau.

West sighed heavily and sat back down on his cot. For the time being, he would have to wait for them to come to him. The government was known for taking its time in everything they did, so he expected this to be a long wait.

"Are you hungry, West?" a familiar voice shouted out to him from outside his cell.

West jumped up. "Stevens, is that you?"

Stevens, a white man in his late thirties, stepped in front of West's cell, holding a tray of breakfast food. He stuck his hand through the bars for a handshake. "Sir, how are you doing?"

West was happy to see an old face. "It's been years, but I would recognize that voice anywhere." West looked him over. "It looks like you finally grew up. When we first met you were a fresh face in the bureau."

"Yes, it's been some years." He handed West the tray of food.

"Listen, if you wanted me to come in to talk with you, guy, you didn't have to set me up and take me out in front of my family like that."

"I know it was kind of harsh, but we were in a hurry. Ernie . . . they found you."

Judge West knew the day would come when he would have to face the group of people he went against and helped put away. "I knew it would only be a matter of time."

"Yeah. They put a huge contract out on your head. Remember what I said the last time we were together?"

"You said that if they ever found me, I would die," West repeated slowly.

"Yes, and because of what happened to your son and his wife, I made a promise on behalf of the bureau that no harm would come to you or your grandson as long as I was alive." Stevens stepped back away from the cell and folded his hands. "We always knew that there was a great possibility that because of your position as a judge we wouldn't be able to keep your identity a secret forever."

"That was a chance that I was willing to take. The number of lives I have helped saved far exceeds me living another day."

"You've always been such a noble man. The day of your arrest we intentionally leaked the story to the newspapers and television stations so that they would be there waiting for you by the time you were brought in for processing."

"But I—"

Stevens held up his hand to stop him.

"We brought you in the back entrance. We set up a decoy that looked just like you to act like you." Stevens held up the newspaper for him to see.

West stared at a snapshot of a man who looked just like him hiding from the press as he is ushered into the county jail. The headline read THE MAN WHO CONVICTED MURDERERS IS ACCUSED OF MURDER.

Steven folded the paper back and stuck it under his arm. "Remember that murder you told us about the black kid that was found stoned to death next to the church?"

West nodded his head yes.

"They are pointing the finger at you as being responsible for that."

"But I told you exactly what happened that night," West protested.

"Yes, we had that story and we were following up on some leads against that story when your name came up."

"What now?" West asked.

"I'm not sure. My superiors have taken me off the case, because they feel as though I'm too close."

"You don't have any additional information you can tell me?" West was anxious for any news he could get. "Stevens, you're just about the only person I trust in the bureau."

"Well, one thing I know for sure is that they hate you. They want you dead. The bounty on your head is for one hundred and twenty-five thousand dollars."

"What about my family? Will they be safe?"

"They haven't made any threats against your grandson, but I'll make sure they keep an ear out for anything suspicious."

"So what's going to happen to me?"

"For now you sit and wait."

At his reply Judge West dropped his head. There was nothing more he could do.

"Excuse me." Danyelle pushed her way through a crowd of college kids loitering in the middle of the registration office. She navigated down several wrong corridors until she found her final destination, the student lounge area.

Anxious to enroll for the spring semester, Danyelle arrived at the Bible College before its doors opened. At seven-thirty in the morning she raced inside to secure her name on the roster for each one of the classes she desired.

Four and a half hours later she was still registering for school. The process wasn't going as smoothly as she had hoped it would. At the start of her day she learned that students who attended last semester had pre-registered, leaving most of the classes she wanted already closed.

Danyelle spotted an empty seat and raced to it before another lazy teenager got to it first. She placed her backpack down by her side and pulled out the school's catalog. She was determined to carry a full load this semester, and she wasn't leaving until she picked out three more elective classes. She focused hard to find classes that revolved around her work schedule, but the girls sitting close to her kept breaking her concentration each time they bobbed their head or snapped their fingers to the music blasting through their earphones. Danyelle sent annoyed looks their way as a hint that they were disturbing her, but they appeared to be in a music-induced coma and never acknowledged her presence.

She scanned her most updated list of available courses. It was a long list, which made it more difficult for her to narrow down which ones were the best.

The aggravation of such a long day gave Danyelle a throbbing headache. She massaged her temples to relieve the pulsating pound against her head, but the suffering continued.

Tired, Danyelle peeked inside her book bag, searching for her medication that could cure all ailments. She breathed a sigh of relief when she spotted the stash she stuck in her bag before leaving home that morning. In a hurry to relax her mind, she raced out the student lounge and into the brisk, cold air.

The temperature outside hovered around the freezing mark, and the weatherman predicted snow for the remainder of the week. Upset because she forgot her gloves, Danyelle wrapped her scarf tight around her neck and pushed her naked, cold hands deep into her coat pockets. The powerful winds pushed her across the courtyard. To shield herself from the cold she ducked behind the library.

A few feet away she saw a cluster of trash dumpsters. *That would be the perfect place for me to get in a few puffs.* Once she was safely behind one huge dumpster, she dropped her bag on the ground and dug for the blunt she rolled that morning. She found it and stuck it in her mouth. It was going to be hard to get a light, so she turned away from the wind. After several tries she finally lit the blunt and inhaled.

After only a few puffs she heard footsteps walking in her direction. She stood still, praying that whoever was coming her way wouldn't notice her. She held the blunt down by her side and listened intently. The footsteps stopped, then the sound of gravel underneath feet alerted her that she was caught.

In a hurry, she extinguished the blunt against the trash dumpster and tried to wave the smoke away. Her heart was beating fast. She was scared she would get caught using drugs on school property. It would be embarrassing to tell her sister that she was kicked out of school before she even attended her first class.

When her unwanted visitor rounded the corner, she was surprised to see a familiar face staring back at her. "Danyelle, I thought that was you." Reverend Montgomery greeted her with a huge smile.

Her eyes were filled with surprise. "Reverend Montgomery, what are you doing here?" Danyelle wrung her jittery hands in front of her pastor.

"I teach here."

It wasn't until he said those words that she remembered that he was a professor at the college.

"I was in the student lounge when I thought I saw you head out the door." He looked around at her surroundings. "What are you doing out here?"

"I um . . ." Danyelle tried to think of an excuse, but her mind went blank.

He was amused and tried to help her out. "Are you registering for classes?"

"Yes. I was registering for classes and it was so stuffy in that building that I had to come outside for some fresh air. I thought maybe if I cleared my head it would help me decide what electives to take."

"Oh! If you need some help, I'll be glad to help you. I have an office on campus. We can go there now and I'll answer any questions you may have."

Reverend Montgomery's generosity made him sexier than usual. Typically, Danyelle wasn't impressed with the reverend, but looking at him now she understood why more than half the single ladies at First Nazareth were chasing him down. He had a physique molded after one of football's greatest running backs, Terrell Owens, and a face that closely resembled basketball sensation Dwayne Wade.

"Are you coming?" he asked when he realized Danyelle hadn't gathered her things to follow him.

"Yes." She quickly grabbed her book bag and followed him to his office.

Unfortunately, Colin's office wasn't in close proximity, and they had to walk to the far end of the campus. As they settled in, Danyelle's teeth chattered from the cold.

"I'm sorry. It's not as warm in here as it is in the registrar's office. Let me get you a cup of hot chocolate."

He disappeared out the office and minutes later returned with two steaming cups of hot chocolate from the vending machine. He placed her cup down in front of her, while she peeled out of her hat and scarf.

Danyelle wrapped her numb fingers around the hot Styrofoam cup. Eager to thaw herself out, she drank. When the hot chocolate reached the back of her throat, she gagged and pushed her lips out. "This stuff is horrible."

Colin rushed to her side and patted her back. "I'm sorry. I know how you feel, but this is the best we have."

Danyelle rolled her eyes and sucked her teeth.

He wasn't offended by her response. In fact, it made him sit up and take notice of how Danyelle's beauty was blossoming right before his eyes. Her curvy body, rosy cheeks, and sexy eyes drew Colin into a trance.

"Rev. Rev." She lightly nudged him with her arm. "Are you ready?"

Lost in his own thoughts he looked around.

"Reverend Montgomery, are you all right? Maybe I should come back another time. I think maybe you were standing out in the cold for too long." She got up to gather her things, but he stopped her.

"No, I'm fine." He reached behind his desk to boot up his computer. "Why don't you show me what you have so far?"

Then they were interrupted when Reverend Baxter barged into his office. "Colin, I have this great opportunity for you and I hope"—He stopped when he saw Danyelle— "I'm sorry. I didn't mean to intrude. Hi." He studied her face for a moment. "I remember you. You're the one with the angelic voice. Don't you attend Reverend Montgomery's church?" He saw her book bag on the floor by her feet. "Are you going to school here this semester?"

She said yes.

"That's great. Isn't that great, Reverend?" He turned to Colin and, for the first time, noticed the look of infatuation in his eyes. It was the same lovesick expression he wore on his face the entire time he courted his wife.

Instantly, he felt like he was intruding on something special. "I'm going to excuse myself and allow the two of you to get back to business. I'm sure the registrar's office could use my help." He quickly let himself out.

Danyelle disregarded Reverend Baxter's odd behavior and pulled out a pile of papers from her bag.

Colin chewed on the end of his pencil while looking over her class schedule.

"You're going to get lead poisoning if you keep doing that." She reached across his desk, pulled the pencil from his mouth, then threw it in the trashcan.

Colin appreciated her gentle chastising. She reminded him of his foster mother. Brassy and bossy. Then he focused his attention back to her schedule. "Why did you pick these three classes?" He pointed with his finger.

"I really didn't have a choice. Most of the classes I wanted were already full. If you could help me find two more classes, then I'll have a full schedule for the spring semester."

He nodded his head while searching through different screens on his computer.

"But it would be great if you could get me morning classes."

He questioned her preference with his eyes.

"I usually work in the afternoons and evenings."

"Would you be interested in this?" He pointed to his screen. "It's a class called 'The facts behind the book of Isaiah.'"

Danyelle jumped up from her seat and looked over the reverend's shoulder. "I tried to sign up for that class, but the counselor at the registrar's office told me it was closed."

"It is closed, but if you get the instructor's permission you can still sit in on his class," Colin educated her.

"Really?" Danyelle knew it would be worth it to hold on and God would open a few doors for her. "Do you know the instructor?"

"You're talking to him. I can lift the closed status long enough to add your name to the roster." He punched a few keys. "And, *ta-da*, you're in."

Danyelle felt God's favor shine down on her. "Thank you, Reverend Montgomery." Without thinking, she wrapped her arms around his neck and kissed him on the cheek. "I really appreciate this." When she noticed how warm his body felt next to her, she quickly stepped back away from him.

"Please." He enjoyed feeling her body so close to his. He placed her hand in his. "You can call me Colin."

His touch placed a fire down in her pants that she had never felt before. Her heart dropped to the bottom of her stomach. Whatever she was feeling scared her enough to run from him. "Reverend—I mean Colin—I have to go." She hurriedly grabbed her book bag to leave.

"What about your other class classes?" he asked.

"That's all right. I'm fine with just three," she hollered out before closing the door behind her.

Colin smiled. He knew there was something special about her.

Chapter 5

Val banged her head against the car's steering wheel three times before her vision became blurred and she had to stop. "What am I doing here?" The rows of headstones surrounding her car pulled her back to reality. This was Julian's final resting place, and she was there to say good-bye.

It was her fifth attempt that week at trying to visit his grave. Each time before, she could never find the strength to get out the car, but this time she prayed for God to hold her hand along the way.

It was hard for her to accept that Julian was gone. In her mind she understood that he was gone, but the gaping hole left in her heart kept growing every day. That's why she was there. She wanted closure. She thought that if she could feel his name etched in his headstone then she would be able to move on.

Not a day passed when she didn't ask God to turn back the hands of time. Just this once, she wanted to play God and change life events.

It was time for her to face her fears. Val swung her car door open. When she stepped out into the brisk air, that's when she noticed her labored breathing. Anxiety swelled in her belly, and doubts filled her head. She wasn't sure if she could do this.

She pulled out a map the groundskeeper had given her from out her pocket. He said it would take her straight to Julian's grave. Her hands shook from nervousness. She set out on her journey and followed the directions through the maze of gravesites until she came upon another visitor who was crying hysterically at their loved one's final resting place.

"I'm so sorry," the girl repeated while lying face down on top of the grave. Her clothes were full of dirt stains, and a small shovel lay by her side. She had just finished planting flowers, and her cries were so loud that she didn't notice she had company.

Val didn't want to intrude. She sympathized with this girl. She understood the kind of grief she was experiencing.

The temperatures were predicted to reach no higher than fifteen degrees. It was far too cold for anyone to be lying out on the ground, and Val began to wonder if this wasn't the Lord's work at hand. She thought perhaps she could have someone to talk to about the way she was feeling.

"Excuse me." Val softly tapped her shoulder. "You look like you could use a friend to talk to."

The girl swept the hair away from her face and sat up. When she turned around, all of Val's sympathy instantly vanished and was replaced with disbelief. Val was stunned to see her face. It was Caitlyn from Seattle. Val's eyes darted to the tombstone of the grave she cried over. It was Julian's.

"How dare you show up here?" Val viciously hollered.

"I-I-I," Caitlyn stuttered.

Then Val hit her with a right hook straight in the jaw. "Why can't you just leave us alone?" Val jumped on top of her and flung her arms wildly at Caitlyn's face.

Caitlyn was powerless against the blows Val threw. She was so full of remorse that all she could do was cry out, "I'm sorry!"

Val beat Caitlyn's face until her fists began to hurt. By the time she stopped, Caitlyn's face was so bloody, she hardly recognized her. She got up off Caitlyn and pointed in her face. "You're not welcome here." Val walked over and pulled out the flowers Caitlyn had planted and flung them as far away from Julian as she could. Then she staggered back to her car and pulled off.

The moment Dean stepped foot in his grandpa's attic he felt like a little boy again. He stared at the low beams he used to swing from and the dusty boxes he would duck behind when playing hide-and-seek with his grandfather. He wiped a few cobwebs out his way so he could get a better look at the place. "Nothing's changed."

"Remind me why we're here again." Olivia stepped up behind him and wrapped her arms around his waist.

"I have to find the deed to the house." Dean broke away from her embrace. "That's the only collateral I have to get my grandpa a lawyer."

"How can you retain a lawyer when your grandpa is still refusing your visits?" Olivia shadowed Dean's every move as he pushed boxes around. "Doesn't it bother you that your grandpa won't talk to anyone? He's turned you and Reverend Simms away. He won't even talk with his public defender."

Dean's eyesight turned blurry and he suddenly felt faint. Scared he was going to fall, he held his hand out to steady himself.

"Are you okay?" Olivia saw that he didn't look too well.

He held on to her hand tight as Olivia led him to sit on a nearby box. "I'm fine. It's so cold up here. I think that blast of cool air caught me off guard." He closed his eyes for a second and squeezed her hand tighter.

"Are you sure there's nothing wrong?" Her voice was full of concern.

He didn't want her to worry about him, so he swiftly pointed the conversation in a different direction. "Do you think he's capable of murder?"

Caught off guard by his question, Olivia answered the best she could. "The first time I heard that news report accusing Judge West of killing a twelve-year-old black boy back in the sixties, I was sure this was some kind of political conspiracy to hurt the black community by filing bogus charges against someone we all love and trust. That man has become our foundation, and if we lose that, our foundation crumbles. Last night I thought he could be protecting somebody. That would help explain why he won't see you. He's probably scared."

"I'm sure he is scared. He's a white man being accused of killing a black kid in the South. I also think he's embarrassed to look anyone in the face." He patted Olivia on her back and stood to his feet. "We need to get started looking for those documents. I promised Bryce we could go to the movies later this afternoon."

"I'll start with those boxes over there." She pointed to a box sitting in the far corner, while Dean began laboring through another box in the opposite corner of the room.

Dean pulled open the flaps and dug his hand deep inside pulling out a mound of Polaroids. He browsed through them, finding snapshots of him he never remembered posing for. Then a picture of his parents brought his journey down memory lane to an abrupt halt. He analyzed the loving picture of his mom and dad together.

This was the closest he had ever been to a picture of his

parents. His grandpa refused to hang any pictures of them in the house. All pictures of his mom and dad were kept locked away. He remembered his grandma telling him that having pictures of his parents around was too painful for his grandpa to handle.

Every so often his grandma would surprise him by pulling out a picture of them. But he was never allowed to keep it for long, and she always made him promise to never tell Grandpa.

His grandma always said he was a carbon copy of his father. This was the first time he got to see for himself the close resemblance. Dean thought they shared the same square jaw line, build and smile. It was obvious where his perfect bronze tan came from. The woman with beautiful dark brown skin and curly hair was no doubt his mother. A shockwave of hurt penetrated his heart. He wished they had lived.

"Olivia, have you found anything yet?" Dean put the pictures away and turned toward his girlfriend.

"No, not too much of anything. Just a lot of photos of white people," she replied.

Dean laughed to himself and started working on another box. Inside he discovered an abundance of official documents and files. Dean's birth certificate, his grandparents' wedding license and a copy of his parents' death decree were the only contents found within the box. As he skimmed through, he realized his grandpa kept his paperwork in order. Every piece of paper was neatly filed and labeled.

"Dean, it's cold up here." Olivia wrapped her arms around herself and rubbed to get warm. "Would you like a cup of hot tea? Oh, Dean! I forgot to tell you. I found a bunch of linens stored away in a box over here. I'm going to leave it by the stairs, and before we leave I need for you to take them downstairs. I figure your grandpa could use them, and if not, I may be able to use them for myself."

Preoccupied with his hunt, Dean said okay. Once Olivia left, Dean threw the documents he held in his hand back in the box. Then he counted the number of boxes they still needed to comb through. There were at least thirty. "God, give me strength!"

Ready to give up, he shoved the box in front of him away. He decided to save this project for another day. He figured they could pick Bryce up early and catch a bit to eat before the matinee. He stood up and maneuvered his way toward the exit. A short lapse in memory almost made him forget about the box Olivia wanted. He did a quick check to make sure the box he was looking in was what she wanted. When he did, he noticed something out of the ordinary about the way the sheets looked. "She did say there were bed linens in this box. Didn't she?"

Dean examined the sheets a little closer before finally holding one up before him. It looked like a Halloween costume. "What is he doing with this?" Dean looked at the backside before turning it around. Stitched over the left hand side of the breast pocket was an emblem. Dean closely studied the white cross set inside a bright red circle. The most interesting detail of the emblem was the red teardrop set in the center of the cross. For some reason his heart rate accelerated and his hands shook uncontrollably. He had never seen this symbol before, but for some reason it scared him.

When Dean blinked his eyes three times what he was looking out became clear to him. In his hands he held a Ku Klux Klan robe. He threw it across the room and dug further down in the box. He found the matching hood. Dean rubbed his forehead. He was confused. *Why is this stuff in my grandpa's attic?*

He tore through the box, searching for an explanation. On the bottom of the box was a manila envelope. Hastily, he ripped it open. Horror surfaced on his face. He stared at a picture of his grandpa posing for the camera along with a bunch of Klansmen. As cool as the room was, Dean couldn't help but sweat with perspiration. Ten men all dressed in white robes with white hoods covering their faces. Judge West and another man were the only two in the picture not in disguise. His grandfather stood right next to the grand wizard and held up a flag bearing the same symbol he found on the robe. "I don't believe this."

"Sorry, it took me so long." Olivia was on her way back up the stairs with their tea. "I added honey to yours, just the way you like it."

Dean hid the robes by throwing them back in the box and stuck the photo in his back pocket. He wasn't ready to tell her what he found.

"Livie, I don't want to spend any more time here. Let's go pick Bryce up from your sister and take him out to eat."

She looked at him strangely. "Okay, but I thought it was so important for you to find that deed."

"It was, but I can get it later." He gestured for her to turn back down the steps.

"What about the box with the linens in it?" she asked.

"I'll pick that stuff up later," he replied.

Chapter 6

Three weeks later

Val reminisced back to her first year in law school. She had one class where the professor would make the entire class act out a mock trial. Each time she played a lawyer she dreamed of the day she'd stand before a real judge in an actual courtroom. Unfortunately, today she was in a courtroom, but not as a lawyer.

The bailiff screamed out Val's name, shaking her from her thoughts. She half-heartedly got up from her seat and stood before the judge.

Olivia sat in the courtroom worried about her cousin's mental state. Val used to be vibrant and so full of life, but after Julian died, she seemed to have lost the will to live. The blue pinstriped blazer with matching skirt looked good on Val, but it wasn't enough to make her look presentable. Her face looked naked and drab without any makeup. The dark circles under her eyes revealed her lack of sleep, and hair that never had a strand out of place was haphazardly piled atop her head.

Olivia prayed that Val would bounce back to her old self, but after she heard about the fight with Caitlyn, it looked like things were getting worse. Then Caitlyn pressed battery charges against Val. Olivia felt helpless and wondered how much more Val could bear before losing all self-control.

The judge pulled her eyeglasses away from her face and lay them down beside her. She recognized Val the moment she walked into the courtroom. Val was one of the law students she'd met with last year. Every year the university asked the judge to speak with a group of law students who were still undecided about what kind of law they wanted to specialize in. The judge remembered Val from that meeting, not because she was the only black woman, but because she was the most focused, detailed, and showed so much empathy for others. Val's passion for law was rare, but refreshing. The judge was very interested in seeing how far Val's ambition would take her.

This morning the judge was disappointed to see that Val had gotten off track and lost sight of her goal. "Ms. Benson, you admit to the court that you are responsible for the bruises on Ms. Haas's face."

"Yes, Your Honor." Val's response was uncaring, cold and lacked remorse.

"Are you sorry for what you did?" The judge wondered what would drive this girl with such a bright future to jeopardize it all.

"No, Your Honor."

Olivia wished she had insisted that Val retain a lawyer. Only a fool would represent herself, and that was exactly what Val looked like.

Across the courtroom sat a slew of lawyers all hired to represent Caitlyn. "Your Honor," one of Caitlyn's lawyers spoke up, "this is not the first time Ms. Benson has attacked my client. They did have an altercation when she"—The uptight Jewish man cut his eyes in Val's direction and turned his nose down—"lived in Seattle. We are asking that the court grant us a restraining order against Ms. Benson."

Olivia stood and yelled from her seat. "This is ridiculous."

The judge's face turned to annoyance when she heard Olivia's outburst. She picked up her gavel to slam it down, but before she could say anything, Olivia pressed on with her protest. "Your Honor, that girl"—She pointed toward Caitlyn—"did nothing but torment my cousin the entire time she lived in Seattle."

The judge questioned Caitlyn's counsel with her eyes. "Is there any truth to this?"

"Your Honor, we are not aware of our client ever being responsible for baiting Ms. Benson in any kind of way."

"Of course you wouldn't." The judge was stern and was losing all patience with both sides. She glared at Caitlyn then noted a few things on the file in front of her before turning to Caitlyn's lawyer. "Is it safe to assume that your client will be returning back to Seattle shortly, since that is her current address?"

"Yes, Your Honor. Ms. Haas has concluded her business here and will be returning to Seattle later this evening," Caitlyn's lawyer replied.

"I'm not sure what the entire story is between the two of you, but I'm going to fine both of you court costs for wasting my time with something that could have been resolved outside of court. Ms. Haas, I feel like you're not entirely innocent in this matter."

Caitlyn shifted uncomfortably under the judge's watchful eye.

"But, Ms. Benson, that doesn't mean you can assault people any time you lose control of your temper. You could have done some permanent damage to her face. Your punishment will be two hundred hours of community service."

The judge dismissed the hearing, and Val strolled out the courtroom with Olivia on her heels.

"I should have hired you as my lawyer," Val cracked a joke.

"I'm sorry, Val. I didn't mean to embarrass you, but I couldn't sit still and allow Caitlyn to make you look like the culprit when she had no right being at the cemetery."

"It's not her fault I lost control."

They stopped at a bench and sat.

"I'm glad you came with me today. I don't think I could handle seeing Caitlyn today without finishing what I started. I think what made me so mad about seeing her again was how guilty I feel about Julian."

"Why would you feel guilty?" Olivia asked.

"I'm the reason Julian died in that crash. I begged him to take that flight. He knew it was too dangerous to fly, but he boarded that plane to please me. If he would have waited for the morning flight, we would be married right now."

"Val, you can't blame yourself for something that was set in motion before we were even born. God called Julian home. It was his time, and you have to let this go. What I'm saying may seem impossible, but if you don't let go of that anger, you will never be able to feel God's love surrounding you." Olivia grabbed hold of her cousin's hands. "Close your eyes. Can you see God's hand reaching out toward you? He wants to stop the hurt, but you won't allow Him to heal you because you're punishing yourself for something that wasn't your fault. Are you going to take God's hand and love, or are you going to leave God hanging?"

Val wiped away the tears that fell from her eyes.

"If you don't move on with your life, then you will never experience the abundance of blessings He has waiting for you."

Danyelle grabbed her duffle bag from the front seat of her car and ran up the church steps. She was running late, and if she didn't hurry, the kids in the children's choir would leave and say it was her fault for being late.

She swung open the church doors out of breath. The church was full of children. There were thirty-two kids in the choir, and today every one of them had shown up for rehearsal. Instead of publicizing her arrival, she took a moment to observe how the children acted without parental supervision. She wasn't pleased.

More than half the children jumped over church pews, ran across the altar and played in the pulpit. The few remaining kids who were serious about rehearsal surrounded the piano exercising their voices.

"That's enough." She stormed inside and dropped her bag on the first pew. "You know better than to play in the house of the Lord."

The children dropped their heads in shame.

"Let's get started."

Everyone quickly shifted into formation like soldiers in the Army. Danyelle handed out copies of a song she had written herself. It was an upbeat a cappella song that she was sure would bring the congregation to their feet.

She softly clapped her hands to establish a beat. At her direction, the choir sang softly and tapped their feet. Danyelle picked the two strongest voices in the choir to sing the lead. When she pointed to them, they performed a duet like Roberta Flack and Peabo Bryson. She was so excited, she couldn't wait for the congregation to hear them Sunday morning. They practiced the song several times before she could finally call it perfect and dismissed rehearsal.

"Well done," a deep voice drifted to her ears from the back of the church.

Danyelle was surprised to see Colin standing behind her. She turned back around embarrassed that he was watching them.

"That was beautiful."

This man is always sneaking up on me when I least expect it.

"Colin, I had no idea you were here."

"I was in my office working, but when I heard the children singing, I had to come witness their divine voices for myself."

"I hope we weren't too loud."

The children raced out the church, and Danyelle cleaned up any papers left behind.

"No. I'm glad for the interruption." Colin shoved his hands in his pocket. "How are you making out at the college? I already know you're the star pupil in my class, but what about your other classes?"

"They're going well." This time Danyelle was ready for him. The last time they were alone together Colin caught her off guard with the way his eyes seduced her, but not this time. If it happened again, she was prepared to give him a dirty look. "Thanks for asking."

His eyes followed her every move.

She abruptly spun around and caught him looking. She marched up to him. "Is there something you wanted?" Danyelle stood eye to eye with Colin.

"Well"—He paused a moment and swallowed hard—"if you're not in a hurry, I was thinking maybe we could get a bite to eat."

"Dinner?" She didn't expect him to ask her out. She was sure he would have backed off from her once he realized she wasn't intimidated by him. "You want to take me out?"

"That is what I said."

In his suit underneath the church's lighting, Colin looked even better than he did on Sunday's or even in class. His sleepy, dark eyes were alluring. She felt like she was under a spell.

Danyelle lightly shook her head to regain consciousness. She playfully wagged her finger at the reverend. "Colin, why are you playing games with me?"

"What? I didn't do anything wrong. All I did was ask a beautiful woman out to dinner."

"Did you forget that you're not only my pastor, but also my teacher?"

He snickered a bit.

"Isn't it against the rules for a professor to date his students?"

"Actually, that is true, and I apologize if I overstepped my boundaries, but you and I are both adults, and like you said, we do attend the same church. Now, if someone saw us out together, they could get the wrong impression and assume you were a straight-A student because we were dating."

"That's why I don't think it's a good idea for us to go out together."

"But, again, we are both adults, and it's only dinner. I just want to get to know Danyelle Benson a little bit better."

Colin's brown eyes made her vulnerable. "I guess dinner would be fine." Danyelle was not sure why she agreed to eat with him, but there was no turning back.

"Great!" He was so excited, he jumped in the air and clicked his heels together.

Danyelle laughed at his animated performance.

"I know a small restaurant that has great food. It's not that fancy, but I like to support the small businesses."

In the car, Colin wouldn't stop talking. When he was nervous he had a tendency to talk for long periods of time. This was an example of one of those times. With Danyelle sitting so close to him he couldn't keep his mouth closed. He talked so fast, he held up both ends of the conversation by himself.

A short ride later, Colin pulled his car over in the heart of North Philly. Danyelle looked around. She was quite familiar with the area. She used to frequent this part of the city often to buy her weed. But, with the rise in violent crime and the drug task force storming the weed corners, it was too much of a risk. She couldn't endanger her life or her freedom over a dime bag of weed. Now, she traveled the short distance to New Jersey to get her stash.

The Cabana Club's sign hung above the front door of the building.

"A club?" Danyelle gave him a critical look.

"It's not just a club. It's also a restaurant."

They got out the car, and before they could enter the establishment, Danyelle heard a familiar voice call her name.

"What's up, girl? I ain't seen you in a while." Javier was walking by and noticed her. He reached out to give her a hug.

Danyelle gave a quick wave of her hand and tried turning away. She prayed he would leave her alone. Danyelle used to be one of his best customers. He would look out for her and often sold her herb at the lowest price.

"Listen, if you need anything, look me up. I just got in a supply and I'm telling you this stuff will set you off." Javier bounced up and down as he talked.

Danyelle could see he was high by his sleepy eyes. Then Javier chuckled to himself and swayed to one side. "I got a few bags on me now if you need something." He dug into his pocket, and Danyelle stopped him before he pulled anything out.

With her eyes she tried to hint to him that this was a bad time, but he was so high he was unaware of what was going on. She knew that standing in front of her pastor with a drug dealer trying to sell her a bag was just as bad as a crack addict trying to buy a bag in front of the cops. She desperately wanted to shake him and scream for him to wake up.

"Excuse me." Colin inched himself between the two of them. "I don't think Danyelle will be buying anything from you tonight. We came here to eat. Nothing more."

Javier looked at him strangely, as if the reverend had just appeared out of thin air.

"Oh, okay." He turned away, but turned back as if he forgot something. "Girl, you know where to find me."

Danyelle slightly nodded her head and rushed into the restaurant. When Colin caught up with her, he acted like nothing happened. He told the hostess they needed a table for two.

"My name is Rosa. I'll be your server for the evening." She led them to a table and placed their menus down.

"If you don't mind I'll order for the both of us," Colin politely requested permission from Danyelle before proceeding. She agreed, and without hesitation Colin ordered them Spanish entrées.

This was Danyelle's first time at a Latino restaurant. Vibrant colors brightened the dining area. Miniature Puerto Rican flags sat on every table, and Latin music playing from the radio filled the air.

"The way you accurately pronounced those Spanish meals, I assume you speak Spanish fluently?" Danyelle snapped her fingers to the beat.

"Yes, I used to live in Spain for two years."

"Rev, it seems like you've done so much to be so young. You haven't lived in Philly long. What brings you to the city of brotherly love?"

"I'm searching for my mother. My parents divorced when I was still an infant, and when my father walked out on my mom she also walked out on me. My grandma raised me, but after she passed away two years ago, I figured it was time I try and find my mom."

"Does she live in Philly?"

"I'm pretty sure she does, but the trail has gone cold."

"Don't give up. God will place her in your path when you least expect it," Danyelle replied.

"That's what I like about you. You have unshakable faith." Colin found something special in Danyelle that most men couldn't appreciate. The day Reverend Simms introduced them he was immediately taken by her enthusiasm for Christ. The way she worked with the youth was endearing, and the passion in her voice put him under a spell.

He wasn't sure what had gotten into him, but a few times he had to scold himself for watching her hips shake from side to side as she walked down the center aisle during Sunday service.

Rosa returned with their meals. Danyelle looked from his plate to hers. Their meals were identical.

"I thought I would order you something simple for your first time." Colin blessed the food, and they dug in.

Right away, Danyelle tasted how spicy and full of flavor her meal was. The rice, beans and meat were filling.

"Are you enjoying the meal?" Colin asked after he saw her plate was half empty.

"It's delicious." Danyelle pushed another mouthful of beans in her mouth.

The table was silent as they ate, and afterwards Rosa came around to clear the table. "Would you like dessert?" she offered.

Danyelle declined, while Colin ordered a cup of coffee.

After Rosa left their table, the proprietor of the place began moving chairs and tables out the way to open up the small dance floor. On Friday and Saturday nights the restaurant turned into a small nightclub. They sat long enough to watch a band set up, and soon that conga sound entered Colin's body and stirred his soul.

He snapped his fingers and bounced his shoulders to the beat. "Can you salsa?"

"There's not much I can't do," she got up and shook her hips seductively.

Colin smiled broadly as he took her hand in his. "Would you care to dance?"

Danyelle was never one to turn down a challenge, but she

had never done the salsa in her life. The two joined several other couples already on the dance floor.

Colin gripped Danyelle's hand tightly and spun her out until she was arm's length away from him. She felt a bit out of place in the midst of seasoned dancers, who obviously knew what they were doing. This music wasn't like the hip-hop music she kept in her car's sound system.

She stood for a moment and watched the reverend move like a well-trained dancer, until he noticed her watching him.

Placing his hands around her waist, he pulled her close to him and this was where their love affair started. He led her in a simple two-step, until the music spoke to her heart through the sounds of each instrument.

Each beat of the drum drew a pattern for their footsteps to follow. The beat was fast, and they worked up a sweat as the music hypnotized every movement of their body. With every backward step taken by Colin, Danyelle would step in.

For thirty minutes they danced like professionals. Then Danyelle's footsteps started to get sluggish. Colin could see she was tired. Salsa dancing could be exhausting. He spun her around once. Twice. Three times. Then he called it quits.

Colin drug Danyelle off the dance floor and back to their table. He gathered their things, tipped the waitress and they departed the restaurant together.

"That was fun." Danyelle danced in her seat. "I enjoyed myself. Thanks for the treat. If I didn't go out with you, I would probably be at home studying."

"No problem. It's good to get out of your usual routine and do something a little different every once in a while." He glanced at her from the corner of his eye. "I haven't done that in a long time." He laughed to himself. "You didn't do so bad yourself. I was kind of worried when I saw you standing their watching everyone else, but you did better than I did my first time."

She smiled.

"Would you like to do it again sometime?"

This time Danyelle's heart dropped. She couldn't believe the reverend was asking her out on another date. "Okay, Colin, what's up with you? In your office you kept looking at me with those sexy bedroom eyes and then you ask me out to dinner. Now you want to see me again? What is going on? You don't have enough women chasing you around church?"

He was shocked at how confrontational she was. "I like you and I want to get to know you better."

Colin pulled his car next to Danyelle's in the church parking lot.

"Okay, I'll go out with you again, but don't think I'm easy."

He laughed. "I never thought that."

"Because, I'll probably be the hardest woman you ever worked for." Those were her final words before she got out the car.

"I never doubted it for a second." Colin watched her get in her car and pull off.

Chapter 7

The steel door slammed shut. "West, get up."

Still in a comatose state, Judge West lifted his head up off the table before closing his eyes and falling back off to sleep.

"Old man, you have to get up." Instead of sitting in one of the other chairs in the room, the federal agent sat on the edge of the table. "Sorry, I'm late. I was in a meeting."

"They brought me down here three hours ago," the judge mumbled.

"West, it's not like you have anywhere to be. I thought you would be happy to get out of that cell for a while."

The judge replied with a sarcastic smirk. "How long am I going to have to stay cooped up in this miserable jail? I thought being in federal custody meant I would be living the good life. For weeks, I've been in solitary confinement. If you didn't know it or not, total isolation is enough to make a man go insane."

"I'm fully aware of that. That's why we have it." The cocky agent winked his eye. "But that's not why we have you in exile from the other inmates."

"Can I make at least one phone call? I've had not one visit."

"That's what protective custody means—No contact with the outside world. We're trying to protect you." He slammed a file folder down on the table. "Listen, if you want to leave, I can call a guard and you'll be released within the hour, but if you leave, I can no longer guarantee the safety of you or your family."

Judge West knew the man was serious. He released an aggravating moan and grabbed at his hair. "How did they find me?"

"I'm not sure, but the important thing is that we got to you before they did. Somebody must have tipped them off that we were bugging their offices, because they started feeding us false information to take us off their trail. They pointed the finger at you for most of the crimes we're trying to tie them to, in particular, the murder of that little boy."

"You must have a mole inside your organization."

"Yes, but that's why we have to be careful of who we talk to. Only the highest-ranking officials in the FBI have access to your case. We have hundreds of agents who don't know the real truth." The agent saw the leery look in West's eyes. "You don't have to worry. The FBI has conducted a comprehensive look into my background. I'm clean."

"Since I've worked with the FBI before, I'm fully aware of the fact that they will only tell me information on an as-needed basis."

"You're right about that." The agent laughed.

"Well, what can you tell me?"

"The brotherhood is fully convinced that you're going to be prosecuted. We leaked incriminating evidence to the press, and if you were to go before a jury they would definitely send you to the chair."

West did a gesture with his hands for him to continue.

"We plan to release you as soon as we get enough evidence to prove that they were ones responsible for that kid's murder in nineteen sixty-one."

West sighed. "After all this is over, am I going to be able to return to the life I had before?"

The agent looked at him and solemnly replied, "Let's hope so." He pulled a letter from the folder and handed it to West. "This came for you sometime last week."

Judge West stared at it a moment before snatching it out the agent's hand. He glanced at the return address. The envelope looked like it had gone through Baghdad before coming to him. It was torn, taped, and the corners were worn. He knew the letter had probably been examined by practically every government agency. "You know once you find out my mail isn't a bomb or death threat from the brotherhood you should give me a chance to read it first."

"West, you know we have to take the necessary precautions to keep you safe."

Judge West skimmed through the letter and threw it back on the table.

"Your grandson said he found out something about your past."

"He couldn't have found out anything to be overly concerned about." Judge West was sure Dean was overreacting.

"I'm not so sure about that. The guy has been up here every day for the past week trying to see you. He knows something." The agent pushed the file folder toward him. "That's what this meeting is about. In this folder we typed up explanation scenarios for you to read through. Once you talk to your grandson, you feed him one of the stories we provided. You may have to add your own spin to make it sound believable, but it's the best we could do."

"So, you want me to tell him a bunch of lies?"

"It's not lies. We just altered the truth."

West rolled his eyes.

"Like I told you before, this is for his safety as well as yours."

"We've set up a special room just for your visit with your grandson. The room is tapped. Everything you say will be monitored." The agent got up and walked toward the door. "Read through the material. I'll tell the guard to give you some time alone in here before taking you back to your cell. It's going to take you a while to read through that."

The door slammed shut again, and Ernest pulled the contents out the folder and began reading.

Dean sat in the county jail visiting room in a dazed state of mind. It was hard for him to clear his mind of the picture he'd found in his grandpa's attic. He studied it from every angle, praying that his eyes were somehow deceiving him.

Before leaving the house, Dean dropped to his knees in prayer. He had to see his grandpa, and only a miracle worker could make that happen. Each time he tried on his own he was turned away, but today he received a pleasant surprise. When he requested to visit with Ernie West, the gates were opened and he was allowed entry.

Dean checked his watch three times. He wondered how much longer it would be before his grandpa arrived. Suddenly, the lock outside the room turned and the door swung open. Judge West entered the room wearing a bright orange jumpsuit and shackles that bound his hands and feet. His prison escort pushed him over to the table across from Dean. Then the guard securely handcuffed his feet to the floor and hands to the table.

Dean stared in astonishment. He could not believe how prison life had changed his grandpa for the worse. The man who stood before him was a stranger. He had dropped ten pounds, his skin was a ghastly white, and his hair had grown so long that strands reached his shoulder.

This wasn't the same man Dean idolized as a child. The Judge West he knew stood up to injustice, but the man who sat before him had accepted defeat and was now a coward.

"How are you doing?"

The judge grunted in response, and silence planted itself at their table.

Dean kept trying to make eye contact with his grandpa, but he refused to look in Dean's direction. "If a man avoids looking you in the eye, that means he can't be trusted."

Judge West glared at his grandson.

"That was one of those precious jewels you preached to me as a kid. You promised it would be beneficial to me when I became an adult." Dean cleared his throat. "We'll, I'm an adult now."

Although Dean was talking to his grandfather in a stern, cold manner he could see how humiliating this was for his grandpa. Dean didn't want to waste any more time. He pulled the picture out his coat pocket, laid it on the table and pushed it in front of his grandpa. "When you were arrested I told myself that it had to be a mistake, that you would never do any of the things that they were accusing you of, but this picture proves otherwise."

The judge lowered his eyes. He wasn't ready to face the truth. It was hard to see his past stare back at him. Judge West picked up the photo and moved it closer to his face. He was immediately taken back in time to the day the picture was taken.

"I thought I knew who you really were, but this photo paints a different picture. Do you know what I see when I look at this sickening picture?" Dean was angry.

"I . . . I . . ." Judge West's voice cracked, and he put his head down momentarily to regain his composure. "I never wanted you to find out this way. I'd give my life to protect you from the truth."

"What is the truth?" Dean pounded his fist against the table.

The urge to confess everything was strong, but if he deviated from the script a horde of federal agents would burst in and cut his visit short. Then they probably wouldn't allow him to have any more while he was in lock up.

"The truth is, at one point in my life I was an active member of the Ku Klux Klan."

Dean shut his eyes to block out his grandpa's upsetting words. "Why?" Dean shook his head, as if to dispel the thoughts from his head.

"I know it's hard to understand, but I was raised in a house that lived and breathed hatred. Both my parents were card-carrying members of the brotherhood. My grandfather was a high-ranking official in the Klan, and my great-great-granddaddy owned at least forty slaves on his plantation. That's the kind of ancestry I inherited from my family."

For the first time in his life Judge West saw disappointment in Dean's eyes.

"From the moment I learned to read, I was forced to study books that depicted whites as the superior race. It consumed my life. Wherever I went, white purity and segregation was preached. 'Don't allow the coloreds to move next door to you, or your property value will fall. Don't allow those Negro children in our schools or your children will turn out dumb just like them.' It went on and on."

"What about the kid you're accused of murdering?"

Repulsed by the sight of that picture, the judge flipped it over face down on the table. "I told you I was brainwashed. I believed I was doing the Lord's work."

"That included killing an innocent kid?" Dean jumped up and kicked his chair across the room. It crashed loudly against the wall. He paced the room hysterically, repeatedly slamming his fist into his bare hands. "I don't know you at all," he shouted. "I've been living with a liar my entire life."

"Dean, I understand you're upset, but I won't allow you to continue disrespecting me. I'm still your grandfather."

"Please! Don't talk to me about respect when you're chained to the table," Dean yelled from across the room.

"Please," his grandpa begged him. "Hear me out?"

Dean wasn't sure if was ready to hear any more. It took him a moment to get control of his feelings. Eventually he picked his chair up from off the floor and sat back at the table.

"Every member initiated that enters the brotherhood must take an oath of secrecy. I vowed to never divulge any information that could harm myself, the order or any members in the brotherhood. That night I accepted a lifetime membership into one of America's most powerful circles. The Grand Wizard made it clear. The only way out was by death.

"When hate simmers it fuels anger, and when you least expect it, that anger will boil over and lash out at the first person you see. That's what happened the night that kid died. They pumped so much hate into me that for me to take that young boy's life meant nothing."

The judge could tell Dean believed every word of his story. He wished he could tell him the real story. "A few days after the"—West chose his words carefully—"incident, pandemonium broke out throughout town. Racial tension was high. Everyone wanted to know who killed that kid. The mayor and governor were under a lot of pressure from the White House to place someone under arrest.

"I steered clear from a lot of my friends for the next few days, then before I knew it, a man I had never met before confessed to the killing and his trial started shortly thereafter. I could not figure out why that guy would admit to a murder that could send him to jail for life. During the trial, I sat in the back of the courtroom thinking it could've been me sitting before a judge and jury.

"I will never forget the prosecution's closing remarks. He called that man names like Satan and the Prince of Darkness. He described the killing as cruel and vile and said that no respectable human being could commit such an act. The prosecutor's words convicted me. The more he talked, the more I felt like he was peeling away layers of who I really was. For the first time in my life I felt unworthy. I didn't even think I deserved to live among society any longer. I thought the brotherhood would revoke my membership and make me an outcast.

"An all-white jury found him guilty, but he was only sentenced to ten years probation. The coloreds were outraged he received such a light punishment, but there was nothing they could do about it."

"Did you ever find out why that guy took the blame for you?" Dean eyes were full of curiosity.

Judge West nodded. "When I exited the courthouse I was surprised at the number of people who had descended upon the courthouse steps. Never in my life had I seen so many people assembled in one place before. It was amazing the crowds this case had attracted. I looked to the left and there were thousands of colored people holding up signs demanding justice, and to right were the whites who wanted the murderer to go free. Straight down the middle, keeping the two groups separated, stood the National Guard in army fatigues, holding rifles in their hands. Ready to point and shoot.

"From the corner of my eye I spotted the Grand Wizard standing behind a pillar, quietly observing the crowd. This was the first time I had ever seen him not adorning that bright red satin robe. When I approached him I started to talk, but he stopped me with his hand. Then he pointed for me to listen. We watched the stylish, educated, and articulate prosecutor step up to the podium.

"I watched him carefully explain to the crowd that justice had been served that afternoon. He said, 'The accused has been found guilty, and although his punishment may seem minimal, it isn't. The state of North Carolina is committed to protecting its people.'

"Hypnotized by his words, the crowd digested his sincerity and walked away believing every word he said. No one questioned or doubted his position. They assumed because he took an oath to uphold equality for all that he had done his job. The Grand Wizard turned to me and said, 'See what he did? He's a lawyer who has mastered the art of persuasion. His body language and voice tone represents a trustworthy man. He is one of our most valuable assets. That's why I couldn't allow you to get charged with killing that boy. One day you're going to be standing at that podium speaking the same words he did today.'

"That next semester I enrolled in law school. The brotherhood paid for every bit of my education. Through huge charitable donations, my entire college education was paid for.

"While I was away at school the one phrase I couldn't get out of my head was when that prosecutor called that man the Prince of Darkness. I wondered if that was how people viewed me. I thought I was doing the Lord's work by upholding racial justice. That is when I did something that I rarely did. I prayed on it. I mean I prayed morning noon and night. I asked God to ease the tension that was bothering me every day.

"After graduation, I was still confused about the purpose for my life. I wasn't sure if I wanted to go back to the brotherhood and do the things they expected me to do. I ran away and that is how I landed in Washington, DC.

"That's where I met your grandmother. She came from a very rich liberal family, and her passion in life was to help the less fortunate. She organized various charity events throughout the city, and it was only because of her that I began to understand that things aren't always what they seem. Your grandmother wasn't a lawyer, but she sure debated like one." He laughed. "She could quote me facts and figures on everything from inequality in education to unfair hiring practices. I loved her passion. That's one of the reasons why I married her." The judge lingered in the moment. "Life was good for us. We were married, bought a house, then along came your father. I couldn't have been happier."

Chapter 8

Spring 2008

"I'm curious. What made you two sign up for a singles retreat?" Danyelle lodged her head between Dean and Olivia. "After close to two years of dating, I consider neither of you single."

Dean glared at Danyelle from behind the wheel of his Lincoln Navigator. Her witty sarcasm was annoying, especially when he knew they had a three-hour road trip ahead of them. He should have listened to Olivia when she suggested Danyelle ride to the resort on the church bus. *It isn't too late*, he thought. Members were still loading the bus, and if Danyelle kept running her mouth, Dean was very close to putting her bags on the curb.

"Dean and I look forward to strengthening our relationship with Christ this weekend. Reverend Simms reminded us how important it is for Christian couples to have Jesus as their foundation." Olivia adjusted her seat belt in the front passenger seat.

"The life we build together will endure a few tremors and probably a few earthquakes that will make us feel like the world is going to swallow us whole. But, if the structure we build is set on solid ground and not sinking sand, we will get through the hard times." Dean caressed Olivia's hand.

"That was corny." Danyelle rolled her eyes. Her suspicions were finally confirmed. Dean was a fool ridiculously in love. Olivia was just as hopeless as her boyfriend. Danyelle watched them smile lovingly at one another. She sucked her teeth.

Danyelle was a pessimist when it came to matters of the heart, and she preferred to live her life according to the teachings of Paul the Apostle. He wrote in the book of Corinthians that it's best to stay unmarried and focus on the work of the Lord. Paul never condemned those who did get married, but Danyelle knew marriage was not for her. She always thought that being married was a full-time job. That was too much work.

Danyelle sat back in her seat and accidentally bumped into Val. "Sorry."

Val never acknowledged Danyelle's apology. Instead, she continued to stare out the window.

Danyelle was fully aware that Val was probably still mourning the death of her boyfriend, but she felt like her own safety was in danger. She feared that Val would unravel at any moment and take her anger out on the wrong person.

Careful not to make any sudden movements, Danyelle cautiously whispered in her sister's ear, "I don't think it's wise for her to be around people." Danyelle nodded her head in Val's direction. "She looks unstable. Look at her."

"She's fine," Olivia insisted. "Aunt Stephie and I agreed it would do her some good to get out the house and immerse herself in some fresh mountain air."

"I haven't heard her speak in weeks," Danyelle replied.

Olivia noticed that since Julian's death Val had turned into a recluse. Everything about her had changed. Buried along with Julian was that friendly, outgoing and confident black woman Olivia admired her whole life, leaving behind someone she didn't recognize. Val had crawled into her own private cocoon and watched the world as it passed her by.

"Danyelle, please sit back and be quiet." Olivia pulled out a book from her bag and shoved it toward her sister. "Here, read this."

"This is Bryce's Winnie the Pooh book," Danyelle complained.

A headache quickly formed at the corners of Olivia's temples from Danyelle's constant chatter. She lay back on the headrest.

Suddenly, she shot straight up from the abrupt knocking on her window. Tressie stood outside waving her hand and motioned for Olivia to roll her window down.

She pushed the power window down. "What are you doing here?" Her eyes settled on the small carry-on luggage bags sitting next to Tressie's feet. Olivia jumped out the truck. "Oh! No! You're not going with us. You told me you didn't want to go on the retreat."

"Dean, could you put my bags in the back please?" Tressie looked over Olivia's shoulder and directed her request toward Dean.

He obediently got out and made room in the trunk for Tressie's things.

"You can't go! There are no more tickets left," Olivia objected. "The church sold out weeks ago."

Tressie dug in her purse and pulled out her ticket, then slowly waved it in Olivia's face.

"Where did you get that from?" Olivia asked.

"Ms. Young." Tressie smacked on a piece of Bubblicious gum. "She said her bunions were giving her trouble and she wasn't up for making the long trip. So I offered to buy her ticket." Tressie cocked her head to the side and gave Olivia an overconfident smile, while ordering Danyelle to scoot over.

Olivia pulled her sunglasses down from the top of her head and over her eyes. Any ideas she had about this being a nice relaxing oasis for her and Dean to escape to were now wiped away. With Danyelle, Val, and now Tressie tagging along, she was bound to get no rest at all.

Their journey up to the mountains was a quiet one. Everyone slept most of the way, and just before they arrived at the resort campgrounds Olivia mentioned to Dean how tired he looked.

"I am tired," he replied. "I need to take a nap before dinner, if that's okay with you."

"Sure. I know how exhausting it was for you to do all the driving. Plus, having to deal with my sister didn't help any." Olivia cracked a smile, but Dean didn't seem amused. He looked like he was worried about something.

"Is everything okay?" she asked.

"I'm fine." He pulled his truck into a parking space right beside the church bus. "We're here," he announced loudly enough to wake up each one of his passengers.

The girls looked around and stretched their arms and legs as much as they could before getting out. Dean unloaded the bags and offered to carry them for the ladies, but Olivia insisted they could carry their own bags.

Dean's lack of energy left Olivia concerned. It may have been his job that was wearing him out, but to be on the safe side she was going to make a doctor's appointment for him when they returned home.

Olivia puckered her lips for the quick peck Dean placed square on her lips then watched as he walked toward the men's cabins, located on the left side of the lake.

Dean walked as if he were carrying a barrel full of adversity on his back. His head hung down low, his shoulders slumped over and his legs wobbled unsteadily. The invisible burden slowed down his journey. With each step he was losing momentum.

She wondered what the burden was that was weighing

him down. It had to be something important because he rarely kept anything from her. They shared everything.

"What did you do that for?" Tressie complained, referring to Dean's offer to carry their bags. "I can't carry all these bags by myself."

"No one told you to bring five pieces of luggage for a three-day trip." Olivia lifted her bags over her shoulder and set out to find their cabin.

After being pointed in the wrong direction several different times, the girls finally found their cabin.

"This is not what I expected when the brochure I read said luxury log cabins," Tressie moaned. "Where is the plush king-size beds, huge garden-style bathtubs, wood-burning fireplace, television and microwave?"

"Do I have to remind you that this is a singles Christian retreat? Your focus is supposed to be on God's will for your life, not the amenities included with this cabin." Olivia pulled out her hiking boots and slipped them on her feet. "Are you ready for our hike?"

"Yes!" Danyelle exclaimed. "This is the best part of the trip."

Hiking to the mountaintop became an annual ritual for the girls since their first visit to the camp three years prior. Olivia called it "A Spiritual Cleansing." Each one of them struggled with uphill battles every day in their personal lives. Every once in a while someone might stumble along the way or stray from their given paths, but fortunately they had God to put them back on track.

The girls started up the steep trail that seemed so much harder to climb than the previous year. They hiked less than a mile before Danyelle rested against a nearby tree. "I'm sorry, but I'm tired. Can't we rest a moment before going any farther?"

"No." Olivia pulled her sister along. "We're not going to stop until we reach the top."

Another half hour passed before Tressie noticed that Olivia was losing her momentum. It was too soon for Olivia to get tired, so Tressie struck up conversation. "Livie, do you think you and Dean will get married soon? You two have been dating for a while and the next step is marriage." Tressie hung onto Danyelle's arm to keep her balance, while Olivia and Val helped one another a few feet behind them.

"I'm not sure. We've talked about marriage, but I think Dean has so much going on, with his grandpa being arrested."

"Has Dean learned anything new?" Danyelle asked between breaths.

"No. Every time I ask him about it he says he doesn't want to talk. A few weeks ago he was determined to find his grandpa the best defense lawyer in the state, and now he acts like he doesn't care."

"Well, until you find out what's up with his family, I think you need to hold off on any marriage plans. I don't need my sister marrying into bigotry," Danyelle screamed. "Plus, I think you need to take my advice."

Olivia gave her a puzzled look.

"Sex. You can't buy a car without giving it a test drive. How can you marry a man without knowing how he is in bed?"

Olivia's face turned red. She gripped Val's hand so tight that Val winced in pain. "Look who's talking. That chastity belt you wear around your waist has never been taken off and, until it is, don't talk to me about sex."

"I'm not ashamed of my virginity," Danyelle proudly announced. "But I'm not walking down that aisle without first getting in that man's pants."

"What would Mommy say if she heard you talking like that?" Olivia shouted.

"I realize we were raised on the 'no sex until after marriage' principle, but times have changed. How many people actually wait?"

"Unfortunately not many, but we should learn from other people's mistakes. We are taught to be wise through Biblical principles," Olivia explained.

"Imagine your wedding day." Danyelle turned to look her sister in the eye. "You, dressed in a flawless white wedding gown that symbolizes your purity. You've saved yourself for this man and are giving him a gift that is priceless. Then comes the honeymoon. You two are in bed, getting ready to get busy, then come to find out he's this big." Danyelle used her thumb and pointer finger to measure an inch. "You ain't feel anything. What are you going to do?"

Everyone was surprised when Val was the first one to laugh out loud. "You know we joke a lot about Danyelle smoking too much weed, but she does come up with some convincing arguments." She turned to Olivia. "Your sister has a point."

"Not you too!" Olivia complained.

"You can't divorce him or send him back to his momma," Danyelle ranted on. "Or would you file for annulment?" Danyelle asked. "What would you do?"

"Marriage is about so much more than sex. When I was with Bryant, we moved so fast that we never got a chance to know one another. I want it to be different with Dean," Olivia defended herself.

Danyelle pressed the issue. "Having sex can only bring the two of you closer. Dean is a cool guy, but he's still a man." Danyelle tilted her head to the side and considered her next words carefully. "Unless Dean's a virgin?" she spat.

Olivia's body instantly turned tense and she stopped climbing. "Not that it's any of your business, but my man is far from a virgin."

"Livie, don't misunderstand my point. I know you're worth the wait and Dean is a great guy, but don't ignore the obvious. For one, he loves you and adores your son. Second, he does everything he can for you. Lastly, he works to give you money, keep gas in your car and help out with your monthly utility bills. How much longer do you think it's going to be before he gets sick of putting all his eggs in your basket without getting anything in return?"

Olivia reflected on Danyelle's mini-sermon. *Am I being selfish?* She never considered the possibility that Dean may want to have sex. Olivia loved Dean and didn't want to lose him. In her heart she knew that sex would never keep a man, but Danyelle's argument sounded so convincing.

"Look!" Tressie pointed to a narrow trail that looked like a shortcut to the top. "We can go through here."

"I don't know, Tressie." Olivia looked skeptical of the path Tressie had found. "I think we should stay on the designated path."

But it was too late. Danyelle was already following Tressie through the thick brush of bushes.

Olivia followed, and it wasn't long before the girls made it to the top.

"See, I told you this was a quicker route," Tressie shouted.

"Yeah, but was it worth it? My arms have scratches from the thorns and pointy sticks," Danyelle complained.

At the mountaintop, each girl found a huge rock to relax on and basked in God's glory. Sunrays trickled down from heaven, painting a beautiful array of pink and yellow light across the sky. Total silence surrounded them.

"If I was you, I would go ahead and enjoy Dean in as many ways as I could," Val said. "If you don't take advantage of the opportunity, it could be snatched away from you and you'll never get to feel the touch of his hands over your body."

Tressie, Danyelle and Olivia looked at one another. They knew Val was regretting her decision to wait until after she was married to consummate her relationship with Julian.

Chapter 9

Anxious to get back to their cabin and get ready for dinner, the girls retreated back down the mountain trail. "Thank God the climb is always easier going down than the climb up," Danyelle hollered, out of breath.

In their absence, the campgrounds grew into a stampede of activity. Buses carrying passengers from different churches passed them by. Men and women, young and old, hauled luggage, duffle bags and coolers in search of their cabins.

"Look at the shortage of men around here," Tressie griped. "I knew I should've stayed home."

The moment the girls stepped foot in their cabin, the bickering between Danyelle and Tressie began. They fussed over who would be the first to take a shower. Then they argued over who would sleep closest to the window. The final straw came when Danyelle threatened to put Tressie's things out.

"Would you two stop it?"

Olivia was tired of hearing them act like children. She snatched her cell phone off her bed and stormed outside to call her son. Pressing the number three speed-dial number on her phone, she called her aunt. "Hey, Auntie, how's everything?" Olivia shouted.

"Olivia!" Val's mom sounded relieved to hear from her. "Did everyone get there safely?" Her aunt wasn't as concerned about everyone as she was about Val. That's why she sounded the way she did.

"We had no problems, and everyone is fine," Olivia replied.

"Good!" She released a sigh of relief. "I know you're anxious to talk with Bryce, so here he is."

"Mommy, we've been waiting for you to call," Bryce sounded upset.

"Why honey? Is everything okay?" Worry filled Olivia's mind.

"Aunt Stephie was going to take me to Chuck E. Cheese, but she said we couldn't leave until after you called. Can we go now?" He spoke away from the phone and toward his aunt.

Olivia could hear her in the background telling Bryce they could leave once he hung up the phone.

"Bryce, I'm not going to hold you up. I just wanted to make sure you were all right and tell you that I miss you."

"I miss you too, Mommy."

She thought he was going to hand the phone back to Aunt Stephie, but he continued to talk.

"Mom, why couldn't Kennedy and Clinton come with me? Aunt Stephie said it was okay."

"Bryce, I explained this to you before we left home. It was time for Kennedy and Clinton to get their shots. The kennel is going to take care of that and give them each a bath. By the time we pick them up on Monday, they will be as good as new."

"Okay, Mommy."

Olivia wasn't sure if he was satisfied with that answer, but he handed the phone back to his aunt and went to the guest room to get his jacket.

"Olivia, don't worry about us," Aunt Stephie said. "We'll

be fine. Enjoy your trip and make sure my daughter has some fun while she's there."

When Olivia hung up the phone, her heart stung a little from the way Bryce brushed her off for Chuck E. Cheese. The hardest part of being a mother was watching her child become so independent. He demonstrated new self-reliance in the mornings by dressing himself and rushing off to class without giving her a kiss good-bye. She could feel him pulling away from her, but there wasn't much she could do about it. Dean warned her that eventually she would have to allow her boy to grow into a man.

After dinner a small group of campers gathered around a bonfire to sing church hymns. The sky was clear, the fire blazed high, and the songs they sang sounded like a professional mass choir. Part of the reason was due to Danyelle. She had taken the initiative to divide everyone into groups and instructed everyone on different song arrangements. When it came to music, Danyelle was a professional.

Late into the night, Olivia announced she was tired. "Danyelle, I'm glad you're the musically inclined one in the family, because I can't sing one more song. My tonsils hurt. I'm going to bed." Olivia placed her hand on Danyelle's shoulder.

"You're leaving already?" Then Danyelle noticed that everyone was leaving. "It's still early."

"It's close to midnight. We're tired." Tressie lifted herself up from off the log she was sitting on.

Olivia ran to catch up with Dean. "Are we still going canoeing in the morning?"

His eyes flashed an affirmative response. "I'll meet you on the dock." They kissed good-night and retired for the night.

"Danyelle, are you going to walk back to the cabin with us?" Tressie asked.

Disheartened that her singers had bailed, Danyelle looked over her shoulder and responded with a no. "I think I'm going to sit out here a bit longer and review a couple pages of notes from class. I have an exam Monday morning, and I need to be prepared for it."

The girls left her alone, and Danyelle picked up a three-ring binder that sat at her feet. She flipped it open to the first page and began testing her memory. To help her relax, she grabbed her book bag and pulled out the only blunt she had brought with her. She used the bonfire to spark it up.

I can study better once I get a few puffs in. Danyelle took a small hit and focused her attention back on her schoolwork.

"Can I join you?" Startled, Danyelle jumped up and dropped her notebook to the ground. It was Colin Montgomery. She quickly hid the blunt behind her back and smiled in his direction. *Why is it that this man always manages to find me when I'm trying to get high?*

"I'm sorry, did I scare you?" He walked around to one of the logs that was positioned around the campfire and picked up her notebook. "I'm glad to see my star pupil is studying. I wish all my students were like you."

Danyelle wanted to respond, but the smoke that filled her lungs prevented her from saying anything. She didn't want to blow smoke in the reverend's face, but she couldn't hold it in any longer. Her eyes began to water. The smoke started to choke her. She finally had to let it out. Loudly, she coughed, bending over to release the smell of marijuana into the air.

"Are you all right?" The reverend patted her on the back. "You know you really shouldn't be smoking out here."

Danyelle cleared her throat, her face red from embarrassment. This was the second time he had caught her. She pushed his hand away and told him she was okay.

An uncomfortable silence filled the air.

"Does it help you to study alone?" He walked around to

the opposite side of the fire, where she could barely see his face.

"Yes, there are fewer disturbances. I can concentrate and retain more. I have this teacher who likes to kill us with scripture." She gave him a playful smile.

"Sounds like a man after my own heart." He walked around the fire closer to her, but she backed away.

She still held the blunt behind her back as it slowly burned.

When he realized she was intentionally avoiding him, he stopped coming toward her. He tried a different approach. "What did Jesus say is the first great commandment?"

"We are commanded to love the Lord with all our heart, mind and soul," she replied with ease.

"And the second?"

"Love our neighbors as ourselves."

Their eyes locked. The bonfire danced around them, and their body temperature rose ten degrees.

Danyelle felt an unfamiliar feeling in the pit of her stomach. She shifted her eyes away from him. It was the first time she felt nervous being the center of attraction.

"Danyelle, you are a mysterious young lady. What made you enroll in Bible College?"

"Although my parents are gone, they left my sister and I with a gift that I consider priceless: a Bible full of God's infinite wisdom." She pointed toward her Bible. "Daddy would often tell us that securing the Lord's Word in our hearts would benefit us later on in life."

"It's obvious that your parents were a big part of your life."

She smiled to herself. "I really wish my dad were around to see my nephew. Bryce walks just like him." She laughed out loud.

"I'm sure they would be so proud of you."

He reached out to hand Danyelle back the notebook

she'd dropped earlier. When she grabbed a hold of it, he used it to pull her closer to him. Then he kissed her.

The feel of lips locked around hers was something she had never experienced before. She closed her eyes and enjoyed the feel of his tongue wrestling with hers.

They kissed for thirty seconds before she abruptly pulled away. She couldn't believe she had just experienced her first kiss and it was with the pastor of her church.

"Reverend, I'm sorry. I don't—" Danyelle stuttered.

"Don't be sorry." He gently kissed her again. "It was my pleasure." He checked the time on his wristwatch. "I have to get back to the cabin. The men are waiting on me to lead them in prayer. Would you like for me to walk you back to your cabin?"

She looked at him with a dumbfounded expression on her face, but he laughed at her response and asked the question again.

This time she replied, "No, Reverend. I'm okay."

Then, as he disappeared into the night she couldn't help but wish he had kissed her again.

Chapter 10

At the midnight hour West tossed from side to side. His sleeping mind replayed the last time he saw his son alive.

"Pop, are you sure you don't want to go?"

"Son, I've been to plenty of these charity events. I've got so many invitations this month that it won't hurt if I miss this one. The same people you see tonight will be the same people I see next month at the next gala event."

"Belinda and I really appreciate this."

"I'm glad to do it. I know how excited she is to finally get out the house. Since she had the baby, you two don't go out anymore. It's okay to get a break and go out to dinner every once in the while." Judge West took his eight-month-old grandson into his arms. "Plus, I think this would be a great place for you to network with other young lawyers."

At that moment Belinda descended the stairs. She looked radiant in a black and silver form-fitting gown that shimmered every time she moved.

"Bye, Dean." She walked over and kissed the baby's fingers. "Don't you cause your grandparents any problems tonight."

"You two get out of here." Judge West shooed them out the door. "Enjoy yourself and don't you two worry about the boy."

His son opened the door and led the way to the limousine waiting by the curb.

After the limousine safely pulled away from the curb West held his grandson up to face him. "Dean, you're going to be a lawyer just like your father and I, but you're going to be better."

Judge West's wife, Martha, interrupted their private conversation, "Ernie, don't put expectations on my grandson. He could be an athlete, an engineer or better yet a billionaire."

"You're right about that. He's a West; he could be whatever he put his mind to," Judge West replied.

"Honey, why don't you take the baby out on the back patio while I make a few glasses of fresh lemonade?"

"Okay." He walked out on the patio and relaxed in his usual lounge chair. Then he heard the phone ring.

"Ernie!" Martha released a loud high-pitched cry. "Ernie!"

He could hear trouble in the way she shouted. He jumped up and raced in the house.

A look of horror covered Martha's face. Her right hand covered her mouth and she used her left hand to hold the phone out to him. When he took the phone she took Dean in her arms.

He listened a moment before he said, "I'll be right there." He hung up the phone and rushed out the door. As he pulled out of their driveway, he could hear Martha yell.

"Ernie, I love you."

When Judge West arrived on the scene, police cars, ambulances, detectives and the media surrounded the limousine that his son and daughter-in-law left in. He stopped his car and ran to the scene.

"Judge West." A detective stopped him. "We need to prepare you—"

Judge West slapped the young detective's arm away from him. When he ran over to the limo the first thing he saw was the limo driver with a gunshot straight to the temple.

West's eyes doubled in size. "What happened here?" West screamed. "Somebody needs to tell me exactly what is going on."

Another police officer, this time a sergeant, came over and pulled West over to the side.

"Apparently, this limo that carried your son and daughter-in-law was ambushed by unknown assailants, who apparently fled the scene, and we have no witnesses. Whoever shot the driver is responsible for the kidnapping of your son and his wife."

"Kidnapped?" Judge West was in shock.

"Yes, they were not killed. We know they were in the car because their identification was left behind. Do you know who would do this?"

Tears welled up in the corner of West's eyes.

"Sir, I don't think that your son and his wife were the intended target."

The judge spun his head in the sergeant's direction.

"We called the charity event, and this limousine was reserved for you and your wife. I think that whoever raided this car was expecting to find you, and when they found your son and his wife, they took them as hostages. Right now our number one priority is to find your son and his wife."

Days passed. The police placed a wire tap on Judge West's phone, and their house was under twenty-four-hour watch by the police, but they heard nothing from the kidnappers. No ransom. No bodies. Nothing. Judge West went into work every day with nothing on his mind except finding who was responsible for the abduction of his grand-son's parent.

Two weeks after their disappearance, the identity of the kidnappers were revealed. Judge West sat in his chambers reviewing cases when he came across a plain manila envelope that he hadn't seen before. He opened it up, and inside were pictures of his son and daughter-in-law blindfolded, their hands tied behind their back. They looked scared, and he could plainly see they were badly beaten. Scrawled on top of the photo were the words: HELP HAINSWORTH OR THEY DIE.

Judge West shifted through the file folders until he came across Darden's file. He was already familiar with the contents of his file. Creighton Hainsworth, a doctor who volunteered his time at the free clinic in one of the poorest sections of the city, had injected over two hundred and thirty babies with HIV. During the trial, Hainsworth showed no remorse for his actions, and when he got on the stand, he blatantly admitted he would do it all over again if he had the chance.

This was a high-profile case that had received national media coverage. The city was in an uproar over it. West was expected to give the doctor the maximum sentence allowed by law, but was confronted with giving him the minimum sentence of eighteen months in jail. If he did anything different than the maximum, every African American and Latino civil rights advocate in the city was ready to storm his office.

West stared at the picture of his son for over an hour. In his heart he knew who was responsible for their disappearance. This was a group of people he was very familiar with. He knew because he used to be one of them. The brotherhood was a powerful organization, and he knew what they could and could not do. He wasn't sure before, but he now knew they were trying to blackmail him into releasing one of their own.

Finally, it was time for him to announce Hainsworth's fate. For the first time in his career, West was still unsure of what would happen to the guilty. He sat down and looked out at the crowd of people. The courtroom was full. West rubbed his temples then began to speak.

"Mr. Hainsworth, would you please stand?"

Hainsworth stood to his feet.

"You have been found guilty of a heinous crime that has crippled an entire generation of children." Judge West paused and took a small sip from his glass. He stared out at the families of each victim then looked at the doctor. Just the mere sight of him made the judge sick. "On behalf of the state of Pennsylvania I am sentencing you to"—He looked out at the families of the victims—"two years in a state correctional facility."

The families gasped and cried out in anger.

West abruptly left the courtroom and rushed back to his chambers. He grabbed his things and told his secretary he had an emergency at home.

When he barged through his front door, he found his wife and grandson sitting in the living room watching television.

"Martha, I know who's responsible for the kidnapping."

"Who?"

At that moment, the nightly news interrupted the program they were watching. The news correspondent reported, "This just in, a few hours ago a fisherman discovered two torched bodies floating in the Chesapeake Bay. Speculation suggests that these could be the bodies of Judge West's missing son and daughter-in-law."

Martha screamed out. "No!"

The judge hugged his wife as she grieved her only child's death.

"I had a feeling they were already dead."

He pushed her away from him and looked her in the eye. "It's the brotherhood."

"Nooooo!" Martha cried. "Not my babies."

"Martha, we have to go. We have to pack our things and leave town."

Martha rushed over to the phone. "Call the police, Ernie. You have to tell the police what you know. They have to pay for what they did to our children."

Ernie walked over and took the receiver out of her hand and placed it back in the phone cradle. "I can't do that."

With her eyes she asked why.

"Our first priority is to take care of the baby. If we point the fingers at anyone in that organization, they will kill us and Dean."

Martha wept in Ernie's arms because she knew he was right.

Suddenly West woke up from out of his sleep. He looked around at his surroundings. It was still dark outside. "Martha," he said out loud, "you were right. I should have turned them in when I had the chance."

Chapter 11

The following morning Olivia rose to her feet at six AM to meet Dean at the dock. Darkness filled the cabin, making it nearly impossible for her to see. She blindly moved around the room, allowing the furniture to guide her to the bathroom. She closed the bathroom door before turning on any lights. She didn't want to wake anyone.

Olivia quickly undressed and slipped underneath the showerhead. This morning was her time to spend alone with Dean, and if one of the girls woke up she was scared they would insist on tagging along.

"Mission accomplished," Olivia sang after she gently pulled the cabin door closed. She was finally free.

When she reached the dock she was surprised to see such a huge crowd of people gathered that early in the morning to go canoeing. Every face she saw was foreign to her, until she spotted Dean talking with a girl.

Olivia quickly sized up the girl and considered her foe, not friend. Her perfect size six fit snug in those pink Daisy Duke shorts, showing off her long, shapely legs, and she batted her fake eyelashes in Dean's face.

Jealously pumped through Olivia's veins. Her first thought was to step directly between the two, but the Holy Spirit kept her in control. If she overreacted, it would only make her look like a fool. So she stood back and watched Dean.

Olivia watched as the girl playfully hit Dean on his shoulder then whispered something in his ear. Whatever she said must have been funny because Dean's smile was so wide, she could count every tooth in his mouth.

The girl then took off her T-shirt to reveal double-D cups stuffed into a bikini top that was no bigger than her hand.

Olivia wished she could crawl into Dean's mind and read his thoughts. Was he turned on by her sex appeal? Did he want to sleep with her? Olivia couldn't tolerate watching them any longer. She rushed over, snuck up behind Dean and tapped him on the shoulder.

When he turned around it was apparent by the joyous expression on his face how happy he was to see her. He wrapped his arms around her and held her like his life depended on it.

The girl had to clear her throat a few times to bring Dean's attention back to her. He introduced Olivia to his new friend, and when they shook hands Olivia could hear Danyelle's words ring in her ears.

"If you don't satisfy him, somebody else will."

The girl politely made small talk with Olivia until she could no longer tolerate the public displays of affection between the couple. She excused herself from their company.

"How long were you going to stand over there watching us before you came over?" Dean busted her.

"You saw me?" She was surprised. "I didn't want to intrude. It looked like you were enjoying her company."

"You know I wasn't interested in her." He laughed at her jealousy. "Come on, let's get going before the line gets too long."

They stood in line for over twenty minutes before it was their turn to climb into the tiny boat for two. Olivia got in first and scooted to the front of the canoe, while Dean sat behind her. Together they stroked the water with paddles.

By the time they reached the middle of the lake, Dean filled Olivia in on the guys he shared a cabin. "Livie, one guy snored so loud, I didn't get a wink of sleep."

"I'm sorry you didn't get any rest. I know how tired you were."

"It's all right." He grabbed Olivia around her waist and pulled her closer to him.

She sat between his legs and laid her head on his chest.

"But as long as you're in my arms, I'm fully energized."

"Good, because you seemed so distant yesterday. I was worried."

"Baby, I'm sorry. I've just a lot on my mind lately," he said.

"Do you want to talk about it?"

"It's not that important to intrude on our time together." He hugged her tighter.

The two sank deep into their own thoughts. Dean's mind was on his grandfather, and Olivia agonized over her relationship with Dean.

The conversation she'd had with the girls on the hike haunted her. To remain celibate until her wedding night was important to her. It scared her to think she could lose Dean to another woman over something as simple as sex.

Olivia prayed most of the night. In her heart she could hear God's voice telling her to sit still and do nothing, but it made her nervous when she saw girls, like the one Dean was talking to earlier, flirting with him. If she waited any longer, she could end up losing Dean and be left with the similar regrets Val now carried around with her. She couldn't allow the same fate to befall her. So she chose to take Val's advice, even if it was against God's will.

Dean's stomach growled. "Baby, I told you we should have stopped at the cafeteria before coming out here. My stomach is screaming, 'Feed me.'"

"Dean"—Olivia took a deep breath—"Do you miss having sex?"

Dean's mouth dropped wide open. He was speechless. It took him a moment to respond to her question. "I wouldn't say I miss it. I haven't thought about it much."

"Why haven't you asked me to go to bed with you?"

Dean's face turned red from embarrassment. "Why are you asking me these questions? We've talked about this already. Bryce's father hurt you, and I would never push you into doing something you don't want to do. I can wait until after we're married."

"I know what I said, but if you want to do it, I will. For you, I will."

"Don't say that. Don't do anything just for me. If we . . . were to do anything, then that would be a decision we would make together."

"Okay." Olivia sighed and relaxed.

A few minutes passed before Dean suggested, "Why don't we get married?"

"What did you say?" Olivia spun around to face him and was blinded by the diamond ring he held in his hand.

"Olivia, will you marry me?"

The huge marquise diamond sparkled under the morning light. Olivia opened her mouth, but the words slid back down her throat. She tried, but her tonsils still failed her.

He gave her a peculiar look as he waited for a response.

"Dean, this comes as a total surprise." With unsteady hands she gently took the ring from his fingers.

"This is what you want? Isn't it?" Dean asked. "Olivia, we planned this. The time has come for us to get married."

Olivia admired the ring for a moment.

"Please say yes." He placed the ring on her finger. "Look at how beautiful it fits on your finger. This ring was made to be worn by you." He kissed the back of her hands. "If you say yes, I want us to get married as soon as possible. Let's say, next week."

"Next week?" she sounded alarmed. "Why so soon?"

He took her hand in his and sat up on the bed next to her. "I love you, and I don't want to wait any longer to spend the rest of my life with you."

Olivia could feel God's favor pouring down on them. She looked up to the sky. "Yes! Yes! Yes!" she screamed. Then she stood up in the canoe to give him a hug.

"No, Olivia," Dean warned, but it was too late.

The canoe tipped over, and they fell over into the water. The lifeguard's whistle blew, and everyone watched as the two kissed in the middle of the lake.

After Dean and Olivia were rescued, they returned to their cabins to change clothes before catching up with their friends in the cafeteria. Olivia was so excited. She couldn't wait to show off her engagement ring and start on the wedding plans, but despite her happiness, she asked Dean to keep their engagement a secret from the others.

Val was still upset and very sensitive over Julian. Olivia wanted to break the news to her in private, so it wouldn't be so upsetting.

"How was the canoe ride?" Danyelle questioned the couple as they approached the table with their trays full of food.

"Fine." Olivia's tone was full of cheer, and it didn't go unnoticed by the girls. "Can you pass me the salt, please?"

Val reached across the table and handed her the salt shaker. Val, Tressie and Danyelle simultaneously turned their head to look at Dean.

He could feel their questioning eyes bearing down on him, but he refused to look up. He was scared to say anything. He couldn't risk Olivia getting mad at him and calling off the engagement.

"Good morning, members of First Nazareth." Colin took a seat next to Dean. "I signed us up for the men's fishing exhibition this afternoon," he told his friend then smiled brightly, wondering why everyone at the table was so quiet. He pounded out a happy beat on the tabletop. When he looked up and caught Danyelle staring at him, he winked his eye at her, and she quickly turned away.

Danyelle looked down and refused to lift her head.

Olivia asked her a question and she answered by talking to the tabletop.

Tressie was used to Danyelle acting odd, but just a few minutes ago she was the loudest one at the table. Suddenly she was reserved. "Are you all right? You're awfully quiet."

Danyelle shrugged her shoulders and played with her food. "I'm fine." Tired of picking over watery eggs, she got up and took her tray to the trashcan.

Colin's eyes followed her. "Man, are you ready to catch some fish? I brought my golden rod. I love fishing. As a kid the boys and girls club used to take us all the time and—"

Dean stopped him with his hand. "Colin, what's up with you this morning? I've adjusted to your upbeat personality, but this morning you act like you've drank twelve cups of coffee."

Colin ignored Dean's questions. The reason he was so happy was because he was in love. "Are you ready? Throw that stuff away." Colin referred to Dean's plate full of food. "Save that appetite for all the fish we're going to catch out on the water."

Dean stood to his feet. "Ladies, we'll see you later." He and Colin left together.

"He is such a nice guy," Olivia said out loud, referring to Colin. "It won't be long before one of the single ladies at our church gets their hooks into him. I wonder who it will be." Olivia finished up her thought just as Danyelle returned to the table.

"Come on. We're going to be late for the afternoon seminar."

"Ladies, I'm glad to see each and every one of your faces here today," an evangelist spoke loudly into the microphone. "Today you are going to be blessed. The spirit is going to pour wisdom into your hearts that is going to enable each of you to correctly choose a good mate. You are going to be able to hear his call when he whispers your name, and most importantly you will learn how to place God first in your lives without neglecting those boyfriends or husbands."

Hundreds of women seated underneath the picnic pavilion hollered out in praise. Enthusiasm pulsated throughout the area.

Every woman there was looking forward to a positive experience, except for one. Val was inconsolable. A faded Phillies baseball cap was pulled so far down on her head that it practically hid the bags underneath her eyes. She'd lost a lot of her inherited Benson curves because her behind was now flat after losing over fifteen pounds. Her grief was stealing her natural beauty.

Val wasn't in the mood to listen to a bunch of women lecture her about what she needed to do to get a man, when God had taken hers away. Unable to withstand the raising cheers, she got up and walked toward the riverbank. She sat on a nearby log and watched the guys across the river fishing for the night's meal.

"Val"—Olivia came up behind her and sat beside her—"I'm sorry, I shouldn't have talked you into coming. I thought you were ready to attend this kind of retreat, but I can see I was wrong. I can be kind of pushy sometimes."

"Sometimes?"

Val chuckled, and Olivia playfully hit her on the shoulder.

"Olivia, I've been through so much, and I know everyone is worried about me, but I'm beginning to worry about myself. Sometimes I don't even know who I am. Each day I get up out of bed, I don't know what to expect. Sometimes I'm sad and I cry all day, but then the very next day I can be so angry that I buy thousands of dollars worth of stuff from the Home Shopping Network. Things I don't even need."

Olivia nodded her head in understanding.

"Other days I'm fine, but I can't get Julian off my mind. I can hear him in my dreams calling my name. Valencia." She mimicked his voice. "I often dream about us making love. Livie, that's why I told you to go ahead and do it. You have no idea how big a hole Julian left in my heart."

Olivia hugged her tightly.

"Livie, I'm ready to go home. If it's all right with you, I'm going to ask Dean to drive me to the train station. I can't take this anymore." She threw a stick she was playing with down on the ground. "Besides, I have to get ready for my big day at the homeless shelter on Monday."

"Honey, I understand."

Val stood up.

"We'll go back to the cabin together and pack your things. Then I'll call Dean on his cell phone."

"Man, I don't believe we've been out here for over an hour and not one fish has nibbled on my line." Dean sat staring at his fishing rod extended into the lake.

Colin laughed. "You're the one who suggested we go fishing. There were other things we could have done, but I thought you were tired of me beating you on the basketball court so that's why you suggested fishing."

"I chose fishing because I thought that didn't require much skill. I guess I was wrong."

Disappointment settled in Dean's eyes, and Colin lightly punched him in the arm to alleviate any pressure Dean put on himself.

"Don't take it so seriously. We're not here to compete against one another. This is about our individual relationship with God," Colin said.

"You're right." Dean turned to Colin. "I'm surprised you decided to participate in this retreat. I thought you hated coming to these kinds of things."

Colin laughed at him.

"Correct me if I'm wrong, but I believe it was you who said that women who attended these types of functions treated it like a hunting expedition for men."

"I said that?" Colin acted confused.

"Yes, man! It was you," Dean reminded him.

Colin looked around to make sure no one else was listening. "I think I found somebody I'm interested in," he whispered.

"Get out of here." Dean had never heard Colin say he was interested in anyone. Colin believed that a man should not pursue any woman unless first led by the spirit. "She must be awfully special if you're interested in her."

"She is," Colin replied.

"Is she here?"

"Why are you asking so many questions about me? What's up with you and Olivia?"

"I love her," Dean admitted. "I've never found anyone more beautiful or perfect. I'm going to marry her."

Colin gave him a startled look. "I didn't know it was that serious."

"I have no doubt in my mind that Olivia was made for me. My soul soars every time she smiles," Dean explained. "If the way you feel about this girl compares in any way to how I feel about Olivia, then I say go for it. Make her yours before somebody else snatches her away."

"I'm working on it," Colin replied.

"I don't know who she is, but I hope she's like Olivia and nothing like her sister," Dean replied.

"Why would you say that? I think Danyelle's cool," Colin subtly replied. He wasn't ready to tell Dean that Danyelle was the woman of his dreams.

"She is cool, when she's drug free," Dean replied. "But when she's high she can get on your nerves. Ask Olivia." Dean heard his cell phone ringing and quickly answered. He listened for a moment. "No, it's fine. I was tired of fishing anyway."

Colin laughed at his friend.

"I'll be right there." He snapped his phone shut. "Man, I have to make a quick run," Dean shouted as he walked away from where they were fishing.

At that moment Colin saw his line move. "It's a good thing you're leaving, because it looks like I've got something." Colin pulled up on his rod and struggled with the fish he caught. "And it looks like this is a big one."

Chapter 12

Later that evening as the sun set behind the mountains, the men returned from their fishing trip with Igloo coolers full of fish.

In the cafeteria, an award was presented to the camper who caught the largest fish.

"Can I get everyone's attention?" A deacon from one of the other churches paced the cafeteria floor with the mic in his hand. "We have a gentleman who has broken the record for the largest fish caught."

A thunderous applause filled the room.

The deacon quickly glanced at the index card in his hand. "Reverend Colin Montgomery caught a trout that weighed seventy-five pounds." He motioned for Colin to join him.

Colin stood and posed for pictures with his fish, just like it was a supermodel. Afterward, he took the mic to leave the crowd with one final thought. "This is a pretty big fish, but I know I'll never catch as many fish as Jesus can."

The crowd laughed and agreed with him. As he walked back to his table various people congratulated him.

When Colin sat down, he overheard Olivia talking to Dean. "Honey, how did you do?"

Colin laughed. "Our friend didn't do as well as others. He didn't catch anything. I don't think fishing is his sport."

"That's all right, baby. I didn't fall in love with you for your fishing ability." Olivia kissed Dean on the cheek while those sitting around jokingly laughed at him.

The men's fishing trip was a success, despite Dean's lack of contributions. They'd caught enough fish to feed everyone that evening, and there were even leftovers. For those who didn't eat fish, the cafeteria staff also served chicken, meatloaf and an assortment of desserts.

Olivia picked up a copy of the retreat itinerary that lay on the table. "Oh, look, they're holding potato sack races across the river. Do you guys want to go?" she asked.

"I'll pass," Tressie replied. "I have a date."

"A date?" Danyelle and Olivia asked in unison. "With whom?"

Tressie's pointer finger led them across the room to a young distinguished gentleman. A pair of black square-rim glasses surrounding his eyes made him look like a scholar. A button-up plaid shirt that perfectly matched his blue Dockers and tan loafers was a change from Tressie's usual dates. "He asked me to take a stroll around the campgrounds with him."

Danyelle placed the back of her hand against Tressie's forehead. "Are you feeling all right? Because that guy standing over there looks a little stuffy and uptight. Definitely not your type," Danyelle assessed. "Besides, I thought no one here would interest you."

"Miracles do happen. He could be 'the one.'"

Tressie then ran off to catch up with her date.

"Come on, baby. Let's go beat everyone at the sack races." Dean stood and held out his hand for Olivia to join him. "Although I already have the trophy."

Olivia beamed. "Danyelle, are you coming?"

Danyelle looked around and noticed she was left all alone. A phone call had pulled Colin away from the table minutes earlier.

"No. I'm going to go for a walk down by the lake," Danyelle replied.

"She's probably going down there to smoke a joint," Dean whispered.

Danyelle overheard what Dean said about her, but this time he was wrong. Tonight her only desire was to spend time alone with her thoughts and God.

When she reached the lake, the sight of two fawns drinking water from the lake made her stop momentarily and enjoy nature.

"It's beautiful out here. Isn't it?"

Danyelle was startled by the sound of Colin's voice. She quickly swung around to face him. "You scared me. I was about to take off running."

"I'm sorry. I hope you don't mind me following you." He stepped in closer to her. "But I was hoping I could spend some time alone with you."

"That's funny"—she laughed—"because I was hoping to spend some time alone with God." She threw him a look full of attitude before switching away.

"Is that your way of telling me to get lost?" He ran to keep up with her.

She stopped and smiled. "No. I was just teasing you. I wanted to see how persistent you would be to follow me."

"I'd chase you all the way to heaven, if that's what it takes for me to get close to you."

She laughed loudly. "That was corny, but you earned points for trying." She stretched her hands up toward the sky and hollered, "Lord, can You please reveal to me this man's true intentions?"

He laughed at her crazy and outrageous behavior. "Why don't you ask me yourself?"

"How can I be sure you're going to be honest with me?"

He gave her a ridiculous look.

"I mean, there are plenty of women at this retreat who would love to have been kissed by you last night, but you chose me. Why?"

"Did my actions scare you?"

"No."

"Good, because I wouldn't want to frighten you off. I apologize for being so forward, but sharing a kiss with you is something I've wanted to do for some time."

She was still very suspicious of his motives.

"When I saw you at the school I was sure it was a sign from God telling me it's time. Time for me to court the woman who will be my wife."

"Wife?" Danyelle laughed. She was now convinced Colin was playing games. "Sorry, Rev, I'm not wifey material."

"If Jesus turned water into wine, I'm sure it would be no problem for him to turn you into my lifelong mate."

"You're funny, Colin." Danyelle laughed and walked away from him. "You almost had me thinking you were serious."

Colin watched her walk back to the campgrounds. "Watch the Lord work wonders in our relationship," he said as she walked away.

Later that night, before the girls laid down for bed, Olivia decided it was a good time to share her engagement. With her legs crossed Indian-style she patiently waited for Tressie to return from the bathroom.

When Tressie slipped underneath her bed sheets, Olivia couldn't hold back any longer. "I have some headline news to share with you ladies. I couldn't tell you earlier because Val was still here and I didn't want to upset her, but Dean asked me to marry him this morning."

The news was so exciting that Tressie screamed out and

ran to Olivia's bed. She wrapped her arms around Olivia's neck so tight, she practically smothered her.

"What?" Danyelle lifted her head from underneath her bed covers. "It sounded like you said you and Dean were getting married."

Olivia nodded her head yes. "That's what I said." Her cheeks were rosy red from smiling so much. "We set a date for two weeks from today. Dean wanted to get married next week, but I convinced him to give me an extra week."

"Livie, don't you think this is kind of sudden?" Danyelle asked.

"No." Olivia's temperamental attitude turned defensive. "On the hike yesterday we talked about how it wouldn't be long before Dean and I got engaged, so why do you sound surprised?"

Danyelle hadn't noticed it at first, but she could clearly see how her response had spoiled her sister's moment. Her sister's happiness was important, but this move was irresponsible. "I'm sorry." She walked over and kissed her sister on the cheek. "I'm just worried about my little sister. You know with everything that happened between you and Bryant I just want for you and my nephew to be safe."

Olivia and Tressie made room for Danyelle on the bed.

"Doesn't it seem odd to you that Dean wants to get married in the midst of all this controversy surrounding his grandpa? The man who has raised him and is like a father to him is behind bars for a crime he supposedly didn't commit, and Dean pushes all that to the side to marry you."

It suddenly dawned on her that Danyelle had valid reasons for being concerned. Instead of agreeing with her sister, Olivia quickly thought of a logical excuse. "As a matter of fact, we did talk about his grandpa, and Dean just wants us to have a reason to celebrate, instead of all the bad news he's been receiving."

Danyelle was skeptical of Olivia's explanation.

Tressie knew the sisters could debate all night long about the pros and cons of getting married, so she tried to move the conversation in a different direction. "Well, since we don't have much time, the moment we get back we have to make an appointment at the bridal boutique to look for dresses."

Danyelle sat across the room and listened as the girls discussed what colors would look best for the season. She was convinced her sister was making a huge mistake. It bothered her that Olivia was being so irresponsible, but there wasn't too much she could do about it then. So she went to bed.

He aggressively yanked her head back by the roots of her hair and forced her mouth open with his tongue. The warmth from his mouth warmed her entire body. She was a prisoner of his passion. He spun her around and planted tender kisses along the back of her neck. He caressed her thighs and massaged her voluptuous breasts.

She released a soft, subtle moan. Individual braids slid down her back like a waterfall. She grinded her backside into his pelvis. She was ready for him to take her. Thoughts of him satisfying her desire drove her crazy. Energy and passion grew until it came to a boiling point. Their breathing was labored.

She gripped the blankets around her, and just as she felt juices flowing from between her legs, Danyelle jumped up and sat straight up in her bed. She looked around and wiped the sweat from her forehead.

It was just a dream.

Danyelle leaned back against her headboard and sighed heavily. She rubbed her thighs together and felt how sticky she was. She never had a wet dream before, and it was embarrassing to think her first wet dream was of her pastor. She lay back in bed. "God, why me?" She rushed into the bathroom to wash all thoughts of Colin away.

* * *

Right before the retreat's final morning church services were about to begin, Colin felt his phone vibrate. He pulled it out and saw that the call was coming from the college. He wondered who would be calling him from the school on a Sunday. Then he thought that something might have been wrong, so he answered.

"Colin." It was Reverend Baxter. "I apologize for calling you on a Sunday morning and I know you're probably still up in the mountains on the retreat, but there is something I need to discuss with you."

Colin looked toward the hundreds of people being seated for Sunday service. He hoped Dean would remember to save him a seat.

"It's alright, Rev. What's up?" Colin figured that whatever he wanted to talk to him about must have been important for him to call him on a Sunday.

"As you know, the Assistant Dean position in our department has been open for a while. I've been trying to get the college to fill that position for months. Finally, after cutting the bureaucratic red tape, the administration finally approved it. I was hoping you would be interested in the position."

"Me?" Colin was surprised.

"Yes. Colin, you haven't been at the college very long, but you have a lot of potential. You're friendly, young, and it's obvious you have a promising future ahead of you."

"I'm shocked. I never thought this kind of opportunity would come my way so soon. I've only been teaching at the school for about a year."

"I realize that, and it's unfair of me to call you without calling anyone else at the school who might be interested, but I really do think you would be a perfect fit for this position."

"Thanks, Reverend Baxter, I appreciate it. I will definitely give it some thought." Colin was flattered.

"It's not too often that you people are offered an opportunity like this."

Colin pulled the phone away from his ear and looked at it. He must have heard his good friend wrong, so he continued to listen.

"I think it's about time we put some brown faces in authoritative positions."

Colin felt a little uneasy with his comment, but he didn't say anything.

"It wasn't until I listened to Judge West talk did I realize how disadvantaged black people are, and I want to do my part to help lift your people up. It's important for me to give to someone who is less fortunate."

Colin was speechless. He had never heard Baxter speak like this before.

"Colin, I'm not going to lie, I don't have a lot of black friends, but me and my wife were talking the other night and I had to tell her that you were okay. You're not like the rest of them. You are definitely a credit to your race. You speak so articulate, and when I look at you I don't see color. It just goes to show you that anyone can succeed if they work hard enough. Plus, think about how comfortable the minority students would feel to have someone like you to speak with. Someone who understands what it's like to be black."

Colin couldn't believe what he was hearing. He started to say something, but when he looked up, he saw Dean waving him over. "Listen, Rev, I appreciate you calling, but I have to go. Church is about to begin. I'll talk with you when I return to work tomorrow morning."

"Oh, okay! Just think about what I said. Maybe we can get the cafeteria to start serving some soul food. It would be nice to have some cornbread and catfish."

Annoyed, Colin disconnected the call and joined his friends.

Chapter 13

"Are you surprised to see me?"

"I am." Embarrassed to look a man he highly respected in the eye, Judge West turned away. "I didn't think they were allowing me any visits.

"They weren't, but you know me. After I threw my weight around they saw the light and allowed me to enter like the parting of the Red Sea," Reverend Simms jokingly boasted.

Judge West chuckled at the reverend's sarcasm.

"So, how have they treating you in here?" the reverend asked.

"You're the second visit I've had in four months."

"I'm surprised Dean hasn't been up here to visit with you."

"Rev, he's upset with me right now, and he has every reason to be. If I told you the truth about my past, you would probably stop speaking to me too."

Reverend Simms got the feeling that Judge West wanted to get something off his chest. "Judge, you know that whatever you tell me is confidential. Being your pastor, I'm bound by an oath."

"I want to tell you, but I'm so ashamed," Judge West confessed.

"West, do you know what I do for a living?" Reverend Simms asked.

"Sure, everyone knows you're a doctor."

"Have you ever wondered why I refuse to treat or give medical advice to anyone at First Nazareth?"

"I always assumed it was because of ethical reasons. You didn't want the burden of being a patient's doctor and pastor."

"No, the reason why I won't treat anyone at the church is because I'm an abortion doctor."

Judge West gave him a startled look.

"That look you're giving me is the exact reason why I haven't told the church my medical specialty."

"Boy, Reverend, I thought I was going to be the one to surprise you today."

"That's my secret. Don't think I don't feel ashamed and that I should confess, but I'm scared that they'll look at me differently or, worse, force me out the church."

"Rev, I don't think the church would do that. They love you."

"People change when they realize you're doing something that they feel isn't aligned with God's will. Once I tell them, they won't want to hear any reasons I have for picking the profession."

"Why did you choose to be an abortion doctor?"

"When I went to medical school I could have been any kind of doctor I wanted to be, but when it was time for me to pick my specialty, I chose to be an OB/GYN and I asked for special training in abortions."

"I don't mean to sound disrespectful, but what would make you pick this expertise?"

"It may be difficult for you to understand, but the number of lost souls I've introduced to Jesus through the clinic far exceeds the number of people who stumble through our church doors. I've counseled teenaged girls who have been raped and molested, married women who are pregnant by their lovers and countless number of other women who are just plain scared. Trust me, at first I thought I was making a mistake by doing this. The number of killings and bomb scares being called into different abortion clinics around the country is frightening, but I couldn't allow death to stop me from what I feel I've been called to do."

It felt good to the Reverend to relieve himself of that burden he'd been carrying around on his back.

"West, I feel so guilty after every procedure. Immediately after, I have to repent, because I know I'm directly responsible for killing one of God's children. I always have to ask myself if what I'm doing is murder."

"Do you counsel any of the girls?"

"Yes, and a lot of them I've convinced to either have their babies or give them up for adoption. The others, I can't get through to be so scared and lost that they go ahead with the procedure. A few of the young ladies from the clinic are now members of our church."

"I'm sorry. I didn't know."

"Now it's your turn. Tell me what burden is on your heart."

Judge West nodded his head and told the reverend every detail about his horrid past.

"Since you're a lawyer and I'm a pastor, we can leave here assured that what we said between us stays between us."

The judge agreed and shook the reverend's hand before their visit was over.

Chapter 14

Val parallel parked her black Mercedes 500 SL across the street from the Sixth Street Mission in North Philly. She thought her days of coming to the north side of the city ended when she graduated from Temple University last June, but because of her anger issues, here she was again. She skittishly glanced around at her surroundings.

Being in North Philly always made her nervous. It didn't matter that the sun was shining brightly, dozens of people were standing around, and it was the middle of the day. Being mugged, robbed or shot was an everyday occurrence in North Philly. She got out of the car and pressed the button to activate her car alarm before darting across the street to the long line of people waiting for a good hot meal.

Unsure of what to expect on her first day as a volunteer, Val nervously chipped the paint off her manicured nails. She remembered the day she received that letter from court. She thought she was hallucinating when it said that the judge had ordered her to serve out her community service by feeding the homeless. It wasn't that she had a problem with helping out those less fortunate than her, but she could barely peel a potato without cutting herself. How in the world was she going to pull off cooking for a multitude of people?

Val stepped inside the mission and noticed that the place looked as dreary on the inside as it did on the outside. The shabby walls, painted a depressing gray, made her want to brighten the place up with different shades of yellow and orange. Her gaze drifted to the ceiling lights. Half of the bulbs were blown out, and the ones that weren't barely provided any light to the facility.

"Can I help you?"

Frightened, Val swung around to face the solider-like voice that spoke directly in her ear.

A tall, slim man with big bulky cornrows, broad shoulders and crossed muscular arms intimidated Val.

"Hi, I'm here to—" she stuttered.

"I know why you're here."

Val did a double take. He was a woman.

"Follow me," she ordered.

Val followed the woman to a door labeled STAFF ONLY. She unlocked the door and allowed Val to look inside. "You can leave your coat and purse in here."

Val carefully hung up her things.

"While you're in there, you might as well grab a new pair of rubber gloves, the ammonia, scrub brush and bucket."

Val did as told then trailed the woman until they stopped in front of the restrooms.

"Your first assignment is to clean the restrooms. The good news is that there's only one to clean because it's a unisex bathroom. The bad news is that it hasn't been cleaned in months, not since the last community service person was relieved of her duties. Kyle is the director of the center and the person you would usually report to, but he's running a little late this afternoon. He left me in charge until he returns. If you need anything, I'm Ms. Ward, and when you're finished here, find me and I'll show you what else needs to be done."

Ms. Ward strutted away like a pimp from the year 1970. Val rolled her eyes and sucked her teeth. She was so angry with herself for kicking Caitlyn's butt that she had to flex her fingers into a clenched fist several times before regaining her self-control and entering the bathroom.

The first scent that greeted her was urine. The smell burned her nostrils and filled her lungs. She quickly grabbed her shirt to cover her nose from the harsh odor. First she inspected the place to see where she should begin. She walked through a sea of used paper towels that covered the sticky floor. The one mirror was filthy, and the soap dispenser was empty. She pushed open the one bathroom stall. Inside she could barely bring herself to look inside at the stained commode. She knew that would be the hardest job for her to do.

She stepped into the bathroom stall with her bucket, gloves and brush. She bent down to begin her duties, but before she could start, she spotted a used tampon lying on the floor. Val's stomach turned. She dropped the brush in the bucket and turned to leave, but the judge's final words drifted through her mind. If she didn't complete the full two hundred hours she would have to serve jail time. She looked around at her surroundings.

"Maybe jail time wouldn't be so bad."

Two hours later Val emerged and stood outside the bathroom gasping for air.

"Valencia." A young man wearing baggy jeans, Timberland boots and dreadlocks in his hair approached Val with an outstretched hand. "I'm Kyle. I'm so glad you could join us." Kyle was a very handsome guy with straight, brilliant white teeth. He even had two dimples that appeared each time he smiled, which was often.

Kyle showed her around and later explained that his responsibility was to make sure that breakfast, lunch and dinner was served to the community on time.

After they had gotten acquainted, Kyle told her that she would probably be working closely with Ms. Ward for the remainder of the day.

Reluctantly, she reported back to Ms. Ward, who had a list of chores that had to be completed before the dinner crowd arrived.

Two hours later Val felt like slave. She had never worked so hard in her life. The joints in her fingers hurt from scrubbing just about every pot in the place. She had been on her feet most the day, and Ms. Ward wouldn't allow her a minute of rest.

Kyle snuck up behind Val and tapped her on the shoulder. "How's it going?" he asked.

Val was in the middle of rinsing out one of the pots used to make soup. "It's going good," she lied. Val prayed that the next five weeks would fly by.

"Val, can you take out the trash?" Ms. Ward, the kitchen sergeant, interrupted their conversation and pointed to the trashcan that was overflowing with debris.

Val looked to Kyle to save her from Ms. Ward's gruesome labor demands, but he simply shrugged his shoulders and walked away. That's when Val realized he was also scared of her.

She peeled off her rubber gloves and gathered the trash bag to take out to the dumpster.

"And when you're done with that, I have something else for you to do," she shouted.

Val grumbled underneath her breath. Ms. Ward treated her like Cinderella. Every time she needed something demeaning done, she called on Val.

Once she replaced the garbage can with a new bag she pushed open the back door and drug the trash out behind her. Ms. Ward sternly warned Val to never leave the trash bag on the ground, because it would attract rats. But when she tried to lift the trash it was too heavy for her to pick up. "I'm not going to throw my back out for a job I'm not even getting paid for." Val slid the bag behind the dumpster. She was sure Ms. Ward wouldn't find it. It was hidden too well.

When she turned to go back inside, her attention was drawn to the sound of metal smashing against the ground. Val couldn't help looking to see what was going on. She stuck her head out in the back alley. There she saw three kids around thirteen years old beating up an old man. Two kids held the man by his arms, while the other took the lid from the metal trashcan and slammed it against his head. Even from where she stood at she could see blood spill from the gash in the man's head.

Without thinking Val screamed out, "Hey, stop it."

The kids got scared when they saw her and took off running. She watched the man fall, curl his body into a fetal position and moan loudly.

Val ran as fast as she could to help him. "Are you all right?"

He looked up at her.

That's when she realized this man wasn't as old as she thought he was. Underneath the smudges of dirt that filled his face and tattered hat that covered his head she found young eyes. She noticed the filthy trench coat on his back, worn sneakers on his feet and gaping holes in his pants. Val had never seen a person her age look so shabby.

"I'm going to go get you some help," she said.

"Daddy?"

From behind an abandoned car that sat nearby a little girl appeared. Her eyes were full of fear. Hesitant to come any closer to her father, she kept a careful eye on Val.

"Hope." He waved for her to come nearer.

She quickly ran to his side. The little girl was so small and beautiful. Val thought she couldn't be any older than three years old. She reminded Val of a chocolate brown morsel with dark brown hair. Hope wrapped her arms around her father and cried. Val watched them for a moment before noticing the light purple spring jacket Hope wore was not enough to keep her warm.

"Listen, you were beat up pretty badly. I can get somebody to help you," Val said.

"No," he screamed. "Just help me get back into that car and I'll be fine," he demanded.

"What will you do if those kids come back? You're too hurt to defend yourself." Val was sure this man wasn't thinking clearly. He was in no condition to take care of himself and a young child.

"Those kids won't be back. They were searching for money. When they didn't find any on me they"—He cut his eyes at Val. "Forget it! Either help me or leave."

Offended by how rude he was, she wanted to leave him lying helpless on the ground. Then she saw his daughter struggling to help her father to his feet. Val's conscience wouldn't allow her to leave without giving a helping hand.

She struggled to lift him to his feet. After a few attempts, they were finally able to stumble over to the passenger side of the car.

"Hope, you lie in the back seat while Daddy sits in the front."

She did as her father asked. Then the man leaned back in the passenger seat and breathed a sigh of relief.

Val was stunned to learn that they were living out of a car. Their home sat on four cinder blocks. The front windshield was cracked, and the hood of the car was missing.

"I appreciate your help," he mumbled, "but you can go now, and please don't mention to anyone that you saw us." He winced in pain.

It was obvious he wasn't from Philadelphia. His thick Southern accent was a dead giveaway.

She stood wishing there was more she could do for them, when she heard Ms. Ward screeching her name.

"Val!"

By the sound of her call, Val knew she needed something else done. Val and the stranger looked at one another one last time before she dashed back toward the mission.

"Girl, where were you? We have dishes piling up in here."

"Sorry," was all Val could muster. She looked behind her one last time and back at the abandoned car before reporting back to the kitchen.

The remainder of the day seemed to drag on for Val. The hands on the clock appeared to have stopped, and Val kept checking her watch to make sure it read the right time.

At last, when Val thought Ms. Ward would never let her go, Kyle told her she could go home.

Anxious to get out of there before Ms. Ward noticed she was gone, Val quickly gathered her things and exited the building through the front door.

During her tour of the facility with Kyle, he'd mentioned that the biggest incentive of working at a mission was the leftover food the workers were rewarded with. Her lips formed a small grin when she looked down at the packages of food she was given from the mission.

Val managed to pack a couple bowls of hot soup, two loaves of bread and a six-pack of bottled water. She was sure Hope and her father would appreciate the food. Once she was outside she snuck around to the back of the building and went straight to where she had left the man and his daughter. She prayed they were still there.

When she walked up to the car she found them both soundly sleeping. She figured they were probably hungry, but she didn't want to disturb them, so she gently placed the food down on the ground and tiptoed away.

"Thanks for not saying anything earlier," the man said, causing Val to jump.

She turned to face him with her hand still on her heart.

"I'm sorry. Did I frighten you?"

"No. It's okay." Her heart was nearly beating out her chest. She pointed to the food she left on the ground. "I left you and Hope some food. It's not a lot, but I thought you might be hungry."

He looked back at his sleeping daughter. "Yeah, she usually gets hungry around this time." He picked up the soup container and took a spoonful. "It's still hot. Thank you."

"You know you are more than welcome to come into the mission to eat. It's all free and it's not half bad," Val joked.

"No, thank you. Hope and I are fine. Besides, Hope and I usually dig through the garbage and get the leftovers anyway."

The man missed the look of disgust that crossed Val's face.

"What's wrong with coming inside? At least you would have someplace dry and warm to eat your meal."

"Listen, I'm not taking my daughter into one of those places." He was hostile and talked to Val like she was the enemy.

"I didn't mean to upset you. I was trying to help," she whispered.

"Don't apologize. Past experiences have taught me that when you go into places like that they try to get all in your business, especially if you have children with you. I'm very private. I don't like people knowing much about me."

"Listen, they probably just want to help you. I'm sure they can probably get you off the street and possibly into your own home."

"We don't need their help." He tried to sit up in his seat, but when he did he cringed in pain.

"I can see that you're still in pain. Those kids put a hurting on you. You may need to see a doctor and have them check for any broken ribs."

"I'll be fine," he shouted.

When he said that, Hope woke up. She rubbed her eyes and glared strangely at Val.

"Hello," Val kindly spoke to the little girl, but Hope never answered back. She simply stared back at her with wide eyes. "She's so pretty. How old is she?" Val asked.

Her father looked at her suspiciously before answering. "She's three." Then he pointed to the driver's seat. "Honey, sit right here so I can feed you." He started talking to Val again. "You're lucky they didn't pull out a gun and kill you," the man said. "What were you thinking when you yelled out for them to stop?"

Val hadn't thought about how dangerous it was for her to interfere. "I wasn't thinking," she replied softly.

"What's your name?" he asked as he gave Hope her first spoonful of soup and a few slices of bread.

"Valencia, but they call me Val," she replied.

"Well, it's nice to meet you, Val. My name is Jonah, and as you already know, the sleeping beauty that has just woke from her slumber is my daughter Hope."

"You two live out here?" Val glanced around.

"Temporarily. We're out here until I come up with a new plan."

A light rain started to fall down around them. Val remembered the weatherman forecasted heavy torrential rains overnight. She couldn't dare go home to a warm bed and leave them to weather the storm all night in that old clunker. "Why don't you come home with me tonight?" Val realized she was being a bit impulsive by inviting a stranger into her home, but she couldn't leave him outside, injured and with a child to care for.

"Thanks for the offer, but we'll be fine. I've been taking care of us since she was eighteen months. We'll be fine."

"You've been on the streets that long?" Val screamed. "You don't have any family I can call to help you out?"

He gave a negative response.

She looked over at Hope. The bottom of her pigtails swept the top of her shoulders. Hope scarfed down her meal as if she hadn't eaten a decent meal in days.

"Do you want to come home with me?" Val asked Hope.

His daughter adamantly shook her head no. Then she didn't think twice before jumping into the safety of her father's lap.

He winced in pain. Hope cried, and so did her dad.

"I don't think your ribs are broken, probably just bruised, but if you come home with me, then I can wrap them up for you," Val suggested again. "If you still want to leave once I'm finished I'll bring you right back," she promised.

He was hesitant to accept help from a stranger, but he agreed, and she helped him out to her car.

Chapter 15

Jonah securely buckled Hope into the back seat before fastening his own seat belt. "How long have you been working at the mission?"

"Today was my first day. I'll be working there as a volunteer for the next few weeks."

"Why would a pretty girl like yourself work at a mission in her spare time?" Jonah had a lot of questions for her.

"It's a long story. One I would prefer to forget."

"Are you a lawyer?" Jonah continued to dig for information.

"What would make you think I was a lawyer?"

"I don't know." He glanced out his window. "I guess I don't know too many jobs that pay enough to drive a car like this."

Val wasn't ready to share her past, so she cleverly danced around his question. "Let's just say that right now I'm trying to find myself."

"The only people I know who use those words are the unemployed kind."

They laughed.

"You drive this expensive car, and I noticed the shoes on your feet probably cost more than it did to feed everyone who came to the mission today. Are you one of those spoiled kids whose parents buy them everything?"

"Are you trying to ask, am I privileged?" Val was more amused than insulted by Jonah's comments.

She made a turn toward Penn's Landing waterfront. This part of the city housed many wealthy celebrities, athletes, prominent city officials, doctors and lawyers. The neighborhood consisted of mostly townhouses and condominiums. It wasn't the ideal place to raise a family, but it was the perfect residence for a young couple just starting out like Val and Julian. That's why they purchased a lovely townhouse built on a small cobblestone lane protected by a huge wrought iron gate.

Val pulled her car up to a small stand that housed the keyboard she needed to unlock the gates. She wound down her window and tapped in the six-digit combination code. Then the mechanical gates opened wide. She drove around to the back of the house.

"It looks dark in there. You should always leave at least one light on in the house to ward off intruders," Jonah warned.

"Thanks for the tip." Val parked and turned off the engine. "I'll keep that in mind."

When they got out the car, they realized Hope had fallen fast asleep in the backseat, her head dropped down in front of her. When she started snoring, Val and Jonah laughed at her.

"Let me get her," Val offered. "You won't be able to carry her." When she scooped Hope into her arms, her eyes opened momentarily. Val was sure Hope would cry. Instead, she laid her head on Val's shoulder and went back to sleep.

When they approached the back door, Val juggled her house keys in one hand and Hope in the other. She tried to insert a key into the lock then realized it wasn't the right one. It had been months since she'd been at the house, and it was hard for her to remember which was the right key.

Jonah watched Val try several different keys before one finally turned the lock.

She pushed the door wide open.

"It looks like you had a hard time finding the right key," Jonah commented.

Val ignored his observation. "It's cold in here. If you don't mind, I can go lay her down in one of the guest bedrooms upstairs and then I'll turn on the heat."

Jonah stared at her holding his baby in his arms. He really didn't want Hope out his sight, but he allowed it. As Val disappeared up the back stairs Jonah switched on a few lights.

By the time she returned, she found him admiring the place.

"This house is an architect's dream. I was going to college for engineering before I had to drop out." He knocked on one of the wooden beams that supported the ceiling. "There's a lot you could do to this place. But by the look of things, you're just getting started." He pointed to the various boxes that were scattered around the room. "I guess you haven't had a chance to go furniture shopping yet."

Val looked around. The house was full of boxes, but there wasn't any furniture. She had forgotten about the boxes that were brought there weeks before her wedding. She and Julian decided not to unpack anything until after the honeymoon. Her mind was suddenly flooded with thoughts of the last time she was in the house.

"Valencia, right after we get married I want to start a family." Julian sat on the gray stone ledge right next to the fireplace with Val perched on his lap.

"I thought we decided to wait until after I finished law school," Val reminded him.

"Baby, I love you so much that I can't wait. I want us to create something that is a part of both you and me."

"You wouldn't happen to be feeling this way because the guy you play with just had a set of twins?"

His face turned guilty.

"Baby, I promise our time will come. Plus, I don't think either of our parents will rest until they hear they have a grandbaby on the way."

"Val. Val."

She looked up and realized she had been caught day-dreaming.

"It looks like you left me for a second."

"No, I'm fine." She noticed Jonah sitting on the steps holding his side. "I'm sorry. I brought you here to get bandages and I'm in my own world. Let me go check the upstairs and see if there's anything here I can use. If not, I'll run to the corner store."

"You don't have to go out your way," Jonah yelled after her.

"It's no problem," Val screamed back. She searched the entire master bathroom but couldn't find one Band-Aid. When she returned to the first floor she began searching for her purse. "I'm gonna have to run out. I won't be long. It should take me no more than ten minutes." She spotted her purse lying on the kitchen counter, picked it up and raced toward the front door.

"I'll be right here." Jonah pointed to where he was sitting. "Val." He stopped her right before she closed the front door behind her. "Can you pick me up some over-the-counter pain killers? My side is throbbing."

Val hurried to the store and within minutes was back home again. "Jonah!" she cried. The last thing he expected to see was him laid out on the floor with his eyes closed. She panicked and dropped everything in her hand. "Oh God, please let him be all right. I knew we should have gone to the hospital." She checked his pulse.

"Hey, you back already?" Jonah opened one eye.

"You had me worried." She breathed a sigh of relief. "I thought you were unconscious."

He laughed. "No. Just tired. This floor is so comfortable. It beats sleeping in an old car any day." He wearily pushed himself up against the nearest wall.

"My offer still stands. You're more than welcome to stay the night. There are four bedrooms upstairs. I don't have much food, but what I have we can share."

"The Bible says, 'Share your food with the hungry and give shelter to the homeless,'" Jonah recited.

"Isaiah 58:7."

Val was shocked that he was familiar with scripture.

"My grandmother was a Sunday School teacher for forty-three years, and as her only grandson, she said it was important for me to memorize verses of wisdom. She said if we carried God's word in our hearts then we would never get lost."

"She sounds like a very wise woman." Val picked up everything she had dropped on the floor and placed them back in the bag.

"I can't get over how beautiful your home is," Jonah commented.

"Yes, it is a nice house."

Jonah heard the sadness in her voice when she referred to the structure as a house and not a home.

She carried all the first-aid items over to him. "Can you take your coat off?"

Jonah slowly slipped out his coat and pulled his shirt up as far as it would go without causing too much pain.

Val knelt down beside him on her knees and wrapped around his ribs with medical tape.

"I would never mistake you as a nurse." He sighed.

"Did I do a bad job?" She tore off the tape and sat back on her knees to admire her work.

"No, but I can hardly breathe." Jonah gasped for air. "Did you tape me up this tight on purpose so that me and my daughter couldn't leave?"

"I'm sorry. Let me try again." She carefully tore the tape away from his body. The second time she was mindful to allow enough room for him to breathe comfortably.

"Hope must really be tired; she doesn't normally sleep this long," Jonah said.

"When's the last time she's slept in a bed?" Val dropped a couple pain pills in her hand and handed them to Jonah.

"It's been a while." He swallowed the pills simultaneously without any water.

"I would have gotten you a bottle of water," Val said.

"Sorry, I guess I'm used to living off the most basic needs. A house, food, water and heat; those are things that most people take for granted."

"Why don't you take my offer to stay the night? If not for yourself, then for your daughter. She looks so peaceful sleeping in that king-size bed."

"I guess it wouldn't hurt for Hope to sleep in a real bed instead of the back seat of that old sixty-nine Chevy."

"Great! I'll go make up the guest bedroom for you and you'll be right across the hall from Hope so if she wakes up you won't be far," Val rattled off.

"That's okay. You don't have to go to any trouble for me. I'll squeeze in the bed right next to Hope."

"Are you sure? Like I said, I have four bedrooms upstairs. I'm sure you would be more comfortable sleeping in your own bed."

Jonah shook his head. "Hope and I are used to roughing it out together; sleeping in a soft comfortable bed for one night will make me soft." Jonah followed her to the room where Hope was sleeping. He took off his shoes and made a comfortable spot for himself in the corner. When he pulled the cap off his head, his hair revealed itself. A mass of un-kempt soft brown curls filled his head.

Val pretended not to notice how ruggedly sexy he looked. "If you need anything just yell." She closed the door behind her and retired to the master bedroom.

"Good-night," Jonah yelled before switching off the lights. In the dark he thought about Val. She was beautiful, intelligent and kind, but it was hard for him to trust any-body. He feared that any strangers trying to get close to him and his daughter would do them harm. He wanted to be-lieve that wasn't the case with Val, but he wasn't sure. That's why he chose to sleep in the same room as Hope. He would have peace of mind that Hope was safe if he slept close to her.

Val locked her bedroom door and collapsed on her king-size bed. The ceiling lights blinded her. She never expected to be back in this house again. Not without Julian. The re-altor called her several times to put the house back on the market per Val's request, but she never returned the call. The house and everything in it was the proof she needed to prove that Julian wasn't just a figment of her imagination. It verified that her dreams were at one time true. She was happy, in love and about to become somebody's wife. Until one day it all vanished. The box with Julian's name scrib-bled in marker taunted her. She ripped it open and the aroma from his cologne drifted past her nose. A box full of his toiletries. Tears gathered in her eyes, but she refused to cry any more. "No more tears." She quickly closed the box, grabbed a blanket and slept in one of the guest bedrooms.

The following morning Jonah lurched forward out of his sleep. He looked around confused at his surroundings. The luxurious silk sheets and brilliant white walls were foreign to him, until he saw Hope sitting in the middle of the floor playing with a stuffed talking dolphin.

"Hey, Daddy." She held up the doll. "See. His name is Ed."

He quickly recollected his thoughts and remembered where he was. "Where's Val at?"

Hope shrugged her shoulders.

As Jonah got up out of bed, he felt a little better. He slightly bent to the side. "My ribs must be healing." He held out his hand. "Come on, honey. Let's go see if we can find Val, so we can tell her good-bye." They wandered around upstairs still unable to find her.

Twenty minutes later Val rushed in the back door. She dropped several shopping bags down on the table and yelled, "Is anyone here?" She listened for sounds of movement in the house, but it was quiet.

"We're up here," she heard Jonah yell from upstairs.

Val followed the sound of his voice to the master bathroom. When she walked in she found Hope up to her neck in bubbles taking a bath.

"I hope you don't mind," Jonah explained. "When we saw how big your bathtub was we couldn't resist. This is like a swimming pool to Hope. She was so excited, I allowed her to take a bath."

Val giggled to herself. "No, that's fine. I'm glad to see you're still here." She turned toward Hope. "Did you get a good night's sleep?"

Hope looked at her with empty eyes and reached out for her father.

"She doesn't like me?" Val said.

"No, don't think that. It takes her a while to warm up to people. It even took her a while to trust me."

Val gave him a strange look. She wondered what he meant by that. *Why would it take his own daughter a while to trust him?* Val's interest in her houseguests just rose through the roof. Val assumed Jonah was just another overprotective father, but there could be other reasons why.

She tried to play it off as if she wasn't suspicious. "I picked us up some breakfast and bought Hope some new clothes. That's what took me so long. I'll go get her things." Val bolted down the stairs. Her cell phone lay on the kitchen table. She thought about calling the police, but she wasn't sure what to tell them. She tapped her foot against the floor. She was running out of time. "Jonah could be a kidnapper. There could be people out there searching for Hope." She stepped toward her phone, but stopped herself. "I need proof. The police won't do anything without evidence. I know what I'll do."

Before returning to the bathroom Val straightened out her composure. "I also picked up a few items for you. I'm not sure if they'll fit, but I figured you could use them."

Jonah helped Hope step out the tub and dry off. "Thanks. If you don't mind, can you help Hope get dressed? I'm going to use the hallway bathroom to wash up and change. It won't take me long."

"Sure." While Val helped Hope get dressed, she figured this may be her only chance at finding out any details about Hope and her father. "Hope, do you know your last name?"

Hope was aloof toward her. She didn't speak and avoided looking in Val's direction.

"Where's your mommy?"

The little girl's eyes were emotionless.

"She's not going to answer you." Jonah snuck up from behind Val. "She still considers you a stranger, and so do I."

"I was just trying to—" Val was at a loss for words.

"You were just trying to find out about me and my daughter. If you wanted to know about her mother you could have asked me." Jonah grabbed Hope's coat and shoes and threw on his own hat, coat and shoes. "Come on, Hope. Let's go."

"Please don't go. I brought you something to eat. At least eat first."

"That's all right. You may try to lift my fingerprints from off the glasses." He grabbed Hope's hand, and they left out the door.

Val watched them walk down her sidewalk, away from the house. She prayed he took Hope somewhere nice with the twenty dollars she slipped inside his coat pocket.

Chapter 16

Colin dribbled the basketball in front of Dean, teasing him. "Come on, Dean. What's the problem?" He grinned. "You're wheezing like an old man."

"Old man." Dean stole the ball out of Colin's hands and stepped around him to make an easy basket.

Dean laughed, threw the ball to Colin and slowly made his way over to the benches. He grabbed his Temple sports bottle and collapsed onto the bench.

It wasn't unusual to find the two men at war on the basketball court any given Saturday. Colin was very athletic and loved all sports. Dean wasn't as competitive as Colin, but there were some sports he excelled at, and one of them was basketball.

"Man, what's up with you?" Colin watched him drink the entire container. "We usually play at least three of four games before you need a break. We haven't even finished the first game."

Dean grinned. "I'm getting old. Everybody can't be as young as you."

Colin sat down next to him.

"So finish telling me what happened when you went into Baxter's office."

"Well, I didn't go in there going ballistic. I prayed that morning and asked the Holy Spirit, 'What would Jesus do?' I really didn't expect God to answer, but He did. When I walked into Baxter's office, I felt tranquility overcome me. It was like being in a room filled with the presence of the Lord. I calmly and professionally explained to Baxter how offended I was by what he said. In the end he apologized and said that he didn't mean anything by it."

"Do you believe him?" Dean wasn't convinced it was that easy. "I mean, there is such a thing as unintentional racism. Some people are bigots and they don't even know it."

"I thought about that when it first happened, but I'm not going to hold this one incident against him. It happened, he apologized, that's the end of it."

"Well, I have some great news to share," Dean stated loudly. "I asked Olivia to marry me."

"Congratulations!" Colin gave Dean a firm handshake. "I knew it would only be a matter of time."

"I couldn't allow her to get away from me. She completes me. Every time I look at her I see my blessing. I can't stop praising God for having favor on me. When she's in my presence, I feel like she has me under a spell, because no other woman can compare."

"Dean, a lot of people don't realize how blessed they are to have a woman like Olivia until it's too late." Colin stood up and dribbled the basketball.

"Man, I'd be honored if you stood up with me as my best man at my wedding."

Colin was caught off guard by Dean's request. He wasn't expecting Dean to ask him to be a part of the wedding. "I wouldn't miss it for the world." He held the basketball in his hand. "What's up with your grandpa? You haven't said anything about his case. You know the whole church stands behind him. Those allegations are preposterous."

"I can't worry about my grandpa. I'm going to go on with my life. I wish him the best."

Colin gave an awkward look. "Man, I know it may be hard to read the horrible things they print in the daily newspaper, but don't allow one reporter's opinion of the case put doubt in your mind about a man who has been like a martyr to the black community."

"What if you put all your trust in my grandpa and he's not what you thought he was?"

Colin guessed there was more to the story than what he knew. "He's only a man, and man shouldn't judge man. We can't expect him not to have made any mistakes. Your grandpa has genuine love in his heart for God and all God's children. Black or white. Latino or Asian. It doesn't matter to him. Maybe you need to do some soul-searching and ask God to reveal what's blinding your heart from seeing the truth. I'll pray for you, and when you're ready to share, I'll be here."

"Colin, there is something I haven't told you yet."

Colin saw fear in his friend's eyes.

Before Dean could say anything, his breathing became erratic. He clutched at his chest and fell to the ground.

"Dean!" Colin hollered out. He tilted Dean's head back and tried to breathe life back into him. He pumped down on his chest for three counts and tried again. Seconds later Dean was gasping for air. Colin pulled his cell phone out his gym bag and dialed 9-1-1.

Colin told the operator where they were, and it seemed like a lifetime before he heard the ambulance sirens in the background. "Hold on, Dean! The paramedics are on the way." Colin could see Dean was still having a hard time breathing on his own.

Finally, the paramedics arrived. They lifted Dean onto a

stretcher and placed an oxygen mask over his face. As they rolled him away, he reached out for Colin and moved the mask from his face.

Colin bent down close to his mouth. Dean whispered Olivia's name. Colin ran to his car, and the first thing he did was call Olivia.

Across town at the bridal boutique Olivia, Val and Danyelle searched for dresses. Olivia searched the racks for the perfect gown. Plus, she had to find dresses for her maid of honor, Danyelle, and bridesmaids, Tressie and Val.

"Val, are you sure you're all right?" Olivia asked from inside the changing room. She worried that Val would have a mental breakdown from being around so many wedding dresses.

"Would you stop asking me that? I'm fine." Val looked around for Danyelle. She spotted her lounging in one of the plush leather chairs. Her feet were propped up on the footstool while drinking sparkling apple cider and munching on sweet strawberries from a fruit tray.

Val walked over and poured herself a glass. "Look what the cat done drug in." Val sipped from her glass and watched Tressie sashay through the store like a runway model.

Danyelle turned around just in time to see Tressie pick up a burgundy bridesmaid dress from off the rack.

"I love this. They have this hanging in the window. This is the dress for me."

Danyelle studied the dress. "It's cute, but they don't have that dress in the color we need."

"We already checked." Val sat down in the lounge chair next to Danyelle.

"Damn." Tressie looked up towards the sky. "Lord, I didn't mean that. Maybe I can get Livie to change the color," Tressie reasoned out loud.

"I don't think so," Danyelle told her. "Anyway, it's too late for Olivia to change the color scheme of the reception."

"I wouldn't change the colors anyway," Olivia hollered from the dressing room, "because it's my wedding."

Tressie sucked her teeth and leaned against the wall.

"Where you been at?" Val asked. "You were supposed to meet us here forty five minutes ago."

"They had me sitting in court all day long for jury selection. It was a complete waste of time," Tressie replied.

"I guess that means you weren't chosen," Danyelle said.

"I think I would have been chosen if it weren't for the fact that every black man that entered the courtroom in shackles and jailhouse clothes I knew."

Val and Danyelle laughed.

"I couldn't believe it. I knew every single one of those guys. It was embarrassing. Once I found the courage to raise my hand, the judge would call me out, and then I had to ask to be excused because I was an acquaintance of the defendant. It got to the point where the judge would start the selection off by asking me, did I know the accused."

Danyelle laughed even harder.

"I even saw Payce's best friend, Darshon, there."

"That goes to show you that you need to start having a better choice of friends," Val said.

"All those people are from my past. It's not my fault that fate brought a bunch of shady characters in my life."

"Don't blame fate for your mistakes," Danyelle replied.

They waited outside the dressing room another ten minutes before Danyelle got tired of eating fruit. She stood up and marched toward the stall Olivia was in. She banged on the dressing room door. "Would you hurry up? Livie, it doesn't take that long to try on no dress."

Customers standing close by turned to look at the commotion Danyelle was causing.

Olivia slightly opened the door and looked around for

her sister. "How can you expect me to do this all by myself? Most of these dresses weigh more than I do. Could you help me out?" She turned around so Danyelle could button up the back of the dress she had on.

"Okay, you two are making a scene." Val stepped in between the two of them. She turned toward Danyelle. "Stop upsetting the bride-to-be."

The perky and vibrant Bridal Boutique sales clerk came over with more dresses for Olivia to try on. "Here you are." She handed Danyelle four more wedding dresses.

"More dresses?" Danyelle questioned.

"Yes, your sister said she would like to try these on, and since you're not only the bride's sister, but also the maid of honor I figured that you could hold the dresses while she tries each one on."

"I thought that was your job," Danyelle dryly replied, but the sales clerk giggled her way to the far end of the store.

Olivia spun around to face the girls. Like children with a staring problem each one of her friends looked at her, but didn't say a word. The smile quickly faded from Olivia's face. "What's wrong?" She stood in front of the mirror. "Does the dress look that bad?" She turned toward them.

Danyelle set the dresses she was holding down on a nearby chair and walked up to her sister with tears in her eyes. "Livie, you look just like Mommy. If I hadn't seen you go into that room, I would have thought you were her."

Olivia was relieved. "You really think so?"

Danyelle turned her sister around to face the mirror. "I think this is the dress for you."

Olivia didn't realize how much this dress resembled her mother's. The simple country linen dress with delicate pearl beading was practically an exact replica.

"Oh, my!" Madge, the sales clerk, walked up and placed her hand over her open mouth. "I have never seen a bride look lovelier. Isn't she breathtaking?" She nudged Danyelle.

"I think I'm going to take it," Olivia said.

"All right." She took one final glance at the dress. "I don't even think it needs any alterations. If you go into the dressing room I'll bag this up for you."

Tressie helped Olivia unsnap the back buttons, and Olivia went back into the dressing room to change.

Olivia admired herself in the mirror. It was still hard for her to believe she was getting married. "Olivia!" Her sister's big mouth frightened her. "What's taking you so long? The sales lady is out here waiting for you."

Olivia pulled the dress over the top of her head and put back on her own clothes. As she was tying up her sneakers, she noticed a missed call on her cell phone.

As she listened to her messages she got scared when she heard Colin's message. He didn't say what happened, but he did say he was on the way to the hospital and that she should get there as soon as possible.

Adrenaline pumped Olivia's heart so fast that she broke out in a sweat. The walls seemed to close in around her and she couldn't breathe. She grabbed hold of the wall and finished putting on her sneakers then dashed out the store and toward her car.

"Olivia! Olivia!" Danyelle called after her sister, but Olivia never turned around.

In the hospital Colin sat next to a sleeping Dean. He hadn't left Dean's side since they arrived. Colin pushed back in his chair. Scenes of how Dean collapsed to the ground flashed before his eyes. That was a scary moment for Colin.

A doctor entered the emergency room cubicle and introduced himself. "Has he been sleeping long?" the doctor asked.

"Since, I've been here," Colin replied.

"I'm not 'sleep." Dean rubbed his eyes to adjust to the bright light. "Just resting my eyes."

"Good. Is it all right if I speak in front of your friend?" After Dean nodded, the doctor sat on the side of Dean's hospital bed. "I spoke with your doctor and he told me that he was very clear when he explained that, because of your condition, you were instructed to take it easy."

"Doc, I was just playing a little ball," Dean complained.

"Basketball is too much for your body to handle. You may have thought the weather was cool enough for you to run up and down the basketball court under the sun, but that drains your energy. That is why you collapsed. You have to get some rest, Mr. West. No more strenuous exercise." He handed Dean a few papers and a pen. "Sign here and you can go."

Dean signed his release forms and threw his legs over the side of the bed.

"Man, what condition is the doctor talking about?" Colin asked.

"Man, I'm sick."

Colin looked down at Colin's shaking hands and knew that Dean was scared. "What's wrong with you?"

Then the white curtain opened up, and in rushed Olivia. "Honey, what happened?" She ran and wrapped her arms around Dean's neck. "Are you all right?"

"I'm fine." He gave Colin a look to keep quiet. "I think we were playing a little bit too hard. The doctor said I was dehydrated and exhausted. He recommended rest."

Olivia helped him down from off the bed. "Well, no more basketball for you."

They walked out the emergency room together, leaving Colin to wonder what was wrong with his friend.

Chapter 17

Reverend Simms repeated a conversation he overheard between a pair of ladies right before the start of service.

"I betcha he's guilty," the one woman said while the other nodded her head in agreement. "All white people are prejudiced."

That woman's words bothered him. Still lost in a daze, Reverend Simms watched the ushers signal to one another that it was time to take collection.

Suddenly, he jumped up from his seat and spoke into the microphone, "Excuse me, before we take collection I would like to take a moment to address the situation with Judge West."

The ushers stopped what they were doing and stood against the far wall.

"The judge and I had a pleasant visit not too long ago, and a handful of you will be glad to know that despite his circumstances he is doing well."

"Amen!" one of the deacons shouted from the first pew.

"I'm sure everyone here has heard about the disturbing accusations against the judge, and I know a lot of people think we should turn our backs on him."

A few people in the audience mumbled, "Yes."

"I'm not standing before you to plead the judge's case, because that's not my job. I'm standing before you because I feel it necessary to remind the members of this church and of this community how much Judge West has done for us."

A lot of condemned souls looked down at the floor, and no one spoke a word.

"Jesus died not just for me and you, but also for the President of the United States. He died for the Taliban and he also died for the skinheads, Klan members and the Nazi party. You may think God only cares about the good people, but He cares about all people, and it doesn't matter what we've done in the past. Once we accept Christ, those sins are wiped clear from the slate."

Reverend Simms tried to look a few people in the eye, but they refused to look his way.

"The only person who can respond to the allegations being brought against Judge West is Judge West, but I thought now would be the perfect time to remind this community of the countless number of times the judge has come through to help us. He has been a pillar of this community. He's stood up for us so many times. Can't we stand behind him right now?"

The audience clapped their hands.

Then Reverend Simms motioned for Reverend Baxter, to join him in the front of the church.

"First Nazareth, it's a pleasure to be here with you again, and I wish it were under better circumstances. Listen, I don't know Judge West that well, but from the few times that we did speak I could tell he was a giving person. Reverend Simms asked me to come here today to tell you about the defense fund I've set up on behalf of Judge West. He is going to need the best representation, and I contributed the first five thousand dollars for the lawyer's retainer fee, but it's going to cost a whole lot more."

"Yes," Reverend Simms spoke loudly into the mic he held in his hand. "That is why I plan to donate this Sunday's offering and a percentage of each Sunday's offering until Judge West is released. First Nazareth, I'm asking you to dig down in your pockets and help us help one of own during his time of need."

Reverend Baxter and Simms watched as people pulled out bills and wrote out checks to put in that morning's offering.

"Reverend Baxter, it looks like every member of my congregation's heart has been open. Why don't we hold a benefit concert in the park on Germantown Avenue? That way, we can get the entire community involved."

Reverend Baxter smiled broadly. "That sounds wonderful, and if you need any assistance with it, please give me a call."

"Which do you want first, the good news or the bad?"

A week had gone by since Val had heard or seen from Jonah and Hope. She worried about them, but there wasn't much she could do. At the mission Val often volunteered to take out the trash. Up to four times a day she would check out the old, abandoned car for any sign of them, but the car remained empty, and it didn't look like they had been back there since she last saw them.

Val gave up all hope of ever seeing either of them again, until Jonah stormed into the mission yelling her name. She was in the middle of mopping the dining hall floor when Jonah charged in her direction. By the look on his face she knew something was seriously wrong. Hope was missing from her father's side.

"They took her," Jonah shouted. "My daughter's gone."

Val dropped the mop and pulled him over to the corner of the room.

Ms. Ward stared at them from the kitchen.

"What happened? Where's Hope?" Val talked very low in an attempt to try to calm Jonah down.

He talked so fast that Val couldn't understand a word he was saying. The more he talked, the louder he got, so she took him by the arm and led him outside so they could talk in private.

Jonah slammed his fist into the palm of his hand and screamed out in anger. "She's gone!" His reaction startled Val.

She watched him pace in front of her like a madman before trying again. "Why don't you relax and tell me what happened?"

Jonah stopped and allowed the cool spring air to caress his face and dry his tears before explaining. "Hope and I found an empty lot to sleep in. It had about six or seven abandoned cars surrounding. The area looked almost like a junkyard. Hope and I were out late last night. She was tired and was getting cranky, so I figured it would be all right if we slept in one of those cars until morning. I planned to leave early enough so that no one would ever know we were there. I woke at dawn and Hope was still sleeping. I knew she was exhausted, so instead of waking her up, I figured I could run to the corner store with the last of that twenty dollars you put in my pocket and get us something to eat."

Val shifted her eyes to hide her guilt.

"I was gone less than twenty minutes. By the time I returned to the lot, she was gone."

"Did you search the area? Maybe she got up and went looking for you."

"No. The entire car was gone. When I returned, I saw a tow truck pulling the car down the street. I yelled to the driver, but he couldn't hear me. There was another tow truck loading up one of the other cars, and I told him that my daughter was in the back seat of that car. He called the other driver on his cell phone, and the guy did stop, checked the car and found Hope."

"Well, where is she at?"

"After he found her, he called the cops. The guy I was talking to said they were required to report any children found in the cars they towed. When I heard that, I got scared and ran." He pulled his hat off his head and threw it on the ground. "They're going to take my daughter, aren't they?"

"I don't know, but I'll do what I can to help you get her back. Stay right here."

Val went to Kyle's office and told him she had to leave because of a family emergency. Then she rushed out of the mission and to her car. She and Jonah left together and went back to her house to make a few phone calls.

"I don't understand why the driver didn't notice a little girl in the car." Val held her cell phone pressed against her ear and was searching in her purse for a pen.

"I can't blame him. He probably never knew she was in there. I told her that if anyone was to ever come up to the car and I wasn't around that she was to hide on the floor and not move until I got back."

"How often do you leave your daughter alone?"

"Not often, but there were times when I would have to steal the things we needed to survive, and I preferred not to do those kinds of things in front of her."

Val contacted the Philadelphia Police Department, and they transferred her to the Department of Family and Children Services. Now she was on hold.

Finally somebody picked up the line who could help her.

"Yes, I'm trying to locate a little girl who may have been placed in your custody earlier today. She was found in the back of an abandoned car," Val explained. "Sure I'll hold." Val rested against the kitchen island. "Yes, you do have her."

Jonah moved closer.

"Well, I'm representing the girl's father as legal counsel, and we would like to petition the court for an immediate custody hearing." Val wrote a few things down on the notepad in front of her. "Thank you. I'll be there tomorrow morning to file the appropriate papers." She disconnected the call.

"You're a lawyer?" he asked.

"Not exactly. I'm taking a break from law school."

"Well, what did they say?"

"We need to file a petition for custody with the Department of Family and Children Services. It's imperative that you find a job and a permanent place to live—today! The first thing the judge is going to want to know is why you were living in an abandoned car with a three-year-old child."

"You sound just like a lawyer," Jonah said.

Val sat on a kitchen stool next to Jonah and took hold of his hand. "Jonah, if there's anything you're not telling me about you and Hope, you have to tell me now."

He looked away, as if the truth could be seen through his eyes.

"If I don't know everything, then you're limiting the amount of help I can offer you and Hope."

Jonah saw sincerity in Val's eyes and knew he had no choice but to trust her. He placed his hands over his head. "I came here from New Orleans. After Katrina hit, we were one of the families who were rescued out of the Ninth Ward. We came to Philly because I was told I could get a job at one of the refineries. When we first arrived, the help the city provided was great. They helped me find a job, a place to live, and they even gave me money to help with daycare, since Hope was still an infant. Then the economy started to slump, and the refineries started cutting back. First, they cut my hours to part time, and then I was laid off indefinitely. I couldn't find another job. Unemployment ran out. The bills started to pile up. I couldn't pay my rent, and we were evicted. That's how we ended up on the streets."

"What about Hope's mother?"

"By the time we realized the storm was a category five, there wasn't anywhere for us to go. We were trapped. The floodwaters started rising, and we had to climb to the roof of my house for safety. It was horrible. Hope's mother held onto me, but the winds were so strong that I couldn't hold on to both her and the baby at the same time." Jonah put emphasis on his words to express how bad it was. "We were on the roof, and the water was around my waist. I held Hope above water and I held on to her mother for as long as I could, but I was losing all my strength. She shouted for me to not let her go, but the baby was crying and I had to either use both hands to save the baby or use both hands to save her. I chose the baby, and when I did the current swept her underwater. I searched for her for weeks. I prayed that she may have possibly survived, but it's been over two years and I still haven't heard anything. That is how I was left with Hope."

Tears formed in Val's eyes. She had seen the devastation of Katrina on television, but to hear an actual survivor tell his story was heartbreaking. She wiped away tears and realized Jonah wasn't a kidnapper. He was a hero. Val commended him for saving his daughter's life. She felt horrible for thinking the worst of him and wanted to help him out.

"Jonah, if you expect to get Hope back, then you'll need a permanent address. You can stay here until you get on your feet, and I'll call around to see if I can hook you up with a job someplace."

"Thanks, Val. I appreciate everything you've done for us so far."

"Don't thank me yet. The battle has just begun."

Chapter 18

"Are you ready?" Val glanced at her watch. It was getting late, and she wanted to make sure they arrived in court on time.

Jonah stood in the bathroom fumbling with his tie.

Val pushed his hands away and neatly fastened the tie. "Are you nervous?" Val could see balls of sweat forming on his forehead.

"No, I'm not nervous. Just anxious to see what the judge is going to say." Jonah brushed past her and descended the stairs.

She heard the back door open then close. He couldn't fool her. She knew he was worried about the hearing.

For days Jonah had scoured the city in search of a job, but like most major cities, Philly was experiencing a decline in the job market. Discouraged, Jonah felt like a failure. He knew how important it was for him to walk into this hearing employed. Being unemployed would prolong the process in getting Hope back.

In the car, Jonah was plagued with worry over Hope. This was the longest they had ever been separated. He prayed for God to keep her safe, but every time he opened the newspaper, there was another story of a child being abused, starved and treated inhumanely.

"God, if You keep her safe, I'll never do anything this stupid again."

When they stepped inside the courtroom doors, Jonah let the door close on her.

"Jonah!"

He looked at her unknowingly.

"You didn't hold the door for me."

"I'm sorry," he replied.

They grabbed two seats on the last row in the courtroom and waited for the hearing to begin.

"Are you hot?" she asked him.

Jonah wiped sweat off his forehead again.

"You've been sweating since we left the house," she replied. "It's probably nerves. Did I tell you how nice you look?"

Jonah smiled for the first time that morning.

Julian's suits were a bit long in the length for Jonah, but Val asked her tailor to hem the pants. Now the suit looked like it was made for him. It felt weird seeing him dressed in Julian's things, but it was for a good cause. Val shrugged off those bad feelings because this was for a good cause. Julian always said to be generous to others.

The closer it got to the eight o'clock hour, the more people piled into the courtroom. By the time a court official entered the room, it was standing room only. Every seat was full, forcing groups of people to line up against the walls.

The court official walked to the front of the room. She spoke loudly enough that she didn't need a microphone to address the crowd. "When I call your name, please gather your things and follow me through that door." She pointed to the door she entered through.

Because of her strong Russian accent it was difficult for Val to understand what the woman was saying. Everyone in the room must have felt the same way, because the room was silent.

Dressed in a dark blue pinstriped suit with matching wedges, the woman scanned her list until she came to her first name. "Rodriguez."

Two women seated in the center aisle excused themselves through the crowd and proceeded through the door.

Three hours later they were still sitting in the blazing courtroom. Val used her hand to fan herself. "I feel like I'm going to melt." She sat up when she saw the Russian woman come out the room. "Please let her call our name."

"Gaines," she yelled then disappeared back behind closed doors.

"What's taking so long?"

"You know how the courts are. These things take time," Val reasoned.

After sitting there for most of the day Jonah's name was finally called. Inside the conference room sat a long cherry wood table. A library of books aligned the left wall, and a huge glass window magnified the Philly skyline. In the corner of the room sat a huge industrial fan that blew hot air across Val's face.

The court official escorted them in and offered them seats before exiting out the rear door.

Seated across the table from them was a man they assumed was the judge, from the official black judicial robe he wore. A woman sitting next to him, scribbled notes on a note pad. The beautiful crown of silver hair that covered her head made her look older than she was.

"I apologize for such a long wait. When I came into work this morning, I found out the air conditioning system malfunctioned overnight. It's just my luck that when the temperatures soar close to ninety degrees there's no air to keep me cool. The whole building has been suffering, but I figured it would be cooler to hold the hearings in here instead of the courtroom."

When the judge smiled, Val could feel the warmth from the sincerity in his voice fill the room. The more she looked at him, the more he reminded her of Santa Claus, because of his huge pot belly and long white beard.

The judge opened a manila folder and reviewed its contents. "I assume you're the father?" He posed his question toward Jonah. "Let me introduce you to Mrs. Chambers. She is the case manager in charge of Hope's case."

"Are you his lawyer?" the judge asked Val.

"No, my name is Valencia Benson. I'm just a friend here for support." She smiled broadly at the misinterpretation. It was flattering to be mistaken for a lawyer. To her that meant she looked the part; all that was missing was her degree.

"Mr. Reynolds, let's begin." The judge cleared his throat. "First, I'm curious about the circumstances that led you to take up residence inside an abandoned car with a small child." The judge's face turned serious.

Val could tell that Judge Cohen was a sweet man, but he was also serious when it came down to business.

Jonah repeated the same story he had told Val. He wrung his hands from nervousness and prayed that the judge would have mercy on him. He missed Hope so much.

"Mr. Reynolds, I understand that when citizens have to rely on assistance from the city that every once in a while some people may slip through the cracks and go unnoticed. Unfortunately, this had to happen to you. I'm sorry for everything you had to endure; however, I can't return Hope to your custody until I'm sure she will be properly taken care of. Now"—He folded his hands in front of him—"what are you going to do to turn this situation around?"

Jonah cleared his throat. "Your Honor. I'm temporarily staying at Ms. Benson's house until I can find a place of my own."

"What about a job?"

"I'm still looking, but it shouldn't be long before some-one hires me."

"Young lady, are you prepared to help him take care of his daughter?" the judge asked Val.

"Yes, Your Honor."

"What is it that you do?"

"Last semester I was in law school, but I'm sitting this se-mester out because of personal reasons."

The judge was puzzled. "So you don't have a job?"

Val shook her head no.

"Your Honor, if it would help Jonah get his daughter back then I can get a job," Val offered.

"No, young lady. The sole responsibility lies on Jonah's shoulders."

He grabbed a pen and talked while he wrote some things down. "Mr. Reynolds, I don't know if the heat is affecting my judgment, but I'm going to give you a chance to right this wrong. First, you have to get a job. Then I'm going to have Mrs. Chambers set up an in-home study to check out your place to make sure it's suitable for a child. Once you submit three consecutive paystubs and you pass a home in-spection, then Hope can go home with you."

Jonah smiled broadly.

"Mrs. Chambers will contact you to let you know when she'll be stopping by."

"Thanks, Your Honor."

"Don't thank me yet. Make me proud and get your daughter back."

As Jonah stood up to leave, Val posed a question toward the judge. "Your Honor, what about visits? Is it possible for Jonah to visit with Hope in the meantime?"

The judge looked to Mrs. Chambers for help with that question.

"I think I can best answer that question." She folded her

hands in front of her. "Hope has already been placed in a foster home with a loving couple. Unfortunately, the couple frowns upon visits with members from the children's family, especially parents. They feel as though it disrupts the stable home they're trying to provide for the child, but I'm sure if I make a phone call they will allow you supervised visits."

"Supervised visits? With my own daughter?"

"Mr. Reynolds, don't forget we're doing you a favor. Either abide by our rules or suffer the consequences. It's up to you."

Val patted Jonah on his arm. "It'll be all right. Just go along with it."

"I apologize for getting out of line like that." He turned to Mrs. Chambers. "Anything you can do will be greatly appreciated."

"I'll give them a call in the morning," she responded before jotting a note down in her daily planner.

Chapter 19

Colin knocked twice on Reverend Simms's office door before rushing in. On the opposite side, Reverend Simms was in deep talk with Dean.

Colin had not spoken to Dean since he was released from the hospital. His calls went unanswered and his messages ignored, but Dean could no longer hide. Today was his wedding.

Reverend Simms greeted Colin with a firm handshake. "Now that the best man has arrived, I'm going to go make sure everything is on schedule in the sanctuary." Reverend Simms left the two of them alone.

"You look good." Colin playfully punched him in the arm. "You haven't been back out on those basketball courts, have you?"

"Man, please don't lecture me. I get enough of that from my doctor."

"That's his job, to keep you as healthy as possible." Colin pulled up a chair. "Are you going to confess and tell me what really went down last week? What put you in the hospital, and why don't you want to tell Olivia?"

Dean sighed. "I have cancer."

Colin's head dropped down in front of him. Dean's revelation was hard to swallow. He couldn't believe it. Colin got
up and walked to the other side of the room.

"The doctors told me I could die if I didn't get any treat-
ment, but those procedures are so exhausting. Afterwards, I
feel sick and sluggish. I might as well be dead because I'm
missing out on life."

"But if that's going to keep you alive, then I think it's
worth it. Don't you?"

"Is it? Is it really worth it? How am I supposed to teach
Bryce how to play baseball? Or make love to my wife when
I can't even muster up the strength to get up out the bed?"

"I'd rather lie in a sick bed than my death bed."

Thirty seconds of silence passed before Colin spoke
again.

"How long have you known?"

"For almost two years. I found out right after I started
dating Olivia," Dean confessed. "When Olivia and Bryce
walked into my life, I knew God had finally answered my
prayers. She's not just a dream come true. She's my reality.
If I acknowledged the cancer, it would put such a strain on
our relationship that I would have to be totally dependent
on Olivia. The Bible says the man is supposed to be the
head of the household. I couldn't do that to her. I would
allow nothing to interfere with fate bringing us to this day."

"And you still haven't told Olivia?"

"No."

"How can you claim to love her and not tell her the kind
of life she's marrying into?"

Dean looked up with tears in his eyes. "Don't think I
haven't thought about telling her, but I have to be sure she's
marrying me because she loves me, not out of pity."

"Olivia loves you, and she deserves the truth." He
grabbed Dean by his arm. "Man, you're making a big mis-

take. There's still time before the ceremony. I'm sure she'll understand."

A light rap at the door interrupted their conversation. "Fellows, it's almost time to begin. We better take our places." Reverend Simms stuck his head inside the room.

Colin and Dean looked at one another.

Then Dean shrugged his shoulders. "I promise I'll talk with her after the ceremony."

Olivia stared at the heavy raindrops that fell outside the limousine window. She prayed the weatherman's forecast for torrential rains was wrong, but the way the rain was pouring from the sky, it didn't look like it was going to stop just for her wedding.

The limousine stopped right outside the church doors. Each one of her bridesmaids dashed out into the rain carrying dresses, shoes and makeup cases.

"Livie, be careful." Aunt Stephie held her umbrella open to protect the bride. "We don't want to get your hair wet."

Olivia carefully climbed out the limo and stopped momentarily when she heard the church bells loudly ringing. The rain washed away any ill feelings she had about her wedding day being a washout. In her heart she knew the Lord was going to bless her union.

"Olivia!" Her aunt gave her a slight nudge. "Hurry, before we both get drenched by the rain."

They ran into the church foyer together.

Her aunt closed the umbrella and pointed down the long corridor. "This way to the dressing room."

Chaos was the only word Olivia could think of when she entered the dressing room. Val rushed past her holding the back of her neck, while Tressie chased behind her apologizing for burning her with the curling iron. Olivia chuckled as she watched Danyelle struggle to get her dress up over her wide hips.

"Now look at your sister. She is well aware that she inherited her big thighs from our side of the family. Why didn't she buy a girdle to wear underneath that dress?" Aunt Stephie rushed over to help Danyelle. "Olivia, go put your things down in the next room, and I'll be there in a minute to help with your hair and makeup."

The adjoining room was reserved especially for the bride. Olivia stepped into serenity. The light blue walls were soothing, and the scent of lavender reminded her of being in an enchanted garden. The room was so comforting that it made her want to pray. She had to take a moment to just give the Lord thanks. The moment she closed her eyes, she was disrupted by her aunt charging through the door, followed by Danyelle, Val and Tressie.

Olivia wasn't mad they were intruding on her time. This was another blessing from the Lord to be surrounded by so many people who loved her. They may have been loud and annoying at times, but He couldn't have chosen a better group of friends.

Val's cell phone rang from the other room and she rushed to answer it.

"Do you think Val has a new love in her life?" Danyelle said.

"Stop gossiping in the church." Aunt Stephie swatted her comb at her.

"I'm not gossiping. Tressie, how many times has Val's phone rung in the last fifteen minutes?" Danyelle asked.

"At least twelve," Tressie said, "and every time she answers, she whispers into the phone and turns away from us."

"I told you." Danyelle smiled at proving her point.

Olivia had to admit, she was curious about Val's mysterious behavior lately. She seemed to have moved past the stage of depression, but something else was occupying her time. Every time she called, Val claimed she couldn't talk. Then while everyone's back was turned, Val moved out of her parent's house. Aunt Stephie was hysterical. Her father was concerned. But Olivia was suspicious of her one-eighty degree change in behavior.

Val walked back in the room carrying a huge bouquet of calla lilies.

"Where did they come from?" Aunt Steph took a huge whiff.

"Me!"

Olivia looked around. Her gorgeous son stood in the doorway beaming with pride. Olivia called him over and gave him a huge hug.

"I hope you like them, Mommy."

"I love them, and you look so adorable in your mini tuxedo." She kissed Bryce on the cheek, leaving traces of her lipstick on his face.

"Dean told me to come and spy on you," her son confessed.

Everyone laughed.

Aunt Stephie took him by the hand and led him toward the exit. "Well, you go back and tell him he is gonna have to wait with everyone else." She turned back toward Olivia. "I'm going to walk him back around to where the fellas are. I'll be right back."

"You look beautiful." Val admired Olivia's makeup. "This will be our last time together with you as a single woman. I'm so happy for you."

The girls embraced with tears in their eyes.

"Val, you know it wouldn't be the same without you, but I hope none of this is going to be upsetting for you." Olivia turned back into her mothering mode.

"No." Val patted her hand. "Listen, I will always love Julian, but he is gone and I can't break down every time somebody else finds happiness." She looked around. "Here comes my mom. I'm going to allow her to help you finish getting dressed."

*   *   *

The organist started to play. On cue, Aunt Stephie sent the girls down the aisle one by one. Dressed in candy apple red gowns, each girl carried a unique look of elegance.

Tressie's sandy brown medium-length hair was neatly curled into a motif of spiral curls. Her slender frame and striking features made her look like a model walking the runway. Everyone admired her beauty.

Like a vision of loveliness floating on a cloud, Val made the way for the maid of honor. Her long tresses were pinned atop her head, and tiny strands of hair cascaded down her back.

Danyelle's transformation was stunning to the guests. Her entrance was grand. The entire church was blinded by her radiance. She never looked lovelier than she did that day. Her eyes twinkled from the bright lights.

Bryce had the most important job. He paved the way for his mom by strutting down the aisle, doing his own version of a pimp walk. He confidently walked up to Dean, slapped his hand and took his place next to him.

Suddenly the tune changed, and everyone stood. The doors at the back of the church swung wide open. Escorted by Val's father, Olivia stepped out surrounded by a reminiscent glow of innocence. Dressed in a cream gown and wearing the same wedding veil her mother wore, she marched down the aisle. Camera bulbs flashed throughout the church.

Olivia looked straight into Dean's eyes. It was the longest journey of her life. The trek down that aisle represented her walking away from life as a single person and stepping into a union with the man of her dreams. When she reached him, he took her hand in his. In her ear she could hear her mother's voice, "A godly man will appreciate and value you." In Dean she had found unconditional love. He unselfishly gave everything he had and never looked for anything in return. She knew he was a blessing.

Reverend Simms greeted the couple then instructed their

guests to be seated. The ceremony began by him explaining the sanctity of marriage. Then he spoke those famous words, "If any person can show just cause why they may not be joined together, let them speak now or forever hold their peace."

Silence filled the church, and Reverend Simms proceeded as usual. As the reverend spoke, Dean reached out for Olivia's hand and squeezed it lightly.

"Dean, please face Olivia and repeat after me."

It was time for them to recite their vows.

"The couple has prepared their own vows, so I will let Dean recite his first." Reverend Simms stepped back.

Happiness covered Dean's face. He had been waiting for this moment since Olivia was in pigtails. He couldn't stop smiling, he was so excited. He took a deep breath.

Then Olivia watched as the smile slowly faded from his face and the joy in his eyes vanished. His eyes rolled up in his head, and he collapsed to the floor.

Olivia screamed in horror.

Colin rushed to his friend's aid. "He's not breathing." He checked for a pulse. "Somebody call an ambulance." He tilted Dean's head back and gave him mouth-to-mouth resuscitation. Olivia cried hysterically into her sister's bosom.

A crowd gathered around. Reverend Simms asked the crowd to stand back.

Ten minutes later the paramedics wheeled a stretcher in. The EMTs frantically tried to revive him. They worked on Dean until he started breathing on his own. Then they rushed him to the hospital.

At the hospital Colin stopped a nurse to ask for an update on Dean's condition. She wouldn't release any information but told him that the doctor would be out to speak with them shortly. Colin immediately took hold of Olivia's shaking hand, and they prayed.

Over an hour passed and they were still waiting on the doctor.

"Colin," her voice was flat and lacked any emotion, "what's wrong with Dean?"

Colin wanted to tell her the truth. He couldn't lie to her.

Tears rolled down her face. "Since the last episode when he passed out from exhaustion I've been making sure he's been getting enough rest and eating healthier." Olivia needed answers. "What's going on?"

"Excuse me." Colin and Olivia looked up.

"I'm Doctor Bell, Dean's physician. Are you his family?" Colin nodded.

"Good! Could you follow me?" He led them to a small conference room, and they gathered around a table. He set a chart down on the table. "Dean was scheduled to have a very important procedure performed this morning and he never showed up."

"We were supposed to be getting married today," Olivia solemnly replied.

Dr. Bell noticed she was still dressed in her wedding gown. "I'm sorry. Did this happen at the church?"

"Yes, in the middle of the ceremony," Colin replied.

The doctor jotted more notes down in his file. "Now I understand why he skipped out on his appointment. After the procedure, he would be so drowsy, he wouldn't have been able to stand, let alone get married."

"What exactly is this procedure for?" Olivia directed her question toward the doctor. "Is Dean sick?"

Colin took her hand. "Livie, Dean has cancer."

She slowly shook her head.

"He told me minutes before the ceremony began. He didn't want to worry you."

Olivia stopped crying and looked at the doctor. "Is it terminal?"

The doctor slowly nodded.

She cried again, and Colin pulled her into his arms.

"He has a rare liver cancer. There is no cure. The only thing we can do is slow down its advancement. It had gone into remission for a while, but it came back. We ran tests today, and the results are not as bad as I suspected, but I still can't offer much hope."

Olivia looked down at the floor.

"He is slowly losing functionality of his liver. This is the calm before the storm. Dean needs to rest as much as possible. No more sports. No lifting anything heavy. He will need all his strength toward the end. I'm going to keep him here for a few days for observation. If his condition improves, I'll release him. Do you have any questions for me?"

"Can we see him now?" Olivia asked.

"Sure." The doctor pulled out one of his business cards. "If you think of anything you want to ask me later on, call me anytime." Then he escorted them to Dean's room.

Olivia gasped loudly when she walked in. The sight of him connected to so many machines and breathing into a facemask was much worse than she envisioned. Her light brown eyes filled with tears.

"God, why him?" she cried loudly.

Colin tried to console her, but she pulled away and stroked the side of Dean's face as he slept.

Olivia wondered why this was happening to them. They were the perfect couple. She had finally found the missing piece to make her life complete, and now she felt like God was punishing them. Or was God punishing her?

Olivia had never forgiven herself for breaking the vow she made to the Lord. Giving her virginity to Bryant was a mistake. A mistake she thought she had paid the price for when her son was kidnapped and nearly sold.

She laid her head down by his side and revisited Reverend Simms's speech about sacrifice. She sat up and wondered what Dean would do if she was the one lying in the hospital. Her heart spoke back to her. Dean would do everything humanly possible to make her happy, and she was going to do the same for him.

They sat with him for over an hour before Dean opened

his eyes. He lifted his eyelids. This was the first time she could actually see how sick he was. It scared her to see him wither away right before her eyes.

"Let's get married," Olivia spit out. "Let's get married, today."

Dean looked at her strangely.

"We already have the marriage license, and Colin is here. He can perform the ceremony."

Dean shook his head. Then he pushed the breathing apparatus away from his face. "No," he said gasping for air, "you deserve a real wedding."

Olivia touched the side of his face. "What I deserve is to be married to you." She giggled. "Now will you lie back and let your future wife take care of things?" She smiled at him. "I have a wedding to prepare for."

"Partner, you better listen to her. I wouldn't go against any woman's wishes," Colin joked.

When Olivia saw the sparkle in Dean's eyes, she knew she was doing the right thing.

"Olivia, I'm going to run home and grab my Bible." Colin checked his watch. "Do you want me to call Danyelle?"

Dean waved his hand to refuse. "I don't want anyone to know about my illness," he whispered.

Olivia looked back at Colin. She really wanted her closest friends and family to witness them getting married, but she didn't want to go against her fiancé's wishes.

"No, that's okay. I can find somebody else to be a witness."

A half hour later, Colin returned to officiate his first wedding ceremony. One of the nurses on the floor agreed to be a witness, and within minutes Olivia and Dean became husband and wife.

Chapter 20

The transition between Val and Jonah moving in to-gether wasn't as easy as they'd anticipated. It was Val who insisted Jonah stay with her until he was able to find a job and decent place for him and Hope, but it wasn't until late one night that she realized she was living in sin. Her parents would die if they knew she was living with a man who wasn't her husband. That's why she hadn't mentioned him to anyone, not even Olivia. Livie was her best friend, and they usually shared everything, but she wasn't ready to explain where Jonah came from.

Jonah respected Olivia and her house. That's why he tried to stay out her way, but it was hard living with such a beautiful sista. He noticed that Val also kept her distance from him, but he thought it was because she wasn't inter-ested in him. She never flirted with him, but her tight clothes, voluptuous curves and perky breasts seemed to ad-dress him every time he looked at her.

He was attracted to her but didn't think it was wise for him to try and get close to her. It was obvious by her home, car and clothes that she was definitely out of his league.

During the day Val spent a lot of her time at the mission fulfilling her obligation to the city. At night she would come home and spend hours on the computer trying to help Jonah find a job. Together they must have applied for over thirty oil refinery and construction jobs. Only two companies were interested in interviewing him.

As luck would have it, as Jonah was walking home from the store one evening, he happened to overhear two guys talking. The gentleman talking wore a security guard's uniform, and he was telling his friend that the hospital he was working at was looking to hire a janitor.

Jonah applied the next day and was hired on the spot.

After several weeks, Jonah had finally fulfilled the requirements the judge had set for him. Mrs. Chambers was expected to drop Hope off at any minute.

When they heard a knock at the door, Jonah charged down the stairs with the energy of a boy rising early on Christmas morning. "I'll get it!" He pulled open the front door, and when Hope saw her father, she broke away from Mrs. Chambers' grasp and leapt into Jonah's arms.

Val could hear Hope squeal with joy at being reunited with her father. She watched the two of them embrace from the kitchen. Hope wrapped her tiny arms around her father's neck and wouldn't let go. Jonah kept trying to pull her back to give her kisses, but she was too scared to let go.

Jonah carried her into the living room.

Mrs. Chambers closed the door behind them and followed. "Let me get a good look at you. It seems like a lifetime since I've last seen you." Mrs. Chambers set down a suitcase full of her things.

"Mrs. Chambers, would you like a seat?" Val offered as Mrs. Chambers admired her decorative living room. She and Jonah had spent most of the morning preparing for Hope's homecoming. The dining room table was full of gifts and a huge chocolate cake, all for Hope.

"No, thank you. It's obvious Hope was missed." She smiled broadly.

"Yes, we are excited to have her back home," Val replied.

"Mr. Reynolds, there are a few forms I need for you to sign, and then I'll be on my way." She pulled a manila folder out of her briefcase and set it down on the coffee table.

Hope hung on to her father so tight that he had a hard time signing the forms, but after some maneuvering he got it done.

"This is a beautiful home," Mrs. Chambers commented.

Val beamed with pride. It wasn't easy furnishing her entire house in less than three weeks, but she got it done. With the help of professional decorators, she selected color patterns and furniture and updated the entire house with the latest in kitchen appliances. The kitchen cabinets were now full of real plates and cups instead of Styrofoam. Pictures of Bryce, Olivia, Danyelle, Tressie and her parents hung throughout the house. It now felt like a real home.

"This is a great neighborhood to raise a child in. The schools are excellent, the streets are clean and there are lots of community events held for children Hope's age," Mrs. Chambers pointed out.

"I recognize I've been blessed." Jonah's gaze fell on Val.

When Val realized he was referring to her, she simply gave an uneasy smile and turned on the television for Hope.

"Well, it appears as though I have everything." Mrs. Chambers gathered the forms. "The background checks that were run on you and Val came back clean, I have three consecutive paychecks, plus references from your supervisor documenting how superior your work ethics are. The only thing I would like to see is where Hope will be sleeping. When I came the first time, the room was still under construction. In my report I documented that she had her own room, but I would like to see the finished project."

"Sure, follow me." Val led her up the back steps.

When she opened Hope's bedroom door, Mrs. Chambers looked impressed. Splashes of lavender paint covered every wall and small pictures of ballerina shoes filled the room. Hanging from walls were ballerina shoes, and sitting on the shelves were baby dolls all waiting to be claimed by Hope.

Jonah and Hope followed close behind them. When he stepped in the room, Hope screamed out and struggled to get down from her father's arms.

Hope's positive reaction put Val's mind at rest. She prayed that Hope would approve of the decorating choices she made.

They watched her run over to her bed and pick up a baby doll and cradle it in her arms.

"This room is fantastic," Mrs. Chambers said.

Jonah walked up beside Val. "I was wondering why every time I walked by this room the door was closed. I thought you were hiding something."

"I wanted it to be a surprise. I knew you had bought Hope a lot of different clothes and toys, but I wanted to do something special for her. Something that came from me."

"Val, you didn't have to go through all this trouble, but I thank you, and so does my daughter. Hope, why don't you come and give Val a hug and kiss for buying you all this stuff?"

Hope turned and looked at her father beckoning her over. She slowly walked toward Jonah.

Val bent down to give her a hug, and Hope reluctantly stood as still as a stone. Afterwards, she turned back toward her father and refused to look in Val's direction.

"She's shy," Jonah replied.

"Well, I'm convinced that I'm leaving Hope in a stable, loving home, but I must remind you that my home visits will continue. If at any time I feel anything suspicious, then your daughter will be immediately placed back in the custody of the state. Do you understand?"

Jonah happily nodded his head. "That was easier than I thought it would be," he whispered in Val's ear.

The following Saturday, Val watched Jonah and Hope watch cartoons together in her living room. She sighed heavily. It hurt that she couldn't establish the same kind of bond Jonah shared with Hope. She realized that he was her father, but Val had tried everything to get Hope to trust her. The little girl acted like she hated her. Jonah asked Val to be patient, but no matter how hard Val tried, Hope left her hopeless.

Hope soared through the air and landed on Jonah's back. He fell over and accidentally knocked over Val's brand-new crystal vase. It fell to the floor and shattered into pieces.

Hope and Jonah looked at the vase, then at Val. Their faces were full of fear. They knew they were in trouble.

"Val, I'm so sorry. We shouldn't have been playing in the house," Jonah said. "I'll replace it when I get paid on Friday."

"Don't worry about it." Val got up to pick up the broken pieces before anyone cut themselves. "I'm not used to having a child living with me. I should have bought cheap vases from the dollar store."

"I know you're probably tired of having us take up your space." Jonah helped her clean up. "It won't be long before I have enough money to move us out of here."

She touched his hand. "Jonah, I enjoy having the two of you here. If it weren't for you, I'd be living in this big house all alone."

They shared a smile.

Then an unexpected knock at the door pulled Val away. When she answered the door she was surprised to see Mrs. Chambers standing on the other side, accompanied by a police officer.

"Hello, Val, is Jonah here?"

Mrs. Chambers' official demeanor scared her. She could feel her heart pump faster. Uneasiness filled her stomach. "Jonah!" She hollered for him.

When Jonah reached the door and saw the cops, he instinctively ran back for his daughter.

Mrs. Chambers and the police officer barged past Val and into the living room.

"Jonah, don't make this any harder than it has to be," Mrs. Chambers tried to reason.

"Is there a problem?" Val could see something was wrong.

"Why don't you ask Jonah that question?" Mrs. Chambers kept her eyes on Jonah. "Someone has made a claim that Hope isn't really your daughter. Is that true?"

Jonah held back the tears and momentarily closed his eyes, as if his worst nightmare had come true.

"Hope will have to remain in our custody until the matter is resolved."

Val couldn't believe what she was hearing. This had to be a mistake.

Mrs. Chambers looked disappointed. "I'm sorry, but we have to take Hope back with us. We have a court order signed by the judge." She pulled out a slip of paper from her pocket and handed it to Val. Then she reached out for Hope.

Hope must have sensed that something was wrong because she screamed out.

Jonah stepped back from Mrs. Chambers and held onto his daughter even tighter.

Then the police intervened. "Sir, don't make this any harder than it already is. We could have you arrested and then take the child."

Val could see that the papers had been drawn up earlier that morning and signed by the judge. She walked over to Jonah and whispered, "Jonah!" She placed a loving hand on his arm and slowly shook her head.

Her eyes said there was nothing they could do. He had to give Hope up. He reluctantly loosened his grip.

Mrs. Chambers pulled Hope from him, and she kicked and screamed for her father. They quickly took her out the house and put her in the police car that was waiting at the curb.

After they left, Jonah paced the living room floor until his anger couldn't be contained any longer and he slammed his fist into a nearby wall. He hit it so hard that he made a hole.

Val had never seen Jonah this angry before. She watched him for moment. The release of all that anger made him stagger over to the fireplace.

"I should have left when I had the chance," he cried. "I stayed too long, and now they've taken my daughter."

Val watched from a distance.

He knew she wanted answers to questions he prayed he would never have to acknowledge.

"Biologically, Hope is not my daughter."

Val listened closely.

"My best friend was a soldier in the army. He was deployed to Iraq, but never came home. He was a casualty of war, leaving behind a wife and baby. They adopted Hope a few months before he left. Once my friend was gone, his wife had nowhere to go. So I invited her to stay with me in New Orleans until she got on her feet."

"Is that who was lost in the storm?" Val asked.

"Yes. After we were rescued, I went to my momma's house in Baton Rouge. We stayed there a few weeks, until one afternoon the police came looking for us. They told my momma that they wanted to talk to me about Hope's parents. I thought the state had found out she didn't belong to me and was going to try and take her from me. I couldn't allow them to place her in foster care. I'm the only family Hope has. So I skipped town. We hid out like thieves, living from town to town, until I caught the bus here."

"I wish you would have told me all of this sooner," Val said.

"I was scared," he replied.

"Is that everything? You didn't leave anything out, did you?"

"No."

"These kind of legal technicalities are beyond my legal expertise, but I'll call a few of my professors and see if they can recommend a lawyer who specializes in family law." Val went to her home office.

West watched a kid who looked like he was fresh out of law school tussle with a mound of files and papers.

"I don't understand," Judge West spoke up. "Didn't they tell you that I already have a lawyer?"

"Yes, a court appointed attorney, and I was hired by the pastor of your church. He insists he only wants what's best for you."

"Who are you again?"

"My name is Joseph Morris, and I work for Myers and Kittering law offices."

"Are you sure you're a lawyer and not a law clerk?"

This kid didn't look polished enough to handle his case. The judge already knew that his was a high profile case and that the lawyer who represented him would have to have experience on how the system worked.

"That's funny, sir." Joseph finally found what he was looking for. He pulled a pen from out the inside of his jacket pocket and sat across from the judge. "I may have just graduated from college, but I did graduate at the top of my class."

"Well, that's good to hear. Where did you go to school?"

"Ankara Law School."

"Where? I've never heard of it? Where's it at?"

"It's in Turkey."

"Are you referring to the country of Turkey?" Judge West laughed to himself. "This has got to be a joke. Are you licensed to practice law in Pennsylvania?"

"Yes, sir. I took the bar exam for Pennsylvania and passed. I'm not from Turkey. I am actually a United States citizen. I was born and raised in Nebraska."

"Why did you choose to go to school in Turkey?"

"I felt like I would do better studying abroad."

Judge West was now convinced that this guy was not ready to represent a client in court.

"And my pastor hired you on my behalf?"

The kid nodded.

Judge West was aware of the fact that Reverend Simms knew a lot of prominent experienced trial lawyers. It made him wonder why he chose this kid.

"Yes, when he came to my office he said he was referred by another pastor." He thought for a second. "A Reverend Baxter."

"Will this be your first case at the firm?" Judge West asked.

"Yes, sir, this will be my first case to ever present before a jury." Joseph pulled out a notepad. "Now, sir, can you please tell me exactly what happened, in your own words?"

Joseph looked harmless. Actually he reminded Judge West of an out-of-place country boy living all alone in the big city of Philadelphia.

"Before we begin, why don't you tell me about back home?" Judge West requested.

"Back home?"

"Yeah, tell me about Nebraska. Since we'll be working together, I want to know as much about you as I can, since you already know a lot about me." The judge was searching for any sign that Joseph may be connected to the brother-hood.

West sat back in his chair and listened to Joseph ramble

on about his strict Mormon upbringing. He was raised on a farm and was the first of eight siblings to leave home.

Once he was finished, West was convinced that this kid wasn't associated with the brotherhood.

"Okay, kid, that's enough talking about you." Judge West looked around. "Where is your tape recorder? Joseph, remember, whenever you meet with a client, you always want to record any conversations you have about details of the charges. It makes it easier for your secretary when it's time for her to transcribe everything."

"Oh, okay." He dug through his briefcase. "I have one of those right here." He set it down in front of them.

West got up to leave. He banged on the door for the guard to take him back to his cell.

"Where are you going?" Joseph questioned the judge as if he were on the stand.

"Listen, kid, go back to your office and call my pastor and tell him I'm all right. I don't need counsel. I'm going to get out of this because I didn't do anything wrong. Please tell Reverend Simms I fired you, and you are free to go."

Joseph looked shocked and disappointed. He couldn't believe he had just lost his first case before it even got started.

Chapter 21

Three days after the wedding, Dean was released from the hospital. Instead of moving into Olivia's small apartment, he suggested that she and Bryce move into his grandpa's Victorian-style home with him. Olivia was hesitant. She didn't want to intrude while Judge West was incarcerated, but Dean assured her it would be all right. Besides, Dean never expected his grandpa to walk freely again.

Their first week in the house, Olivia kept busy. Never one to complain, she cooked dinner, washed dishes, kept the house clean and made certain her husband abided by the doctor's stern instructions to get plenty of rest, take his meds every three hours and drink plenty of water.

Bryce adjusted to the change well. He loved going to a new school, living in a new house and especially having a backyard to play in. Olivia wished Kennedy and Clinton, her dogs, were more open to their new environment. This unfamiliar environment resulted in them going to the bathroom throughout the house. It was frustrating every time she found more dog doo-doo in inconspicuous places.

Thankful that Colin offered to take Bryce for a few days,

Olivia planned to spend plenty of time alone with her husband. Dean was getting stronger every day, but he was still not physically able to consummate their marriage. So to compensate for the lack of intimacy in their marriage, Olivia did other things.

She lit scented candles in the bedroom and gave him a sponge bath every night. They would watch a movie or read a book together. Most nights they would simply sit up late at night and talk.

"Livie, when I go, I want to make sure you and Bryce are taken care of," Dean said.

Olivia lay against his chest. She turned to face him. "Let's not talk about the future. Instead, let's focus on the present."

"I've set up a trust fund for Bryce when he goes to college," Dean told her.

"Dean, it's good to know you're saving for our son's future, but you're going to be here to see him graduate from college, get married and even make us grandparents. You're not leaving me yet. You just got here."

He gave her a quick peck on the lips. "I hope you're right." Then he closed his eyes and drifted off to sleep.

A week later, Olivia sat in the living room folding laundry. Colin had just called her to let her know he was bringing Bryce home. She couldn't wait to see him. She hated being separated from her little boy.

When her cell phone rang she assumed it was Colin, until she looked at the caller ID and saw it was her sister. Olivia pushed the button to send the call straight to voice mail. Danyelle had been calling and leaving Olivia messages all week, each message sounding angrier.

Olivia understood why she was so upset. She had gotten married and hadn't bothered to call anyone to let them know. None of her family knew she was married, except for her son. It bothered her that the people closest to her couldn't be there when she got married, but she had to respect Dean's privacy. He still didn't want anyone to know about the cancer.

That's why it was taking her so long to return any calls. She was avoiding their questions. She didn't want to lie to them, but she couldn't tell them the truth.

Olivia folded the last of Bryce's clothes and put them away in his room. She looked in on Dean, who was sound asleep, and walked back into the living room. Then she walked toward the laundry room, took clothes out the washer and headed out the back door to hang clothes on the line.

She whistled for Kennedy and Clinton to follow her. She thought it would be good for them to get some fresh air.

Taking a few white T-shirts out the basket, she hung them by clothespins on the line. She failed to notice her sister standing right behind her.

"Why have you been ducking my calls?" Danyelle shouted in Olivia's ear.

Startled, Olivia looked around. When she realized who it was, she realized it was time to face the music. It was only a matter of time before Danyelle came looking for her.

"I was going to call you, but I've been busy."

"You left me a message telling me to leave Bryce over Aunt Stephie's. That was the day of the wedding. Since then I haven't heard from you. You couldn't even call and update me on Dean's condition? I would have thought he was dead if it hadn't been for the fact that Reverend Simms told everyone you two had gotten married at the hospital."

Olivia turned her eyes away and stepped farther away from her sister. Again, she started to hang up clothes, but Danyelle stopped her.

"What is going on with you?"

Olivia was an awful liar. The one thing she hated doing

was keeping things from those she loved, but this was one secret she couldn't share with her sister.

"Livie, you owe me some kind of explanation. You can't ignore me."

"What do you want me to say?" Olivia shouted.

"I want you to explain why I had to find out through a third party that my sister was married," Danyelle screamed. "Tell me why you moved out of your apartment and didn't bother to tell me"—She pointed to herself—"Val"—She counted off on her fingers—"or Aunt Stephie. Why is this such a big secret?"

"It's not a secret. I told you I've been busy."

The two sounded like they were at a screaming match.

The sound of Olivia's back door opening caught both of their attention. Bryce stuck his small head out the screen door. "Hey, Mommy! I'm home."

"Hey, honey."

Bryce ran out to give her a hug. "Reverend Colin is looking for you. Hey, Auntie Danyelle." He ran back toward the house and yelled out to his mother just before he went inside. "Oh! Mommy, I forgot to tell you that Dean is calling for you."

"Okay, baby, tell him I'll be right there."

Olivia stepped forward, but Danyelle blocked her path.

"Is Dean here? If you won't tell me what's going on, then maybe he will."

Olivia dug her fingernails into Danyelle's arm. "Danyelle, I think you've overstayed your welcome." Olivia stared her sister in the eye. "Please leave. I won't have you bothering my husband."

Danyelle had never heard her sister sound so cold. Olivia tried her best to disguise the fear on her face as overprotectiveness, but Danyelle could see through her façade.

"Fine, but don't think we're finished." Danyelle marched off.

Colin peeked into the storage closet. Danyelle stood in the midst of church supplies. "You summoned me?" Colin stepped inside the closet with her. "I knew you'd come looking for me one day. I just didn't think it would be this soon." He took and kissed her hand.

She snatched it away. "Would you stop it? I called you down here for answers." She pulled a hanger from out of the closet and slid on one of the children's choir robes.

"Oh! Is that all? I thought you called me down here to smoke a blunt with you. I mean, this is where you go to sneak in a few puffs on those days when we have morning and afternoon services."

"Colin, we are not talking about me, we are talking about them." She picked up another robe from out of the pile left on the floor and tried to put it on its hanger, but she was so mad that the hanger slipped out her hand and she ended up throwing the robe back on the ground.

"Why don't you calm down?" Then he pulled Danyelle out of the closet and pointed for her to sit in a nearby chair. "Why don't you tell me what the problem is?"

"It's my sister's marriage."

Colin studied her facial expressions. He tried to figure out what was bothering her.

"My sister is hiding something from me, and I need to know what it is."

"Have you tried talking with her?"

"She won't talk with me. I want to let it go, but something is nagging at my soul. I can't let it rest."

He grabbed a hold of her hands.

"I wish she would talk to me."

"She will when she's ready. Don't push. Give her some space."

"She's telling everyone that Dean passed out from exhaustion. Is that true?"

Colin stared into the eyes of the woman he loved. He was sworn to secrecy by Dean. "The doctor says that Dean was overexerting himself and that he needed plenty of rest."

"Well, I'm glad to hear that. I was beginning to think he had some kind of life-threatening disease," Danyelle replied.

Colin loved looking at her. He wished he could be this close to her all the time. He pulled her face closer to his. He wanted to kiss her. He stroked the side of her face.

"Ms. Danyelle," a child's voice screamed. Then the patter of little feet ran through the church hallways. A young boy came to a halt when he saw the adults so close. "Ooooh, Ms. Danyelle and Reverend Colin are in love," he shouted. He sprinted up to where they were sitting and dropped his robe in Danyelle's lap before disappearing out the room.

Colin and Danyelle laughed at the little boy's reaction.

Danyelle stood on the front steps at Judge West's home. It was the Friday before Mother's Day, and she was ready to make amends with her sister. The last time she left, Danyelle was so angry she vowed to never return until Olivia called and apologized. That was two weeks ago, and she was still waiting on that call.

Danyelle had no idea how she ended up back at the judge's house. She had a strict itinerary set for the day. Her plans were to study for her finals, get some laundry done and meet Colin for dinner later that evening. Then as she drove to the cleaners she heard a commercial on the radio advertising the release of *Horton Hears a Who*. It was in the movie theaters, and Bryce had been bugging her to take him when it came out. She couldn't break a promise to her nephew. Before she knew what she was doing, she turned the car around and was pulling into Judge West's driveway.

She rang the doorbell. No answer. Danyelle placed her ear up against the door. She could hear music blaring in the background and Olivia hollering for Bryce. Danyelle tried the front door and it opened. She stepped into a maze of boxes. Again, she heard her sister screaming for Bryce to bring her a rag.

Danyelle stepped around and over huge boxes. They were piled so high on top of one another that Danyelle thought she would never find her way out. Fortunately, Olivia had a habit of talking to herself when no one was around and it led Danyelle straight to her. She found her sister on her knees scrubbing the inside of the oven. Through the sliding glass doors Danyelle could see Bryce in the backyard playing with Clinton and Kennedy.

Here was the perfect opportunity for them to make up while there was no one around to disrupt them. "I've come to make a truce."

Frightened by the sound of her sister's voice, Olivia lifted her head and banged it hard against the inside of the oven. She crawled out the oven, rubbing the back of her head.

"I'm sorry. I overreacted the last time I was here."

Olivia heard the sincerity in her sister's voice. She was glad Danyelle had come by because she couldn't take another day of them not speaking. Olivia opened up her arms, and the two hugged.

"I'm sorry, too," Olivia said.

"I knew you missed me," Danyelle boasted. "Now where is my new brother-in-law? I would like to properly welcome him into the family."

"He and Colin are moving boxes from my place."

Danyelle smiled to herself when she heard Colin's name. Their relationship was still a secret, but she wondered how much longer they were going to be able to keep it up.

"They should be back any second."

"Well, can I take Bryce off your hands?" Danyelle didn't want to be there when Colin returned. "I promised him we would go to the movies to see *Horton Hears a Who* and it was released yesterday."

"I know. That's all he keeps talking about. I'll go get him for you."

While Olivia was gone, Danyelle snooped in a few boxes. The boxes were full of things from Olivia's apartment.

She was still looking for a clue that would explain why Olivia and Dean married so quickly, but to keep the peace she decided to let the issue rest for the moment.

Hours after Danyelle left, Dean held the front door for Colin as he stumbled in with an armful of boxes.

"Colin, do you need any help?" Olivia cleared boxes out of Colin's path so he wouldn't trip over anything.

"I told him I could carry something, but he wouldn't let me." Dean sounded agitated.

"Thank you for telling my husband no," Olivia said. "He doesn't seem to understand that just because he's not laid up in the hospital or in bed that he's still sick."

"No problem, Livie. Where would you like these boxes?" Colin asked.

"You can set them down right here." Olivia pointed to the only open spot in front of her. "I might as well try to empty as many boxes as possible." She dug through and revealed a vast collection of paintings and prints. "I love Cidne Wallace's work. She immortalizes the attributes of every black woman so tastefully."

She placed the print to the side and searched the box again. "This painting used to belong to my daddy. It's called 'The Resurrection of Lazarus.' " Olivia held it up so the guys could get a good look at it. "It's a reprint done by Henry Tanner. He—"

Colin cut her off. "He was a prominent African American painter in the country who was raised in Philadelphia and his father was an A.M.E. minister. His mother escaped slavery through the Underground Railroad."

"You've heard of him." Olivia was glad someone loved art as much as she did.

"I studied his work while in college." Colin had never seen an actual reprint this close before. He studied how Tanner captured the realness of Lazarus wakening from death. "This is priceless."

"I've never seen any of these pictures hanging in your apartment," Dean added.

"No. There was never enough room for them with Bryce's pictures filling my walls. I kept them stored away. I promised myself that when I bought a house I would have enough room to display them all." Olivia admired the lovely images of black people being artistic. "These pictures have such a warm feeling; it will make this place really feel like home."

Dean walked over and kissed her on the forehead. "If that will make you happy, then I'm happy." Then he noticed how quiet it was. "Where's Bryce?"

"Oh, Danyelle was here."

Dean looked surprised.

"She came and took him to the movies." Olivia checked the time on her watch. "As a matter of fact I have to go pick him up from her apartment."

"Don't worry. I'll stay with Dean until you get back." Colin put her mind at ease.

"Thanks." She grabbed her purse and car keys.

"I'm not an invalid. I can be alone in the house."

"We know." She gave him a quick peck. "But I feel better knowing someone is here with you." She rushed out the door.

As Dean's eyes followed her vision he became dizzy. He reached out for Colin.

"Are you all right?" Colin led him to the couch and went to the kitchen to get him a glass of water.

"I'm okay. I think maybe my legs were getting a little tired."

"Man, I told you to take it easy." Colin sat on a nearby box. "Do you want me to call your doctor?"

Dean shook his head no. "Don't do that. It'll just upset Olivia. Plus, there's something I want to talk to you about now that Olivia is gone."

Colin listened closely. He was sure Dean was going to confide in him his last wishes in case anything were to happen to him.

"Remember the day I was rushed to the hospital and we were talking about my grandpa?"

Colin said yes.

"Well, I found out something that may change your mind at how you look at him as a man."

Colin waited for him to tell him more.

"I have to show you something." Dean got up. "I'll be right back." He left out the room and went into one of the back rooms.

A few minutes later he walked back into the living room wearing the white-hooded Ku Klux Klan uniform. The only thing that could be seen was the whites of his eyes.

When Colin saw him he was startled and started to run for the door, but stopped when he noticed it was Dean underneath that getup. "Man, what are you doing?"

Dean pulled off the hood. "I thought if I tried it on, maybe I could figure out what would make my grandpa join such a hateful organization."

Colin looked at Dean and then at the white sheets and slowly shook his head.

Chapter 22

Val unbuckled her seatbelt and turned toward her passenger. "Are you ready?" It was Wednesday night, and her Bible study group was scheduled to meet that evening. The girls had gotten used to holding Bible study at one another's apartment, but Val specifically asked them to meet her at the church. She felt like she and Jonah both needed to dwell in the house of the Lord, with everything they had been going through.

"The last time I was in a church was the night before Katrina hit New Orleans. Our pastor brought in a small portable radio into the sanctuary to keep us abreast of the storm's progress. The pews were packed. People were laid out on the floor and on the altar. It was barely enough room to stand. I guess everyone felt church was the safest place to be that night."

"There is no better person to turn to than Jesus in the midst of a storm," Val said.

They got out and walked into the church together, but there was no one there.

"Olivia." Val expected everyone to be waiting for her. Instead, the church was empty, but she knew they couldn't be far because she saw two cars parked outside. "Danyelle!" she hollered.

"Val, we're downstairs. We'll be there in a minute," Olivia yelled from the basement.

Val and Jonah sat on the pews nearest to them.

Seconds later Olivia climbed the back steps and stepped into the sanctuary dusting herself off. "Girl, I was downstairs looking for Sunday School workbooks for Bryce's class. You know Ms. Young can't ever find anything and she"—Olivia looked up from dusting off her clothes and stopped mid-sentence when she saw Jonah sitting next to Val.

Danyelle was so close behind her that she didn't notice her sister had stopped walking and ran straight into her.

"Girl, what is your problem?" Her eyes followed Olivia's gaze, and she too noticed Jonah.

Val giggled at their reaction. She knew they would be shocked to see her with a man. Val had never been with any other man except for Julian, so for her to bring someone to church with her meant he was something special.

"Where's Tressie?" Val asked.

"She's out of town on business again," Danyelle replied. "I think she had to go to Nebraska."

Val said okay and introduced everyone to Jonah. She wasn't the least bit surprised when Danyelle started to playfully tease her.

"So, Val, is this your new man?" Danyelle asked.

Olivia's face turned red from embarrassment. Sometimes her sister took things to the extreme. "Danyelle, would you stop it?"

"I betcha my sister didn't bother to call and tell you the latest newsflash," Danyelle instigated.

"What is she talking about?" Val hadn't really kept up with Olivia and what was going on with her and Dean.

"Does this have anything to do with the wedding? You and Dean are still getting married, right?"

Olivia smiled and tried to shrug off her questions. "We'll talk later." She cut her eyes in Jonah's direction. "When we're alone."

Now it was time for Danyelle to interrogate their guest. "Jonah? That's a biblical name. I like it. Do you know about Jonah in the Bible?"

"Yes, ma'am," Jonah replied.

"Listen to his country accent." She laughed loudly in his face. "You have to be from down South because nobody says, 'Yes, ma'am', from these parts," Danyelle mocked him.

"I'm from New Orleans," he boldly declared.

"What can you tell me about Jonah in the Bible?" Danyelle grilled him.

"Would you leave him alone?" Olivia scolded her sister. "He didn't come here to explain anything to you."

"Hush! I'm just trying to make conversation," Danyelle replied.

"No, it's fine. I don't mind answering her question." He turned in Danyelle's direction. "Jonah ran from God. He was running from being obedient to God, and whenever a person runs from God, they end up being eaten by a big fish."

Val could see that Danyelle was impressed.

"Well, this country boy does know his Bible," Danyelle replied. "So, Jonah, are you running from something?" Danyelle's face turned serious. "Perhaps from God?"

"Danyelle?" Olivia gave Danyelle a stern look, warning her to cut it out. "That's a personal question." She looked at Jonah. "You don't have to answer that."

"What? I just asked him a question."

"You don't know this man," Olivia pointed out. "What makes you think he's running from God?"

"Let's just say it's intuition," Danyelle said.

"I'm sorry," Olivia said to Jonah. "What may seem like odd behavior to you is normal for her."

"No. That's all right, I have nothing to hide." He looked Danyelle straight in the eye. "As a matter of fact, I'm not running from God, I'm running toward Him. I endured the disasters of Katrina, and that is only because I knew Jesus was right there with me as I hung on to my rooftop with one hand and my daughter in the other. When I left my home in New Orleans I wasn't running from God, I was following him. He brought me here to make a new friend." He glanced at Val.

Olivia knew Jonah's answer impressed Danyelle, because afterwards she stopped with the questions and opened the meeting in prayer.

Chapter 23

On Friday afternoon, Val, Jonah and Mr. Lawson, their lawyer, entered the courthouse together and took the elevator to the fifth floor.

The moment they stepped off the elevators, a security guard greeted them.

"Good afternoon. Could each of you please sign in?" He pointed to a lined piece of paper on the table.

Afterward, he searched the computer for their names. "Please follow me," he said to Mr. Lawson. "The judge has closed the hearing to the public to protect the child."

They made a left down another hallway.

"You are the last party. The hearing should begin as soon as you get in there." He stopped and allowed them to pass through a huge wood door. The security guard closed the door behind them and returned to his post.

Together they walked toward the defense table, and as Val proceeded down the center aisle, she could feel a pair of eyes watching her. When she looked up she abruptly stopped in her tracks. Sitting at the table across from theirs was Caitlyn and her lawyer.

When Caitlyn realized she had Val's attention, she gave a sly grin and whispered something into her lawyer's ear. The lawyer turned over his shoulder to look at Val, and the two began whispering again.

"Val, what's wrong?" Jonah came up behind her. "Is everything all right?" He was concerned.

Val couldn't take her eyes off Caitlyn.

He looked to where Val was staring. "Come on, let's not keep Mr. Lawson waiting."

The two of them grabbed a seat next to Mr. Lawson and waited for the judge to enter.

Val kept sneaking looks in Caitlyn's direction. She wondered what she was doing here.

When Judge Cohen walked into the courtroom, everyone stood. "You may all be seated," he announced. He sat down in his chair and picked up the papers set before him. When he saw Jonah's name, he dropped the papers back down on his desk. "Mr. Reynolds," he proclaimed, "what are you doing back in my courtroom? Did I make a mistake by returning Hope to your custody?"

"No, Your Honor." Jonah's eyes pleaded with Mr. Lawson to step in.

"Your Honor, there seems to be a question of the child's *maternity*," Mr. Lawson stressed the last word.

"Now, I'm confused. Can someone please tell me what is going on?" the judge asked out loud.

Caitlyn's lawyer stood up to speak, "Well, Your Honor, my client has reason to believe that Mr. Reynolds is not the child's biological father. This is the biological mother." He pointed to Caitlyn. "She gave the baby up for adoption, and since then both adoptive parents have died and she would now like to get her daughter back."

The judge turned toward Jonah, and he could see by the look in Jonah's eyes that there was some truth to Caitlyn's story.

"Well, I don't think I've ever had to rule on a case this complex," Judge Cohen commented.

"As you can see, I have provided a copy of Ms. Haas's financial records for the past three years. I have provided depositions from her friends and associates that can vouch for her character."

Caitlyn's overzealous lawyer tried to charm Judge Cohen with his flattering words. He mentioned a lot of prominent people in Seattle who were associates of Caitlyn's, but Judge Cohen seemed unmoved.

"Ms. Haas, where is Hope's father?" Judge Cohen asked.

"Well," Caitlyn cleared her throat before stealing a glance in Val's direction, "her father played for the NBA, but he was killed not too long ago in a plane crash."

"Julian Pennington?" the judge questioned.

Caitlyn affirmed by nodding her head yes.

Val sat up in her seat and stared at Caitlyn. She was sure she had heard her incorrectly. At first she thought this was another one of Caitlyn's sick jokes. A vicious lie she had concocted to hurt her.

Then the weight of Caitlyn's words started to affect Val in a negative way. Her mouth turned dry, and her stomach turned. The room spun around her. The well-ventilated courtroom was now suffocating, and Val felt like she couldn't breathe. She grabbed for her purse and rushed out the courtroom doors.

As she left, she could hear Jonah call out her name, but that didn't stop her. Val ran to her car and jumped into the driver's seat. She watched her hands shake. Her heart raced with fear. She noticed her doors were unlocked, and she slammed her hand down on the lock button.

Val was intimidated by Caitlyn's courtroom revelation. She didn't know why her lies would shake her to the core. There was no doubt in her mind how much Julian loved her, but Val felt like Caitlyn had won because she'd had his baby. From the parking lot she stared at the courthouse. She couldn't stay any longer because she wasn't emotionally prepared to face Caitlyn again.

She started her Mercedes and spun rubber to get out the parking lot as fast as she could. Val drove through the streets of Philly erratically. The Mercedes cut off trucks, ran through red lights and barely yielded at stop signs. She wasn't sure where she was going. Her subconscious took over control of the car.

The car came to an abrupt stop in front of First Nazareth A.M.E. He had safely directed her to His house. The Lord's house.

She struggled to get out of her seatbelt and staggered up the church doors. Inside, the church was empty. Val didn't wonder why no one was around. She knew He planned it this way. When she needed to talk with Him at one of her most vulnerable times in her life He made His altar available. She ran to the altar and prayed earnestly. The word that kept crying out from her soul was *"Why?"*

At that moment a lot of truths were revealed to her heart. Since Julian's accident, she hadn't prayed at all. Months had passed since the last time she came to the Lord with love in her heart or praise on her lips. In her heart she could hear God asking her, "Why?" Why hadn't He heard from her? He was delighted each time she called on Him, but lately He missed the sound of her voice. He wanted her to pour out her sorrows to Him.

Val knew what God wanted, and without hesitation she handed her troubles over to Him. Her soul immediately felt light. "Thank you, Jesus, for Your grace and Your mercy."

Val heard the reassuring sound of his voice telling her, "Everything is gonna be all right."

With that thought she closed her eyes and envisioned God holding her tight in His arms. She simply laid her head on the altar—which in her mind was God's shoulder—and smiled, to herself.

Back inside the courtroom Caitlyn's lawyer was still trying to get the judge to side with his client. "Judge Cohen, as you can see from Caitlyn's references, she comes from a very good family. There is no doubt she can provide for the child financially. The child will attend the best schools and have all the advantages a child needs. We ask that the court stop wasting taxpayers' money by humoring Mr. Reynolds and his need to seek custody of a child he has no claims to. Ms. Haas would like to expedite the matter as quickly as possible so that she may be a mother to her daughter."

Offended by the lawyer's remarks, Judge Cohen became increasingly leery of the lawyer's true intentions as time moved on. The young experienced lawyer lacked respect for the court and spoke to the judge as if he were a peon.

"Ms. Haas, what was your reason for giving your daughter up in the first place?" the judge asked.

Her lawyer sighed when he realized the judge had disregarded his remarks.

"Your Honor, I'm not sure," she stuttered. "I guess I felt like I was too young to care for a baby."

"Is it safe to assume the father felt the same as you?" Judge Cohen dug deep for answers.

"No." Uncertain of what to do, she searched her lawyer's eyes for an answer. "He never knew he had a daughter."

Judge Cohen stopped writing and set his pen down in front of him. "You mean to tell me Julian Pennington never knew he had a daughter?"

Caitlyn halfheartedly shook her head no.

"Your Honor," Caitlyn's lawyer tried to intercede on her behalf. "If you don't mind—"

"I do mind." He was tired of the lawyer's nonsense. Then he shifted the focus back to Caitlyn. "Why would you keep something like that a secret?" The judge sounded like a stern father reprimanding his child for doing wrong.

Caitlyn shrugged her shoulders in response.

Frustrated with the entire case, Judge Cohen sighed. "Ms. Haas, you carry very impressive references." He handed the bailiff a folder to give back to Caitlyn's lawyer. "You also come from a very good family, but none of that means much in my courtroom. I'm going to put in an immediate order for DNA testing. Ms. Haas, Hope and Mr. Reynolds will all have to be tested. It's only fair to Hope to know her true lineage. Once the results are in, they will be returned to my office. At that time I will contact all parties through their lawyers. We will meet back here, and I will not only read the results out loud, but also grant full custody to either Mr. Reynolds or Ms. Haas. In the meantime, I'm going to grant both you and Ms. Haas visitation to Hope at the group home where she is currently living." He picked up the gavel and slammed it hard against the sounding block.

Val slid her key into the lock that opened her front door. She entered, and from the kitchen she could hear Jonah talking with Mr. Lawson. The screen door slipped out her hands and slammed shut, creating a noise so loud, she felt like an intruder in her own home.

Jonah jumped from his seat and rushed into the foyer. "Hey!" He opened up his arms wide and embraced her with so much love, she thought she was going to start crying again. "I was worried when I couldn't find you at the courthouse. I tried to reach you on your cell phone, but it kept going straight to voice mail."

"I'm sorry," she whispered. "I wasn't feeling well and I

left to come home. But I thought maybe I just needed some fresh air, so I went out to the park."

Jonah looked at her strangely. "Are you feeling all right? I thought something else was wrong." Jonah pressed her for information.

"No." Val straightened out her clothes.

At the park, Val calculated the amount of time that had passed since Caitlyn and Julian were last together. She subtracted out nine months and ended up with a three-year-old child. Val added and subtracted months, weeks and years from every angle. It all turned out the same. There was a great possibility that Julian was Hope's father. If Hope really was Julian's child, that meant his seed had been living in her house, eating her food and sharing the same air as her.

Val closed her eyes and prayed this was all a dream. This couldn't be happening. Having to deal with Caitlyn was enough, but caring for Julian's daughter was too much.

"Val." Jonah touched her lightly to wake her from her thoughts.

"I'm fine." Val turned toward the kitchen and saw Mr. Lawson watching them. "Mr. Lawson, I apologize for leaving so suddenly at the courthouse. Sit down while I get you another cup of coffee, and you can tell me about the hearing."

Jonah watched Val strut past him and toward Mr. Lawson. He could sense that there was something wrong with her. What that was, he wasn't sure.

The following morning Val left the house when the sun was still down. She hadn't slept a wink all night. All she could think about was Caitlyn being Hope's biological mother.

After her talk with Mr. Lawson, Val volunteered to help in any way she could. That's why she was the first person in the law library that morning. She was determined to find any information to help Jonah keep Hope.

On her computer screen was a list of adoptive cases similar to Jonah's, but none denied the birth mother custody. In each case the child was always returned to the biological mother, except in instances of child abuse or neglect. She tapped a few keys and read through another list of cases. The database listed over three hundred cases, and she planned on going through every one.

After five hours of research, Val was tired. She couldn't take it any longer and needed help. Val sought assistance from the librarian. Mr. Lawson had warned her that this would be a hard case to win, but Val was determined to find at least one case of precedence. She put her trust in God and knew that with Him anything is possible.

Chapter 24

The fragrance of lavender-scented candles saturated the air, Will Downing's sultry voice adding a bit of spice to the evening and Olivia's sheer Calvin Klein dress was the finishing touch she needed to a perfectly planned rendezvous. This was the night she had been dreaming of since Dean's discharge from the hospital.

Over the past few weeks Dean had regained his strength. A good dose of rehab, rest, good cooking and lots of love from Olivia and Bryce were all contributing factors to his speedy recovery. He even felt strong enough to return back to work.

But tonight would be the night they would consummate their marriage. Olivia designated that night as their honeymoon, since they never got a chance to have one like most couples.

Olivia fanned her hands back and forth to dry her freshly painted nails while she waited for Dean to come home from work.

The timer on the stove alerted her to remove a pan of pasta shells stuffed with ricotta cheese and tomato sauce.

The enticing aroma swept past Olivia's nose and caused her stomach to growl. After taking the contents out the pan, she neatly arranged the main course on a serving platter. She placed everything on the dining room table and took one final look. Olivia excitedly tapped her right foot on the rug. "It's perfect! This is a night he will never forget," she said out loud. Then she grabbed a wineglass full of sparkling cider and relaxed until Dean arrived.

Fifteen minutes later Dean walked in the door unaware of what his wife had planned for the evening. She greeted him in the living room. The first thing he noticed was how low-cut her dress was.

"What's going on? Did I forget something? I know your birthday isn't until October." Dean was worried.

Olivia led him to the dining room table set for two with the fine china that belonged to her mother. "I thought we deserved to spend a quiet evening alone."

"Where's Bryce?" He sat across from her at the table.

"He's staying the night with my sister."

Worry lines formed along Dean's forehead.

"It's okay. Bryce is at that age where he tells everything he sees. If Danyelle does anything I won't like, he will tell me."

Olivia served her husband as if he were king. She looked stunning, and the candlelight seemed to only enhance her beauty. Once again he thanked the Lord for sending him a wife who possessed every quality he ever desired in a woman.

"What did you do with Clinton and Kennedy?" Dean looked around for the pooches. They usually welcomed him home.

"I put them outside for the night. I know they're used to sleeping in the house, but it won't hurt for them to sleep outside for one night."

"I miss their daily routine of jumping up on me when I come home from work." He smiled.

The couple ate their dinner in silence. The only sound they heard came from the knives and forks hitting their plates.

Dean practically cleared his plate before he took a hold of Olivia's hands. "Livie, don't think I don't appreciate everything you do for me." Dean didn't let a day go by without telling Olivia how much he loved her, but tonight was different. She had gone through a lot of trouble to make this night special. The candlelit dinner and sensual atmosphere were something he would cherish for the rest of his days.

"Listen, I know I've asked you to do some things you wouldn't typically do, like marry me without your family and then keep secrets from them, but if it gets to be too much, you have to let me know. I wouldn't want you to carry a burden that's too heavy for you."

With tears in her eyes she said, "I love you."

After they finished eating, Dean volunteered to clear the dishes from the table.

While he was busy cleaning up, Olivia slipped into their bedroom to change clothes. She opened her top dresser drawer and pulled out the red-and-black negligee Tressie helped her pick out earlier that day.

Olivia walked out and found Dean sitting comfortably on the living room sofa waiting for her to return. She cleared her throat. The dazed look on Dean's face visibly said he was confused and didn't know what was going on. Embarrassed, Olivia's face turned red. She timidly forced herself to stand directly in front of him.

Dean never knew Olivia had such a voluptuous body. Her curvy hips and ample thighs shouted out to him. He wanted to reach out and touch her long vanilla legs that were unblemished. He couldn't believe anyone that alluring could be real because he was sure she was a dream.

"Olivia." Dean reached out to caress her waist, but when he touched her she jumped away. He realized she was nervous. "We don't have to do this." He didn't want her to feel obligated to be with him.

"Why? Are you not feeling well?" Olivia grew concerned.

"No, I feel fine. Better than I have in weeks. But if you're not comfortable, then I can wait. I want us both to want this."

She may have been a little scared, but she was ready to be with her husband. Olivia took a deep breath and closed her eyes and climbed on top of him. That was her way of saying she was ready.

Dean rubbed her thighs. He was sure he would enjoy the rest of the evening. She climbed off him and led him to their bedroom. The look in his eyes said he had been waiting for this moment for a long time.

Bubbles greeted them as they entered the room together. Dean stopped and thought he had entered into Fantasy Island. Their bedroom had been transformed into an enchanted garden.

Olivia hoped she was seducing Dean the right way. Tressie often shared intimate details of things she did to set the mood for her ex-boyfriend Payce. She had to give it to the girl. Tressie did some creative things with candles, feathers and rose petals; but Olivia wanted something different. That's when the idea of bubbles came to her. Bryce had a bubble machine that Olivia used to fill the room with bubbles. She decorated the room with a few plants. The final touch was the soft pink lightbulb that illuminated the room.

Olivia was pleased that every minor detail went as planned. She loved Dean, and it was important for their first night together to be unforgettable. She wanted to give him just her body, but also a part of her soul.

As they sat on the side of the bed. Olivia waited for him to touch her, but he never did. Instead, he avoided looking at her by staring at the far wall.

Dean hadn't been with a woman in such a long time, he was just as nervous as she was.

Once she realized he wasn't going to make the first move, she took his hands and wrapped them around her waist. Pulling him down on top of her, she kissed him passionately.

Instantly the intensity grew between them. His hands roamed her body, and within minutes they were both unclothed. Dean gently laid her down on the bed, and the two of them made love late into the night.

After hours of lovemaking, the newlyweds passed out in a loving embrace. With bed sheets twisted around their naked bodies, dreams of their night together filled their mind.

Hours later Olivia, never a sound sleeper, woke at the sound of something crackling in the distance. It wasn't a loud noise, but it was enough to wake her. She turned over and pulled the pillow over her head, hoping it would block out the sound. The disturbance continued. Then she was forced to get up and investigate.

She looked around the bedroom and then over at Dean. The darkness of the room gave it an eerie feel. For the first time since they had moved into the house she felt vulnerable and unsafe.

Throwing on her robe and slippers she went into Bryce's room out of habit. She became alarmed when she found his bed empty, until she remembered he was staying with Danyelle. She walked back into her bedroom and climbed back into bed. She leaned over to kiss Dean and hopefully wake him for another sex session when she saw a bright light glowing from outside their bedroom window. She got up slowly and tiptoed toward the window. When she looked outside she screamed.

"Dean!"

The high-pitched way she yelled his name scared him. He lifted his head and jumped up when he saw the distress on his wife's face.

She called his name again and waved him over so he

could see what she saw.Olivia pulled the blinds up and watched a wooden cross burn on their front lawn.

Dean grabbed Olivia's hand, and they raced down the stairs. They had to get out of that house. He pulled open the front door and was ready to run out when he was stopped by the startling sight of Olivia's two shih tzus. The dogs had nooses tied around their necks and hung suspended from the rafters. Their fur had been burnt off, and blood dripped off their bodies.

Olivia screamed, and Dean ordered her back inside. She ran toward the phone and called the police.

Before Dean rushed back inside he saw the taillights of a pickup truck pull off a few feet away from the house.

Ten minutes later, the police and fire department had arrived and took statements. The firemen hosed down the burning cross and took it down.

Detective Craig Denali stared at the racial slurs that had been written on the front of the house in blood. Then he went to speak with Dean.

"Mr. West, I know this must be upsetting for you and your family. The police department is going to follow all leads to find out who is responsible for this, but I don't think this is just a random act of hate. I would bet my badge that Judge West's home was targeted on purpose."

Dean took a seat on the curb and watched the police take samples of blood from the house and place them in a small petri dish. He was afraid to tell anyone else his secret. He wasn't sure if he could trust the police to protect him and his family.

"I'm going to post a car out here to watch the house for the rest of the night," the detective said. "We have all units searching the area for any suspicious persons, but if you need anything, give us a call." He handed Dean his card and walked away.

Chapter 25

Val pressed both hands against her temples to try and stop the throbbing headache that had haunted her all morning and most of the afternoon. She popped two aspirins in her mouth and waited for relief. She couldn't believe how bad her head hurt. Val crossed the floor to the librarian's desk.

"Hi. Did you happen to find any of the information I was looking for?" Val hoped the librarian had some luck, because she was running out of options.

The librarian knelt down and placed a pile of books on the counter. "This is all we have in this library. Honey, if you don't find what you're looking for in here, then I doubt you'll ever find it."

Val pulled the pile of books closer to her, but the librarian stopped her.

"You don't look well. Your eyes are really red."

"I have a headache," Val told her.

"Is it hurting your eyes?"

"A little," Val replied.

"Why don't you go home? You've been the first person in

this library every day for the past couple weeks, and you stay until it closes. I know lawyers like to burn the midnight oil, but everyone deserves a little rest." She pulled the books back toward her. "Now go! I'll save these books for you."

Val reluctantly went back to the table and gathered her things. She didn't want to leave, but the librarian had a point. If she went home and got some rest, she could return in the morning refreshed. A clear mind and fresh eyes may have been preventing her from finding the right precedence case.

As Val exited through the revolving doors, some college kid bumped into her. He almost knocked her to the ground. Val wouldn't have cared, if it wasn't for the fact that she got a huge whiff of the sandwich he was carrying. Her stomach growled from the pastrami and cheese on toasted roll. It was her favorite.

"That looks so good." Her gaze followed the boy and his sandwich until they disappeared out of sight.

Instead of heading toward the parking lot, Val strolled toward the nearest deli. She had to get a sandwich. On her way she passed by a children's boutique that happened to have a sign outside advertising their grand opening. From the sidewalk, dresses, skirts and tiny little patent leather shoes called her inside. Instantly, she fell in love with what the store had to offer.

An hour later Val emerged with both arms loaded with packages. She was now starving, but there was one more thing she had to get. She walked a few feet and entered the toy store. Hope had plenty of toys at the house, but Val had her heart set on something special for Julian's only daughter.

She walked straight to an aisle full of teddy bears, all wearing New York Knicks jerseys with Julian's number. After Julian died, the bears were sold throughout the city in remembrance of his life. She was glad the stuffed toys were still being stocked and even happier that she was able to find one so easily. She knelt down to grab a bear from off the bottom shelf, one that hadn't been touched. Then a pair of legs wearing white tights and a short purple skirt walked up to her.

"Do you need any help?" the stranger offered.

"No, actually I think I got what I came for." Val stood up and looked straight into Caitlyn's eyes and at her shopping cart full of toys.

Val was weary. She didn't trust Caitlyn.

Caitlyn stepped up closer to her and pointed her finger in her face. "Are you going to hit me? Go ahead. I want you to. I would love to tell the judge how Hope's father's girlfriend violated the restraining order I have against her."

Val ground her teeth together to remain calm. "Caitlyn, why are you here?"

Caitlyn sucked her teeth. "This is not about you. I came here to buy my daughter a few toys." Caitlyn looked at the bears sitting on the shelf. "It's obvious you also were shopping for my child. Val, let me give you a bit of advice—Don't bother. As soon as those test results come back, my daughter will be coming home with me. She won't need anything from you. I can provide all her needs, especially when I get back to Seattle."

"What do you think your family is going to say when you return home with a black daughter?" Val's patience was about to blow. "They will disown you and cut you off financially, and I'm sure you could never live with that," Val said.

Caitlyn gave her a smirk. "I hear jealousy in your voice. The same kind I heard when you found out Julian chose me over you. Are you jealous? Jealous of the fact that I had Julian's child and you didn't?"

Val was tired of talking and tried to walk around her, but Caitlyn stood in her path.

"No. You're going to listen to every word I have to say."

Val was surprised by her boldness.

"You should have seen your face when you walked into that courtroom and realized I was Hope's mother." Caitlyn laughed. "You know, I paid one thousand dollars for my plane ticket here, and my lawyer charges me seven hundred and fifty dollars an hour, but the look you gave when you found out Julian was the father was priceless." She laughed in Val's face. "The only thing that would have made that moment better was if Julian was here to tell you himself."

"Julian didn't know about Hope." Val sounded unsure of herself. "He would have never abandoned his child."

Caitlyn giggled, turned her back to Val and picked up a teddy bear from off the shelf. "No, Julian didn't know about the baby. I was going to tell him, but my family didn't think it was wise. Having his baby may have tarnished my family's name."

"What?" Val couldn't believe what she was hearing.

"My uncle didn't think Julian was good enough to be counted among the greats like Charles Barkley, Isaiah Thomas or Larry Bird. That's why he didn't have any problems trading him when Julian asked. When I found out I was pregnant, no one was more shocked than me. I knew that you and Julian were back together, and I was so far along that an abortion was not an option. So I settled for adoption."

"So why do you want her back now? How can you tear her away from the only father she has ever known?"

"Isn't it obvious? I love my daughter and I want her with me." Caitlyn's words sounded empty and uncaring. "When I take Hope back to Seattle with me, don't fret, because I plan to leave you with something to remember me by." Caitlyn's sincere smile turned to a smirk. "A broken heart—because, rest assured, I'll have a seat sitting next to me for that handsome Jonah."

Val rolled her eyes.

"Just like old times."

* * *

Val pulled her car into its regular space in the garage. She pushed the button to turn off her ignition and rested a minute before going inside. Laying her head back on the headrest, she closed her eyes to slow her adrenaline down. Caitlyn was the one person who always managed to bring out the worst in her. She sat for a second and prayed that the Lord would take over her spirit. After she finished, she took a deep breath and realized it had been a while since she'd last spoken with Olivia. They were way overdue for one of their heart-to-heart talks.

Val set her things down in the living room. The faint sound of a radio playing in the distance and the clanging sound of weights made her stop what she was doing and listen carefully. It sounded like it was coming from the basement. She slipped off her high-heeled shoes and attempted to go downstairs when the house phone rang.

Val picked up the kitchen extension. She was surprised. It was Julian's mother on the other end. "Hey, Val, it's Mrs. McCormick. I was just calling to find out how you were doing."

Val's heart nearly jumped out her chest. It shouldn't have been a surprise to hear from the woman who would have been her mother-in-law. Julian's mother worried about her almost as much as her own mother, but her call was so unexpected. What if Jonah would have picked up the phone instead of her? How would she explain that one?

"I'm doing well. How about you?" Val had to cut this phone call short.

"I'm trying to keep busy. Mr. McCormick wants to go away on vacation, but I'm not sure I'm ready to leave home."

Val listened to Mrs. McCormick talk, but she was too deep in thought to comprehend a word she was saying. All she could think about was Hope. How would she explain to Julian's mother that she has a three-year-old granddaughter? She held the phone to her ear, wondering if she should tell her about Hope now or later.

"Mrs. McCormick," Val interrupted her mid-sentence. "Do you ever feel like Julian left a piece of himself here with us on earth?"

Silence filled the line, and it took Mrs. McCormick a moment to respond. She found it strange that Val would ask such a question. "Yes, I do."

Val was caught off-guard by her answer.

"I know I sound like a grieving mother, but I carry my son with me everywhere I go. Whether it be the supermarket, the park or work, I carry him in my heart."

That was not the response Val was looking for. Then she was reminded of Jonah by the sound of him rapping in the basement. Val quickly ditched her idea to tell Mrs. Mc-Cormick anything. First, she had to tell Jonah about Julian.

"Mrs. McCormick, I have to go, but I promise I'll call you later on in the week." Val hung up the phone and bolted down the steps to the finished basement.

When she reached the bottom step she was stunned at the sight of Jonah's bare chest glistening with sweat under the bright lights. He lay on a bench press lifting one hundred and seventy-five pounds. Val watched his bulging arm muscles flex. She watched for a moment before clearing her throat.

He looked up. "Hey, I didn't hear your car pull up. I hope you don't mind me using the weights. I found them pushed in the corner and I needed to work off some steam."

Val looked around at all the equipment laid out on the floor. They were Julian's weights. "I'm surprised to find you home."

Over the past couple weeks Jonah had stayed busy. He spent close to sixteen hours a day at work and at least four hours at the children's home with Hope. The remaining four hours of the day he used to sleep.

"Did you forget? We're supposed to meet with Mr. Lawson tonight. He wants to discuss details of the case with us tonight over dinner."

She threw her hand to her mouth. "It must have slipped my mind."

Just a minute ago she was all ready to tell Jonah everything about Julian, but something stopped her. She couldn't bring herself to do it. Her past relationship with Hope's biological father could complicate things, and she couldn't risk Jonah losing faith in her.

"I bought some clothes for Hope. You can take them to her the next time you visit," Val said.

"Thanks." He got up to load the bar down with more weights. "I'll take them tomorrow." He started pumping iron again.

Val was mesmerized by the sight of Jonah's muscular body. He noticed her watching him and stopped lifting. She couldn't pull her eyes away, and before she realized what was happening, Jonah stood directly in front of her. Her hands quivered and he pulled her lips toward him. He softly brushed his lips against hers. She savored his touch and she felt her heart flutter. She felt something for Jonah that was foreign. It was different than her love for Julian.

He pulled her closer by embracing her waist and kissed her a little deeper. She opened her mouth and allowed his tongue to enter. A soft moan released itself from her. She abruptly pulled away from him.

"I'm sorry," he apologized. "I shouldn't have . . . I thought that . . ."

"No, it's not your fault. I . . ." She looked away and thought about Julian. Guilt flooded her conscience. She scolded herself for being so weak and betraying her love for

Julian. "I need to go get ready. We don't want to be late." She disappeared up the stairs.

A tall slender hostess escorted Jonah and Val to the table where Mr. Lawson was already seated and enjoying a huge lobster tail. He wore a bright red plastic bib that extended from his neck down to his huge protruding belly. When he saw Val and Jonah walking his way, he waved them over with one hand and used the other to take a swig of beer from his mug. Jonah pulled out a chair for Val and, once they were seated, placed their orders with the waitress.

"Folks, I'm sorry to be the bearer of bad news." Mr. Lawson didn't waste any time. He cracked open a lobster claw and gazed at the meat momentarily before shoving it in his mouth. "I've studied practically every adoption case in the state of Pennsylvania, Washington and Louisiana, and I can't find one that has not returned a child to its birth mother.

Jonah cupped his head in his hands and let out a low discouraging groan. Mr. Lawson had confirmed his worst fears. He was going to lose his daughter.

"The only instances I found where a birth mother was denied custody of their child was if the mother was a drug addict or lived the kind of life that would put the child in physical danger. I even went as far as to get a few people I know to look into the girl's past. She came back clean. A few parking tickets and they were settled by her family lawyer. She wasn't lying when she said that her family practically owned Seattle." Mr. Lawson looked toward Val. "Did you come across anything at the library that could possibly help us?"

Val's eyes offered him no hope.

Val knew in her heart that Caitlyn was an opportunist and gold-digger, but she doubted that Caitlyn had any skeletons in her closet worth uncovering. If she did, the

Haas family would have them buried so deep, it would take decades to uncover them.

Mr. Lawson's cell phone rang loudly. He answered and quickly placed his hand over the mouthpiece. "I wanted to tell the both of you in person that I don't think there is anything else I can do for you." He threw his napkin down on the table. "But don't think I've given up. I'm going to work on this until the very end." He pointed toward the phone. "This is a close business associate of mine. I have to get going, but anything you order is on me. So enjoy."

Val and Jonah thanked him, and as Mr. Lawson walked away he spoke into the phone, "Reverend Baxter, what can I do for you?"

Once their meal arrived, Jonah and Val ate their dinner in silence. "Do you want to talk about what happened between us earlier today?" Jonah played with his food.

"No, not really." She pointed across the table. "Can you pass me the salt?"

He handed her the saltshaker. "Val, I feel something special whenever I'm near you, and I know you feel the same." He touched her hand. "You're the most beautiful, intelligent and generous woman I know, and it's rare to find a woman as pretty as you who isn't conceited, stuck-up or selfish."

She couldn't help but smile. She threw her napkin at him playfully.

"I'm just kidding, but can you do me a favor?"

She nodded her head yes.

"Would you go out with me and Hope this Saturday?"

"Are you sure?" Val was honored that he wanted to share his time with Hope. "I don't want to intrude on your time together."

He nodded his head. "The last time I visited with her she asked me"—he pointed to himself—"to ask you"—He pointed toward her—"to go out with us, and I told her I would."

Val eyed him suspiciously. "She did not say that."

"No." He laughed. "Those weren't her exact words, but we did talk about asking you to go out with us on Saturday. It's the first time social services are going to allow me to visit with her away from the home. I thought it would be fun if you came along. She's grown so much since the last time you've seen her. We figured that if we treated you to lunch that would be a start at thanking you for everything you've done for us."

Val pushed the broccoli around on her plate. Jonah's request warmed her heart. It felt good to be wanted by someone. "I would love to go out with the two of you on Saturday."

"Great. I know exactly where we'll go. I promise you will enjoy yourself. So it's a date. I'll pick you up at one o'clock sharp in your living room." They looked at one another and laughed heartily.

Chapter 26

Dean wanted to come to the jail alone. He wanted to confront his grandpa in private about the vandalism that happened at the house, but Colin thought it was a bad idea. He knew how upset Dean was and he didn't want things to get out of hand. So he offered to tag along to make sure things went smoothly.

"I appreciate you coming with me," Dean said after they sat down in the visiting room.

"I'll do whatever I can to help you out." Colin gave him a brotherly hug before Judge West was escorted in.

"Congratulations!" the judge shouted. "I heard you and Olivia got married. I always said she was a good woman. I'm so glad you made it official. You made a good choice."

"How did you find out?" Dean wasn't going to tell him anything about the wedding.

"Reverend Simms told me. He still comes to visit at least once a week." Then he turned to Colin. "I guess your partner told you everything."

Colin nodded his head yes.

"Are you disappointed?"

Colin wasn't sure what to say. "Judge West, I love you. What you did in the past has nothing to do with right now. As far as I'm concerned, your slate is wiped clean with me." Colin turned toward Dean. "It's others who may not be as forgiving."

Judge West understood then spoke to his grandson. "I thought you were finished with me for good. What brings you back to this hellhole?"

"As if you don't know."

The judge looked at him confused.

"Your friends left a burning cross on our front lawn? What do your people want? Why are they harassing me and my family?"

The judge inhaled a few times, and when he was finally ready to talk, he had tears in his eyes. "At first I thought they just wanted payback against me because I had left the brotherhood, but after the letter I got the other day, now I know they want more."

He had Colin and Dean's full attention.

"The brotherhood accused me of abandoning them. They told me I was a thief, because I took their money for law school and they were never compensated for paying my way."

"So this is about money," Colin said.

"I wish it were that easy, but I think this is their way of warning me not to implicate any of them in the murder of that boy. If I try to cut a deal with the feds or cooperate with them in any way, they will reach out to hurt my family."

"Damn!" Dean slammed his fist down on the table. "I can't believe this could affect my family." He pointed in his grandpa's face. "Nothing better not happen to my wife or I'll kill you myself."

"Dean . . ." Judge West was at a loss for words.

"Judge, is there anything we can do to stop them?" Colin intervened.

"I did get a letter the other day and they offered to have all the charges against me dropped," Judge West said.

"They can't do that," Dean said. "The feds are the ones prosecuting you."

"Don't you understand? They *are* the government. I told you that they have connections everywhere. Don't under-estimate the power of the brotherhood. A lot of liberals think that racism has ceased to exist, that it died off after the civil rights movement. That is far from the truth. Trust me, it's alive and well." He folded his arms in front of him. "Just because they don't lynch people from trees any longer does-n't mean that minorities in this country aren't still being lynched. Millions of narrow-minded people run this coun-try. They come in all forms. It could be that lovely real es-tate agent who is so nice and has done everything she could to help you find the perfect house, but she only shows you the homes in the black neighborhoods because they don't want your kind living next door to them. What about the school guidance counselor who insists that your child is not smart enough to keep up in the regular classes? Then your child is labeled as a special education case until graduation."

"What do they want you to do?" Colin asked.

"They've asked me to rejoin them. They want to rein-state my membership and have me do the work I was sup-posed to do when I left the brotherhood."

"Yo, man," Dean was talking to Colin, "I told you this was some sick stuff. So I guess this means you're going to rejoin them."

"If it means keeping you and your family safe, then I'll do what I have to do," Judge West replied.

"Man, I can't take any more of this." Dean tapped Colin on the arm. "I'll wait for you out in the car." He left the room.

"Colin, you have to understand I'm just trying to do what's right, so that no one gets hurt. I know what kind of power that organization has and what they can do. They'll kill him if I don't cooperate."

"Don't worry, Judge, I'll talk to him. But what about you? This has to be hard for you."

"I've been beating myself up over being so dumb."

"You were a kid. You didn't know any better. It's a good thing God doesn't hold us accountable for the things we did before we were covered with the blood." Colin could see how sad he was. He needed some reassuring words.

"Some days I feel so ashamed of what I did in the past that I can't even get out of bed. I cover my head with blankets to try and hide my disappointment from God."

"Let's pray!" Colin spoke a powerful prayer asking God to heal all hearts surrounding the matter.

Together they ended the prayer with, "Amen."

"What do you do now?" Colin stared into the old man's aging bloodshot eyes.

"Nothing. I wait for them to get in touch with me. That's when I'll tell them that I'll rejoin them." He looked Colin in the eye. "Please don't think less of me because of what I'm doing. I could never again believe in what they represent. I may have to do some unethical things to keep my family safe, but in my heart, I love all God's children." He looked away.

"I figure the first thing they'll want me to do is work on this bill the Black Caucus is trying to pass. They sent me newspaper clippings describing the bill in detail. Ultimately, the bill will reopen hundreds of closed murder cases that occurred during the civil rights area. In more than ninety-five percent of those cases no one was ever charged. Each case, no matter what the evidence suggested, was automatically classified as a suicide or accidental death." Judge West slowly shook his head. "I'll probably have to move back to Washington."

"But it would take more than your vote to kill the bill," Colin told him.

"They wouldn't want me to be a part of this for nothing. I'm sure they already have several members strategically in place to assist me. I'm just a small piece to the puzzle. I'm sure they have Charles Seale, Joel Watkins, Eddie Frist and Henry Sellers working for them."

"Who are they?" Colin wondered out loud.

"They were guys just like me. The brotherhood put them through law school, and I know that each of them have become very successful in Washington. I've followed each of their careers, and I can tell by the things that they've advocated against and for that they are still active members of the brotherhood. One guy is even a part of Congress. They have people throughout this country shaping it into what they feel it should be."

Colin looked at his watch. "Listen, Judge, I have to go, but I promise I'll be back to visit you some time next week." He got up, and the two hugged.

"Colin, can you keep an eye on my grandson? I can see how this ordeal is taking a toll on his health. He looks so thin."

Colin looked into his eyes and remembered that Judge West didn't know about Dean's illness. "Yes, sir. I'll do that." He then left out the door.

"Colin, what's wrong? You haven't said much since you picked me up."

Danyelle and Colin held hands as they strolled along the Penn's Landing waterfront.

He smiled before kissing her hand. "I'm just enjoying the evening with one beautiful lady."

"Olivia told me you and Dean went to visit with Judge West this afternoon. How did it go?" she asked.

"It was nice."

His words were empty, and his face was so emotionless, Danyelle guessed that the visit was heavy on Colin's mind.

They walked a few more feet before Danyelle stopped and turned toward him. She grabbed both his hands. "You can tell me anything. I'm here for you whenever you need."

Colin's heart formed a smile. It felt so good to know that Danyelle did care about him, but he couldn't let her know that. "Why you being so nice to me?" He looked at her suspiciously. "This is not the same hard, cold girl that brushes me off every time I speak to her."

She pushed his hands away from her.

"The Danyelle I know would have hung up on me when I called."

"I'm worried about you."

Her words were full of sincere warmth that confirmed Colin's thoughts that she was the one for him.

"If that were true, then I wouldn't feel like you and I were secret lovers."

Danyelle's face turned guilty.

"No one knows how I feel about you, and you act like you want to keep it a secret from your family and friends when I'm ready to tell the whole world." He pulled her closer to him. "Can you put a little trust in me? I wasn't lying when I told you that I love you."

"I want to believe you, but it's hard for me to put one hundred percent of myself into what we have. I'm scared that if I start caring for you that I might lose sight of God's vision for my life. I know the Father will provide all my needs, but I can't afford to lose favor with Him. He's brought me so far. I finally have a prosperous outlook on life."

"Do you think I would get in the way of that?" Colin asked.

"Not intentionally, but it comes naturally for a woman to

want to nurture her man. Right now I only have room for one man, and that's God."

Colin was disappointed, but he understood. "I would try and change your mind, but I'm not going to do that. You may not know it yet, but God has already told me that we belong together. So I'm going to pray on it, and one day you will be mine." He pulled the back of her hand up to his lips.

Chapter 27

Saturdays were generally hectic at the children's home, and this Saturday wasn't any different. Jonah opened the lobby door for Val.

Mrs. Chambers smiled when she saw the couple enter together. While balancing the phone in one ear, she turned to another staff member. "Can you please go get Hope Reynolds from the rec room? I remember seeing her in there watching cartoons."

The girl dashed off and Mrs. Chambers spoke to Jonah. "You are one of the more reliable parents. You haven't missed a Saturday," she said.

"I miss her," Jonah replied.

Children screamed, phones rang and chaos was erupting in every direction.

"Jonah, I have to apologize again for not being able to get that overnight pass for you, but my supervisor wouldn't approve it because of the questions surrounding Hope's maternity."

"That's okay, Mrs. Chambers. I appreciate being able to spend the afternoon with her."

"She's excited. One of the aids was helping her get dressed

this morning and she bragged about the new clothes you bought for her. Today she's wearing your favorite color."

"Yellow," Jonah said.

"Yes, but don't tell her I told you."

Whoever had Mrs. Chambers on hold returned back to her.

"Daddy!" Hope screamed and ran into her father's arms.

"Don't you look pretty? And you're wearing my favorite color."

She delightfully nodded her head up and down.

He turned toward Val. "Aren't you going to say hi to Ms. Val?"

She glanced at Val and hid her face in her father's neck.

Val knew Hope hadn't seen her in a while. She prayed their outing today would make her feel more comfortable around her.

Jonah signed Hope out, and they left.

"Where are we headed?" Val asked once they were in the car.

"Have you ever heard of the Please Touch Museum?" Jonah studied a few Internet printouts.

"Yes, Olivia takes her son there all the time. I've never been, but I heard it's a great place for kids." Val merged into traffic.

"It was listed as one of the city's best places for children. I figured Hope would like it. She likes to explore."

Val glanced at Hope in her rearview mirror. She sat quietly in her car seat checking out the new doll her father bought her. "I think you're right. She'll love it."

The Please Touch Museum was built especially for young children. It encourages youngsters to touch the displays while at the same time providing a playful learning experience. Both Jonah and Val felt like children. The trio browsed the aisle of the mini supermarket and later had tea with Alice in Wonderland.

During the course of the day Hope's attitude toward Val

changed little. By the smiles on their faces, any stranger would assume they were a happy family. They laughed and played together, but when Val tried to get close to Hope, the little girl got stiff. Her body would tense up, she avoided even looking in Val's direction and would run to the safety of her father's arms.

Upset that she couldn't connect with Hope, Val stepped back and watched how Jonah interacted with his daughter.

He saw her watching them. He told Hope she could continue playing in the pool of balls just as long as he could see her. Then he went to rest next to Val.

He took a seat. "What's up?"

"Nothing. It's been a long day, and I'm getting tired. I don't want to ruin your time with Hope, so I think maybe I'll leave and allow you to spend some time alone with her."

"Listen, I told you it's going to take some time for Hope to trust you. I've seen how distant she is toward you. Stop being so anxious. She'll come around when you least expect it. Are you hungry?" Jonah didn't want her to leave. He grabbed Val's hand and wouldn't let it go. He called Hope over, and the three of them left. "Where shall we get something to eat?"

They stood outside the museum contemplating their next move.

"Why don't we let Hope pick?" Val suggested.

"Nope! Not this time. We invited you out. We always eat wherever Hope wants, and it's usually pizza."

Hope squeezed her father's hand.

"Okay." Val laughed. "I don't really like fast food. Let's see if we can find a restaurant close by where we can sit down and eat."

They turned to stroll down the surrounding streets when Val's body froze at the sound of her name. She would recognize that voice anywhere. She turned around and stood face to face with Julian's mom and stepfather.

"Hi!" Val sang.

Mrs. McCormick reached out to give Val a hug, then her eyes did a beeline straight to Jonah and Hope.

"I told my husband that was you." She smiled. "I would recognize those hips anywhere."

"What are you doing out here?" Val's body temperature was steadily rising.

"We were taking a walk in the park, and I think he's getting a little dehydrated because he started getting a little sluggish during that last mile." She reached out and patted her husband on the stomach. "We're going to the convenience store to get him a Gatorade."

"You two have to be careful out here. Summer is fast approaching. We don't want either of you to hurt yourselves."

There was an uncomfortable silence as everyone searched for something to say.

Mrs. McCormick knelt down in front of Hope. "You are such a pretty little girl."

Val couldn't believe Hope's reaction. She let go of Jonah's hand and leapt into Mrs. McCormick's arms.

"And friendly. Look, honey," she said to her husband. "Isn't she cute?"

He nodded his head yes.

"She doesn't do that with just anybody," Jonah said. "I'm her father, and this is my daughter Hope."

Val looked like she was in a daze. Jonah wondered why she hadn't introduced them to her friends.

"It's a pleasure to meet you."

They shook hands.

"Were you at the Please Touch Museum?" Mrs. McCormick asked.

"Yes, and I shopped at the supermarket and I got this." Hope held up the trinkets she bought at the museum store.

Val was stunned. She not only went to Mrs. McCormick, but she also talked to her. The little girl wouldn't even speak to her.

"She is adorable," Mrs. McCormick said. "Val, you have to bring them by the house for dinner."

"I would like that," Jonah replied.

Val smiled. "Sure, Mrs. McCormick. I'll give you a call." And she stepped backward, hinting it was time for them to leave.

Jonah held out his hand for Hope, they said their good-byes and left.

"Y ou were unusually quiet at the restaurant." Val hadn't even noticed Jonah had gotten back in the car. "Did you see how she reacted to Mrs. McCormick? Hope doesn't even know her."

"I told you Hope is funny like that. Some people she takes to more readily than others. Plus, that lady reminded me of the grandmotherly type."

"How did it go when you took Hope inside?" Val wanted to change the subject.

"She cried and reached out for me. One of the staff members had to pull her away. We go through the same thing every week. It's hard leaving her behind. I hope Mr. Lawson finds a way for us to be together."

Val could hear how hard it was for Jonah to leave his daughter behind. She rubbed his back. "Listen, don't give up. Stay prayerful. I don't know what's in the Lord's plans, but I know He won't let you down."

Val backed out of the parking lot, and they headed home.

"Mr. and Mrs. McCormick seem like a really nice couple. Mrs. McCormick talked like she's known you for a long time," Jonah said.

Val kept her eyes straight ahead. She was not ready to have this conversation, but she knew this was the perfect opportunity for her to come clean.

"Why do I feel like there's tension in the air?" Jonah asked.

Val swallowed hard. "I was engaged to their son."

"Oh! Now I understand why you were acting so nervous," he replied. "You kept playing with your hands and shuffling your feet."

"I was not." She laughed.

"Well, I guess we won't be going there for dinner."

"I don't think so."

"Why didn't you tell me you were engaged?"

"There's not much to tell. Weddings are called off every day. I don't want to act like my broken engagement was something special."

"Yeah, but I'm sure it hurt. Is that whose clothes were packed away at the house?"

Val nodded her head yes.

"I don't know what happened, but I can see it was painful. I won't mention it again."

Val sighed. "I appreciate that."

When they entered the house Val laid her keys down on the kitchen table and went toward the stairs to take a hot shower and change clothes.

Jonah stopped her and walked up close to her. Their lips were inches apart.

"Thank you," he whispered.

Val could feel the intensity of the moment. When he looked at her she could feel her heart being drawn in his direction. Her palms perspired. She wiped them along her pants, and before she knew it, he pressed his lips to her and pulled her into his embrace. Val couldn't stop herself from wanting more kisses. She kissed him back, and her arms caressed his back. The kisses quickly rose in passion, and through his pants Val could feel his erection.

She pulled away from him. "We have to stop."

But Jonah didn't want to stop. "We don't have to." He tried grabbing at her.

"No." She backed away. "Good night, Jonah." Val turned and retreated to her bedroom.

Chapter 28

Colin swung his office keys in his left hand and snapped a beat with his right hand. He picked up his pace. He had to drop his things off at his office before his first class started. A quick glance at his watch showed he only had ten minutes before he would be late.

On his office door someone had posted a bright yellow note with his name scrawled across the front. He snatched it off and read it.

PLEASE SEE ME AFTER YOUR FIRST CLASS—REVEREND BAXTER.

The urgent box in the far left-hand corner of the note was checked.

Enthusiasm grew. Colin had a good idea what the reverend wanted to see him about. It had to be about the Assistant Dean position he applied for weeks ago. It was about time Reverend Baxter appointed someone to that position.

With his spirits high, he opened the door and placed his briefcase down. He grabbed the books he would need, then dashed back out the door. On his way to class he couldn't help but smile.

Colin was friends with just about every candidate who applied for the position, but the difference between him and them was their true intentions for wanting the position. The thirty-thousand-dollar pay raise was a huge incentive for many, but Colin wasn't in it for the money. He loved to teach, and this new position would allow him to develop new programs, and enhance the Christian learning experience.

When Colin arrived to class, his students were waiting on him. He walked to the head of the classroom and handed out a pop quiz. His students sulked and moaned in response, but he whistled happily as he gave them thirty minutes to complete the test.

A half hour later, he instructed those who weren't finished to hand in their papers. Then he gave his students a rare treat–an early dismissal. Colin was anxious to get over to Baxter's office.

Colin set out on foot to Baxter's office. Although he had to travel over a mile, it didn't matter. His long legs got him there in no time.

He entered the building and walked the long corridor that led to Baxter's office. When he reached his destination he saw that Baxter's office door was partially ajar. He could hear voices inside. One was Baxter's, the other was unfamiliar to him. Out of respect, Colin didn't want to interrupt their conversation, so he stepped away from the door and chose to wait out in the hall.

A few feet away Colin was sure he heard the two men mention his name. He crept back toward the door and eavesdropped on their conversation. He was dying to know if he had gotten the job or not.

"So you're really going to offer Montgomery that Assistant Dean position?" the stranger asked.

"He is the most qualified. Plus, it looks good for the school. He would be the first African American in the history of the school to be appointed to such a high position, not to mention the increase in federal grant money from the government for promoting a minority." He laughed. "Of course, I've already arranged to have my cut taken off the top. The school wouldn't be getting these extra dollars if it weren't for my brilliant thinking."

"Make sure you keep that coon in check. You know how they get when they get a little bit of power. They start thinking they're in charge."

They chuckled together.

"Times certainly have changed. My ancestors were slave owners. They actually owned blacks, and now they have more rights than we do," Baxter replied.

Colin couldn't believe what he was hearing. Professor Baxter was someone he considered a friend. They had a good relationship. Colin never suspected the man was a racist. He had eaten at this man's dinner table, played golf with him and even got into serious debates about the different mysteries of the Bible. Colin was stunned.

"What happened with Eddie Frist?"

That name sounded familiar to Colin, but he couldn't remember where he had heard it before.

"The feds didn't even have enough evidence to hold him, but we're still working on Ernie West, and I can just about guarantee he'll side with us. He would rather die first than let anything happen to that black grandson."

"I still can't believe you're the one who found West after all these years."

"Neither can I. Imagine my surprise when I visited Montgomery's church and I saw him sitting out in the congregation. The only white face among a sea of blacks. I had to return a second time just to make sure it was him. But it was smart of him to hide out all these years in the black community. I would have never thought to find him there. I got a call from the former Grand Wizard, and he said that he would make sure I was generously rewarded at the banquet ceremony. Are you going?"

"Yup. I just received my invitation," the man replied. "Isn't it set for next week at the Claymont Country Club?"

"Yes, the brotherhood is not only moving up in the world, but also out into the open." Baxter gave a hearty laugh.

Colin slumped against the brick wall. *How does he know Judge West?* Colin's mind was in a daze. He stumbled toward the men's room to splash some cold water on his face. He drenched his face three times before drying off with a towel. *What am I going to do?*

The door to the bathroom opened, and Reverend Baxter entered.

"Colin, I was just talking about you to a colleague of mine. I assume you got my note that's why you're here."

Colin gave him a blank stare.

"Is everything all right with you?"

Colin turned back toward the mirror. In it he could see both of their reflections, and for the first time Reverend Baxter did not look anything like the godly man he had grown to trust. Baxter's features transformed right before his eyes.

In the blink of an eye, the professor's pale skin turned a shade of dark red. His eyebrows arched up, and the pupils in his eyes lost their color. Colin could feel wickedness in the room.

He jumped back and tumbled over the trashcan. Everything, including him, fell to the ground.

Baxter went to help him up.

"No." Colin shielded himself from any help.

"Colin, you don't look too well."

"I-I have to go." Colin dashed out.

"Don't worry about the rest of your classes. I'll find someone to cover for you."

Baxter yelled out after him, but Colin never heard him. He was already out the door and over to the music arts building.

He rushed in and searched several classrooms before he found who he was looking for.

He charged into the classroom. He wrapped his fingers around Danyelle's arm and pushed her out the room.

"Colin!" Danyelle shrieked. "What are you doing?"

He pulled Danyelle outside into the hallway. "I need to talk with you, and it's important." He paced in front of her, waving his hands like a madman.

She had never seen him act like this before. She stopped him and took his hand. "Tell me what's going on."

He sighed heavily. It was strange how, at a time when he had just heard the worst news possible, all he could think about was how much he loved Danyelle. He moved one of her golden brown micro braids away from her face and caressed her cheek. He didn't think it was possible to love another human being as much as he loved her.

This was all for her. The advantages this new position would bring him would be meaningless without Danyelle. He thought about what he would have to give up if he turned the position down and resigned from teaching. He couldn't work for a man like that. The biggest disappointment he would have to endure would be postponing his future with Danyelle.

That meant he would have to look for another job, and he was sure he would have to take a significant pay cut.

He thought he needed to talk to Danyelle, but he changed his mind. He needed to talk with God.

"Colin, are you going to tell me what's on your mind?" Danyelle asked again.

"Nothing is wrong with me. I was just having a bad day,

and seeing your pretty face just made it a whole lot better. Now since I've already interrupted your class, why don't we go down to the cafeteria and grab something to eat?"

Although Danyelle wasn't totally convinced of his answer, she decided to let it go. She knew he would talk to her when he was ready. Until then she would wait.

Chapter 29

The risqué scene that erupted between Jonah and Val left them afraid to be alone together. For days the two tried to avoid all contact, but it was hard. They stopped talking, eating meals together, and they barely spoke to one another.

It was weird for Val. The kiss, the passion and desire that raced through her body when Jonah touched her were something she wasn't expecting. It was like she had been drugged with a poison that she couldn't control. She was so ashamed of her lustful desires that she repented daily. Her feelings frightened her so much that she locked herself in her bedroom and only came out when Jonah wasn't at home.

Jonah also had a bunch of feelings that left him confused. His behavior the other night was so unexpected. He had never acted like that before. It's not like he had never been with a woman before, but holding Val and caressing her soft body made him insane. He would have laid her down on the spot.

Now he regretted his actions. Things were so different

between them. Val put so much distance between them, he didn't know if he would ever get close to her again.

Jonah stood outside of Val's bedroom door all ready to go spend the afternoon with his daughter. He'd promised Hope he would pick her up early, but he didn't want to leave without Val. They had so much fun together the week before, he wanted to do it all over again.

Jonah stared at her closed bedroom door, contemplating his next move. Should he knock and ask her to go, or should he go alone? He checked his watch. If he didn't get going he was going to miss the next bus. He turned to leave and glanced back over his shoulder one last time before racing out the front door.

Val stood on the opposite side of the door with her ear pressed up against the door. Jonah usually spent his Saturdays with Hope, and Val had been up for hours waiting for him to leave the house. She was still hiding from him, but today she had plans. Olivia had invited her over for lunch. Val couldn't wait to see her. She needed somebody to talk to.

Val waited another twenty minutes before driving over to Judge West's home.

"Where is my godson?' Val dropped her purse and car keys down on the coffee table. Then she looked around strangely. "Why are all your things here?" She pointed to an African mask hanging on the far wall. "And why did you ask me to meet you here instead of at your apartment?"

Olivia gave her a sly smile. "Sit down." Olivia pointed to the seat next to her on the couch.

Olivia finally confessed that her and Dean had been married for weeks.

Val thought Olivia was joking with her, until she looked down at the wedding band on her left hand.

"Why didn't anyone call to tell me?" Val pulled Olivia's hand up closer to her face so she could get a good look at her ring.

"Because you never answer the phone. Besides, I asked everyone to try and keep it quiet. I wanted to tell you myself."

"Have I been that consumed in my own life that I haven't had time to hear about my cousin's wedding?" Val felt guilty for only thinking about herself for the past few weeks.

Olivia patted her hand. "It's not your fault. We've all been busy."

"So when Dean passed out at the church, what brought that on? You never got around to telling me the details."

Olivia wasn't sure how to respond. Val was the first person to come straight out and ask her about Dean's condition. Her usual response to anyone who asked about her husband's health was, "He's doing fine."

That simple answer wouldn't go over well with Val. She was expecting a logical doctor explanation.

"Stress," Olivia blurted out. "It was just stress, and the doctor gave him a clean bill of health."

Satisfied with Olivia's response, Val got to the point of her visit. "Livie, I also have some surprising news to share with you."

Olivia waited with bated breath. She was sure this had something to do with Jonah.

"Jonah and I have been doing more than spending time together."

"I figured you two were getting serious. You should have seen the way he looked at you when we were at the church. Danyelle couldn't believe you would ever get over Julian and she—"

Val cut her off mid-sentence. "We are living together."

"Did I hear you correctly? You and Jonah are living together? As in living in the same house—under the same roof?" Olivia pressed the back of her hand against Val's forehead. "Are you sick?"

This wasn't the kind of response Val was expecting.

"You moved in with him?"

"No. He moved in with me."

Olivia knew Val was acting a little strange lately, but this was insane.

"We're staying at the house Julian and I bought just before the accident."

"Okay, now I'm worried. You're doing things that you normally wouldn't do. This relationship is moving way too fast. How well do you know this man to ask him to move in with you? It's only been"—She thought back—"a few weeks," she shouted.

"Olivia, calm down!" Val pleaded.

"Don't you remember what happened to me when I allowed a man to move in I hardly knew?" Olivia reminded her.

"Let me explain!"

Val gave Olivia a quick recap of how she met Jonah and Hope, her confrontations with Caitlyn, and then she unveiled the biggest secret.

"Hope is Julian and Caitlyn's little girl."

After she was finished, Olivia was speechless.

"Wow! That's an amazing story. It's weird how God works. What are the chances of you taking Julian's daughter into your home?"

"I had the same thoughts. I wish God could tell me how this is going to end. I would hate for Caitlyn to get custody of Hope."

"How do you feel about Julian having a daughter?" Olivia asked.

"I can't help but love her. Even if I wanted to hate her, I couldn't. I must admit it felt strange when I first found out she was Julian's child, but I never felt any resentment toward her. I see her as a blessing. Julian's gone, but he still managed to leave a part of himself behind." Val's eyes danced with joy as she talked about Hope. "Livie, you should see her. She's adorable, but I'm not sure she likes me. She's very cold and withdrawn when I'm around."

"How do you know for sure she's Julian's child?"

"Every time I look at her I see glimpses of him," Val replied. "I know that I shouldn't take Caitlyn's word on anything, but I guess the only way we'll know for sure is to get Mrs. McCormick to take a DNA test."

"What did she say when you told her she has a grandchild?"

Val took her tongue and wet her lips, then avoided the question by looking down at her watch.

"You didn't tell her?" Olivia was livid.

"I was going to, but if I did that, then I would have to tell Jonah about Julian, and I'm still trying to figure out how to do that."

Olivia opened her mouth to complain, but Val held up her hand.

"I'm scared. I'm not sure how he is going to react once he finds out I was engaged to Hope's biological father. He may think I was trying to trick him or take Hope away from him. I need to make sure he understands how much I care about him and it has nothing to do with Hope. He doesn't trust too many people these days, and I happen to be one of the few he does trust."

"Oh! So you care about Jonah. Is something going on between the two of you?"

Again Val put her head down. She was guilty.

"I knew it!" Olivia jumped up from her seat. "It was so obvious when you brought him to church." Olivia danced around.

"Don't get so excited. My life isn't as grand as yours. You might be mad at me after I tell you how I've been acting."

Val then told her about the kiss they shared and how she had been avoiding him.

"Why are you hiding from the man?" Olivia placed her hands on her hips with attitude.

"I think I'm falling in love with him."

"It's okay to have feelings for another man so soon after Julian. He wouldn't want you to be by yourself. You're too beautiful for that, but I am concerned about your living arrangements."

"Don't worry about that. I'm not going to do anything I don't want to do," Val said.

"That's what worries me. Once that lust settles in, it's so much easier to give in than stand up for your beliefs." Olivia sighed. "Girl, whatever you do, don't give in. If Jonah is as real as he portrayed himself to be when he was at Bible study, then he'll wait. Plus, I know you wouldn't fall in love with just anybody."

Her eyes followed Jonah up the steps and into the building. She was ready to give the performance of a lifetime.

When Jonah emerged from the group home with Hope in his arms, Caitlyn jumped out of her car and ran over to them.

"Hey, Jonah!" Caitlyn waved. "And there's my little girl."

Hope frowned her face when Caitlyn pinched her cheeks.

"I thought today was my Saturday." She threw Jonah an innocent look.

"No, I'm pretty sure it's *my* Saturday, but I could be wrong. Let me go back inside and check with Mrs. Chambers."

He turned to go back inside, but Caitlyn stopped him.

"There's no need to do that." Caitlyn was the master of manipulation. "You already signed her out, so you two go ahead and enjoy your time together. I'm a little disappointed that we won't be able to fly the kites I bought, but we can do that next Saturday."

Caitlyn faked disappointment and sulked as she turned away.

"Why don't you join us?" Jonah didn't want her to feel left out. Jonah hated to see any woman upset. Besides, he knew how he would feel if he couldn't spend any time with Hope. "There's no reason why we can't spend time with her together."

Caitlyn played like she didn't want to intrude, but a little prodding from Jonah and she easily gave in.

They climbed into her car and headed toward the park.

Hope, Jonah and Caitlyn looked like a family together at the park. Hope jumped for joy at the different kites her father flew in the air.

Later, they walked over to the playground and allowed Hope to play in the sandbox while Jonah and Caitlyn talked.

"How many kites did you buy?" Jonah's arms were tired. "Every time I thought we were finally done, you pulled another one out your bag."

Caitlyn laughed. "I bought one of every kind at the toy store."

Jonah giggled to himself.

"I know you're probably thinking I'm trying to buy Hope's affection, but that's not true. Material things are the only way I know how to show someone that I care. That's how I was raised. I know nothing else."

Jonah felt sorry for her. "Hope and I were homeless for almost six months. For her last birthday, I bought her a lollipop. That was the only thing I could afford. I felt like a failure. But to her it was the best present in the world. She wrapped her arms around my neck and planted a huge kiss on my cheek. Then she told me I was the best daddy ever." The pleasant memory left a smile on his face.

"You really love her, don't you?" Caitlyn could hear in his voice how much he loved her.

They watched Hope play with another little girl in the sandbox.

"You can come visit her when we move back to Seattle."

Jonah twisted his head in Caitlyn's direction at warp speed. "How can you be so sure you're going to win this case?" He stormed away, regretting that he'd invited her along.

"I didn't mean to upset you." She walked up behind him. "But I know she's my child."

"I'll do anything. Please don't take her from me. She needs me," Jonah pleaded.

"What about me? Don't you think I want what's best for my daughter? A little girl needs her mother. There are things that only a mother can teach her child."

"We were fine," Jonah said more to himself than to her. "Me, her and Val."

Hearing Val's name made Caitlyn's blood boil. "Do you think I would allow Val to be a mother to my child?" Caitlyn spat. "That will never happen. She may have gotten Hope's father, but she will never get Hope."

Caitlyn stomped off toward the sandbox.

A moment passed before Jonah realized what she said, and he ran to catch her. He spun her around to face him. "What did you mean by Val had Hope's father?"

"Julian. She took Julian from me. They were planning to get married, but his plane crashed and . . ."

Astonishment covered Jonah's face. It was apparent he wasn't aware of Val's relationship with Julian. He walked a few feet away from her.

"She didn't tell you about Julian?"

"She . . ." he stuttered. "She told me she was engaged, but she didn't say to whom."

A fury of excitement danced around inside of Caitlyn. She couldn't believe her luck. There's nothing like the taste of sweet revenge. She had waited a long time for this day, and she didn't even have to arrange for this to happen.

"I'm not surprised she kept who she really was a secret. If it weren't for her, I think Julian and I would have stayed together, and I would have never put Hope up for adoption."

"Can you tell me what happened?" Jonah had to know their history.

Right before Caitlyn began her story, Hope ran over to tell her father she was hungry.

"Why don't we go get something to eat and then take

Hope back to the children's home?" Caitlyn suggested. "Afterward, I'll answer any questions you have for me."

Three hours later, Jonah and Caitlyn sat on the sofa in her hotel suite.

"Julian and I were in love." This was the story Caitlyn had concocted in her mind. "As a matter of fact, I'm still in love with him. Julian started his career playing for the Seattle Supersonics. We met at a mixer that my uncle, who happens to own the team, threw for the entire basketball organization. We were hot and heavy from the start." She stood up and walked over to the bar to pour herself a drink. "There was nothing tame, innocent or endearing about our courtship. From our first night together, we both knew we were meant to be together; except there was one problem."

"Val?"

"Yes." Caitlyn took a sip from her glass. "They were already engaged, but it wasn't going to last. They were having their share of problems. So we kept our relationship hidden from her, until the tabloids took a picture of us together in Aspen. Our picture was plastered on every newsstand in the country.

"Once our relationship was out in the open, Julian asked Val to move out of the house. When she moved out, I moved in. The morning I found out I was pregnant, Val came back to the house and physically attacked me."

Jonah gave her a strange look.

"Yes, she pushed me to the ground, jumped on top of me and slammed my head into the floor until it bled." Fake tears poured from her eyes. "I was terrified. Luckily, Julian had come home early and pulled her off me."

"That sounds nothing like the Val I know," Jonah replied.

"Then you really don't know her. My lawyers issued a restraining order against her a few months ago because she attacked me again! At the cemetery! That girl is crazy."

Jonah couldn't believe they were talking about the same woman. "So what happened between you and Julian?"

"We were happy, but all that changed when the league found out he was using steroids during the regular season. Our life was turned upside down. He lost everything: his endorsements, his teammates turned against him, and there were rumors going around that the organization was trying to trade him. He was humiliated, and after the league temporarily suspended him, he fell into a depressed state."

Caitlyn sat back down next to him. "Determined to stand by my man, I told him that my love for him couldn't be swayed. Then my uncle came by the house to let him know he had been traded to New York. He was furious, and that's when he turned on me. He thought I knew about the trade and accused me of deceiving him. I know he was just upset, but what he said hurt," she cried. "He threw me out the house and moved back to the East Coast. I never saw him again. That's why he didn't know about the baby. I never got a chance to tell him, and he wouldn't take any of my calls. I wish I did get a chance to tell him because maybe, if I did, we could have been a family. I would have never given Hope away, and he would never have been on that plane."

Caitlyn played the wounded actress well. The tears flowed freely. Everything she told Jonah was a lie, but he believed every word of it.

"I'm sorry. It sounds like you've been through a lot."

"That's why I say you can't trust Val." Caitlyn dried her tears with the back of her hand. "I suspect she had something to do with the NBA finding out about Julian's steroid use."

"Why would she do that?" Jonah couldn't believe she would be that vengeful.

"Val was so angry when she left Seattle, I think she would have shot us both if someone had given her a pistol." She sat up straight. "After Julian left Seattle, I moved back in with my parents. I overheard my uncle telling my father that the request to have Julian's urine tested came straight from the

NBA offices in New York. It's rare that they would do something like that.

"Who else would tip off the NBA? I know it was her. That's why I say be careful. She is a very conniving person."

Jonah had so many thoughts going through his mind. The biggest question he kept asking himself was, Why did Val keep her fiancé's identity a secret from him? He didn't want to believe that she was responsible for the downfall of her fiancé, but if she could ruin the man she loved, what would she do to him? Jonah wasn't sure what he should do. He had confided with her in her some personal aspects of his life. *Would she use that against me?* He needed time to think.

"Do you mind if I sleep here tonight?" Jonah looked like he was about to cry. "I mean, I'll sleep out here on the couch, but I don't think I want to go back to Val's tonight."

"Sure, that's no problem. I'll go get you some extra blankets from out the bedroom." On her way out the room Caitlyn thought to herself, *Once again I win, and this time Val won't get a second chance to take what's rightfully mine.*

Val felt rejuvenated after her visit with Olivia. Spending time with her cousin had always been therapeutic for her. She entered her house and called out for Jonah. It was quiet. "He must still be out with Hope."

She kicked off her sneakers at the door and turned to her favorite channel, Lifetime. While watching television, she decided to take Olivia's advice and tell Jonah about her and Julian.

Lately, God had been speaking to her heart about being honest, but she kept pushing the Lord out her head. Today, He put Olivia in her face to tell her what she already knew. It was time to come clean. She had waited long enough. *Besides, what's the worst that could happen?*

Stretched out on her fluffy couch pillows, she drifted off to sleep.

When she awoke it was morning and the television was still on. The women from the sitcom *The Golden Girls* were gathered in their living room talking. She got up and turned the television off. "I must have been tired. I didn't even hear Jonah come in last night."

She climbed the stairs and went straight to his bedroom. She knocked on the door. When he didn't answer, she knocked again, but still no answer. She slowly cracked open the door and called out his name. Stepping inside his bedroom, she saw that his bed hadn't been slept in.

The worst entered her mind. There was a lot of crime in Philadelphia. She prayed nothing happened to him. He could have been shot, robbed or mugged. Anything was possible living in the city.

She raced back down the stairs to find her cell phone. If he called and she didn't answer, she was sure he would have left a message. When she reached the kitchen, she heard the back door swing open. It was Jonah.

She ran and wrapped her arms around him. "I'm so glad you're all right. I was worried when I couldn't find you."

Jonah gave her the cold shoulder and merely brushed past her. He started up the stairs.

Val followed. "Jonah, there is something really important I need to speak with you about."

Jonah glanced over his shoulder and gave her an ugly look, but he didn't stop his stride.

"Jonah! I'm trying to talk to you."

When he walked into his room he grabbed a handful of clothes and stuffed them in his duffel bag. Then he gathered his sneakers and work clothes.

"Jonah, what's going on? Why are you packing your things?" Val was confused.

"I can't live here any longer," he shouted at her.

She stepped back. He was angry, but she had no idea why. "Jonah, what's wrong? You can talk to me about anything."

"Why don't we talk about how you were engaged to Hope's biological father?" His unsuspecting words were hurled in her face.

How did he find out? "Jonah, I was going to tell you, but—"

He charged toward her and pointed in her face. "If you were going to tell me, then why did I have to hear it from Caitlyn? Stop with the lies. What were you trying to do? Play me for a fool? Were you going to set me up and try to take my daughter from me? Tell me, what was the game?"

"Jonah, I," she hesitated, "I wanted to tell you, but when we first met I was trying to erase all memories of Julian from my life. Then came the revelation about Hope's true paternity. It took me a few days to believe it was true."

"That's why you left the courtroom in such a hurry that morning."

Val confirmed his suspicions.

"And now. What's your excuse for not saying anything after all these weeks of being together? I've been confiding in you, trusting you, inviting you to spend time with me and my daughter."

Val wanted to tell him that she was scared, but at the moment he didn't look like he would be sympathetic to her needs. She had never seen him this angry.

He raced back down the stairs.

Val stood in the middle of his bedroom, her heart beating out of control. An overwhelmingly frightening feeling took over her body. She knew that if she allowed Jonah to leave her house, she would never see him again. She chased after him.

"Where are you going?" she cried. "You can't leave me."

"I'm going to go stay with Caitlyn."

Val's face turned to horror.

"It looks like she's the only person who can be honest with me."

Flashbacks of when Julian betrayed her to be with Caitlyn played out right before her eyes. "Jonah, I don't know what's going on, but I do know that she can not be trusted."

"That's funny, because she said the same thing about you. Besides, she made me an offer I can't refuse. We already know that once the DNA results come back that Caitlyn is going to get full custody of Hope. So she has graciously invited me to move back to Seattle with her, so that I could be close to Hope. I'll be living with her."

"Is that where you stayed last night?"

Jonah rolled his eyes. "Not that it's any of your business." He stressed his words. "But if you must know, I did stay the night with her last night." He picked up a few of Hope's toys from out the living room.

She couldn't believe he had fallen for Caitlyn's tricks. Still in a daze, she heard a knock at the door.

When she answered, Caitlyn stood on her back step with a taunting smile on her lips.

"Hi! Is Jonah around?"

Caitlyn's innocent, sweet voice was a disguise. She tried to sound completely harmless, but Val was on to her. Val slammed the door in her face and walked away.

Jonah witnessed everything. He practically knocked over Val to open the door.

"Don't be mad with her." he said to Val. "She just did what was right."

Jonah apologized for Val's rude behavior. "It's okay."

Then Caitlyn whispered, "I told you she was violent." She took the bags he held in his hand. "I'll take these out to the car."

"Okay! I'll just be a few more minutes. I need to double-check to make sure I have everything." Jonah jogged back up the stairs.

When he did, Val caught up with Caitlyn out by the car.

"Whatever you're planning, it's not going to work."

"It looks like it already did. This must feel like déjà vu to you, losing yet another man to me." She pointed to herself. "Don't worry. This time you won't be getting him back." She turned and walked away.

"That's what you think. Game on."

Caitlyn and Jonah pulled off in the car. "Are you all right?" she asked.

"Yeah! I'm fine. I feel like I was living with the enemy. It's scary because I had no idea she could be so nasty."

"Jonah, I think you made the right decision to get away from her. At any time she could have gotten Julian's family to come and take Hope away from you and there is nothing you could have done about it." Caitlyn hit the gas pedal to beat the red light. "Thankfully, his family has no chance of taking her from me. From now on, you and I will be Hope's parents. Why don't we get married?"

Jonah stared at her strangely.

"Let's do it. We'll get married, and then you can legally adopt Hope and we can be a family."

Jonah was hesitant to go along with Caitlyn's suggestion, but he spoke without thinking.

"Okay, let's do it."

"Great. When I get back to the hotel, I'll call my lawyer and have him call the judge. The sooner Hope is in our custody, the sooner we can go back to Seattle."

Chapter 30

Frustrated, Colin sat with his head in his hands. He spent the past few hours combing through every religious book in his home library. There had to be one book that would tell him how to dispel the strong feelings of hate he experienced every time he ran into Baxter at the college. He rubbed his tired, red eyes and looked down at the concordance flipped open on his desk. His computer screen listed several scriptures that talked about hate.

"Matthew 5:44—Love your enemies and pray for those who persecute you."

He stared at the scripture and repeated it in his mind. "God, I've never had to pray for anyone who hated me because of the color of my skin."

The question, Why? burned inside Colin's soul. Why did hate seep into his body and spread like the plague? It ran through his veins like a fresh, rolling stream. It was so strong that it frightened him.

Then Satan kept putting thoughts of revenge in his head. Images of Baxter being tied to a tree while Colin flogged him repeatedly with a bamboo whip flashed in his mind. He smiled when he envisioned Baxter crying out to the Most High God as he ripped open his flesh.

This evil was consuming him.

Colin picked up the phone to see how his friend was doing.

"The cancer came out of remission." Olivia looked over her shoulder to check on her husband resting comfortably on the sofa. "We just came from the hospital, and of course they wanted to keep Dean overnight, but he refused."

"Did the doctors say what happened?" Colin couldn't take any more bad news. "I thought they had it under control with the radiation and chemotherapy."

"His body is not responding to the treatments. He waited too long. The joints of his arms and legs are swollen and in pain. He can barely walk. What scares me the most is his difficulty in breathing. Colin, he's getting sicker." Olivia tried to hold back the tears. She didn't want to cry in front of Dean.

"Who's that you're talking to on the phone?" Dean heard his wife whispering. He hoped she wasn't talking about him to one of her friends.

"It's Colin." She brought the phone closer to him. "Do you want to speak with him?"

He took the phone from her. "Hey, man, what's up?" Dean sounded tired.

"Man, I didn't mean to call and interrupt your rest," Colin apologized.

"No. It's fine. This is just a minor setback. What's on your mind?"

Colin called to find out when was the last time Dean spoke with Judge West, but under the current circumstances, Colin decided not to worry his friend with something he could handle on his own.

"Man, I called to wish you a speedy recovery. I'm going

to try and make it over there one day this week so you can cheat me in a game of chess."

Dean laughed. "I look forward to it."

Judge West knelt down beside his bunk with his hands cupped before him. He had repeated the same ritual for the past twenty years. Being locked away in a jail cell hadn't changed anything. He would still give thanks to the Lord, because whatever this trial and whatever the reason, he knew there was a purpose.

Two FBI agents walked toward his cell, both wearing dark blue suits with plain matching ties. Their wing-tipped shoes tapped hard against the concrete floor as they moved closer to West's cell.

One gentleman cleared his throat to acknowledge their arrival.

West didn't budge as he continued to pray.

The man cleared his throat again, except a little louder. Still no response from West.

He opened his mouth to bark at West, but the other agent stopped him and shook his head no. He was respectful of God and understood that every man deserves time to commune with God.

They waited until West lifted up from off his knees.

He turned to face his guests. "What can I do for you gentlemen?"

"We heard what you told your grandson and that preacher during that last time they came to visit. You were never given permission to release that much information. What you told them was confidential."

"I'm tired of being a puppet for the federal government. I've done everything you've asked, and you couldn't even keep my family safe. I'm tired of it all. I'm going to reactivate my membership with the brotherhood." Judge West picked up his Bible and shook it at the two agents. "If Christ willingly gave His life for me, I can't see how I wouldn't give up mine for my flesh and blood." He pointed his finger at them. "I hope you're not here to change my mind because, if so, you're wasting your time." The judge gave them a stern stare as if to dare them to say anything.

The tallest agent walked up to the cell and stuck his hand out to give West a handshake.

"Welcome back to the brotherhood."

The judge gazed at his outstretched hand a moment. He looked into the agent's eyes. He should have known the brotherhood would send someone to make certain he was telling the truth.

"What's the matter, aren't you going to shake my hand?" A sly grin formed on the agent's face. "That's all right. I was told to expect your unfriendly demeanor." He pulled his hand back. "Now that we know you're on board, when I get back to the office I'll make a few calls, and you'll be out of here in no time."

The agents looked at one another and in soldier-like synchronization marched away.

"Wait a minute," West screamed. "I have some questions for you."

The agents ignored his cries and kept on stepping until they were outside the jail and back in their car.

Chapter 31

Val cultivated the soil then dug a five-inch hole. This was her first attempt at trying to make her front yard look professionally landscaped like her neighbors' yards. Her house was the only one on the block that looked like a barren desert. Every garden tool she bought from Home Depot lay scattered around her.

She grabbed another flower bulb from the three dozen she had bought earlier that day and set it down in the small hole. She covered it with soil. She wiped the sweat from the bridge of her nose. It was high noon, and the summer heat was quickly approaching.

"I've only planted one and I'm already tired, hungry and thirsty." She laughed at her efforts at manual labor. She knew she should have gone with her original plans to call a gardener.

The reason she'd decided to do it herself was to get Jonah off her mind. She missed him. He had only been gone for a few days, and the house seemed so quiet without him. She often daydreamed that he would come back, but her mind kept telling her he was gone for good.

Mr. Lawson called the house early that morning to let her know the court clerk called his office. They were scheduled to meet in the Judge Cohen's courtroom Friday afternoon. She told Mr. Lawson he could contact Jonah at work. As for herself, she didn't think she would be attending the hearing. She no longer had anything to do with the case.

"Excuse me."

Startled, Val looked up at the owner of green eyes and sandy blonde hair.

"I was told Jonah Reynolds lives here." Even in his casual blue Dockers, off-white polo shirt and loafers, he was still good-looking.

Val stood to her feet and brushed her hands off before offering her hand to him. "He's not here right now. Is there something I can help you with?" Val wasn't sure if this guy was from the courts or social services, but she guessed it had something to do with Hope.

"My name is Cole Haas, and I have a very important matter that I would like to discuss with him."

Val's attitude quickly changed from friendly to untrusting. For some reason, she didn't trust this guy.

"It's concerning his daughter . . . Hope."

Her leery looks made him continue talking.

"Are you his wife?"

"No, I'm just a close friend. I'm Valencia Benson."

"I knew you looked familiar. I remember seeing you at a few of the Sonics parties held by my uncle. You were dating Julian Pennington."

She slowly nodded her head and finally realized who he was.

"You're part of the Haas family." Her voice turned threatening. Then she felt frightened. She thought Caitlyn had sent him to harm her. "If you're here to harass me, I'm calling the cops."

She turned to run into the house, but before she got far, Cole grabbed her arm.

Val swiftly put to use her self-defense moves she learned in college. She gripped his wrist and twisted it so far that she flipped his entire body over her. He hit the ground hard.

"Please, don't hurt me," he yelled. "I'm not here to cause you any trouble."

"Then what do you want?" Val had her sneaker lodged in the crease of Cole's neck.

"I want to help Jonah get his daughter back."

"Why would you do something like that?" Val was convinced he was lying.

"Please." Cole could barely talk. "If you let me up, I'll explain everything."

It took a few seconds before Val decided to give the man a chance to plead his case. She released her foot from his throat and allowed him to get up from the ground.

He tried to brush off the abuse he had just incurred. Then he sat on her front steps and chuckled to himself.

Val switched to her professional legal persona. "Mr. Haas, I'm sorry, but I fail to see any amusement in anything that's happening right now."

"I'm sorry for laughing"—He rubbed his neck—"but I forgot that my sister and you share a turbulent past. You've experienced firsthand how manipulative and conniving Caitlyn can be." Then he turned serious. "Val, I'm here to save you from any further trouble from my sister."

"You're a few days late. Hurricane Caitlyn has already blown through here and left behind massive destruction."

Cole dropped his head in front of him, disappointed. "It's not too late. We can still stop her," he said.

"I'm telling you it's too late." Val looked out. "She's beaten me this time."

"You may not feel that way after I tell you what I know."

Val turned toward him with a glimmer of *hope* in her eyes.

"The reason I'm here is because our grandfather passed away a few months ago. He was the founder of our family empire. Every Haas I know is an entrepreneur. We own a newspaper, a basketball team, hotels. Anything you can think of, someone in my family owns at least a piece of it."

Val sighed loudly. "I already know how rich your family is. Can you get to the point?"

"Okay, I'm getting to that," he fussed. "Anyway, like I said, every Haas I know is an entrepreneur, except for my lazy sister. Caitlyn has never worked a day in her life. My parents had her so spoiled that I believe she really thinks there's a money tree in my family's backyard.

"About a year ago my parents cut her off from all financial support. They told her it was time for her to grow up and get a job. Vowing to never speak to my parents or anyone in my family again, my lowly sister departed the Emerald City in search of her own fortune. Then we heard she started dating some baseball player out in California. That didn't last long. So I suppose she was broke again. Then my grandfather passed away. She missed the funeral, but managed to make it back to Seattle for the reading of the will. My entire family was aware that Grandfather was going to leave his fortune to the oldest grandchild, which is me."

Val signaled her hand to tell him to wrap his long story up.

"Okay, listen to this. There was a clause in the will that none of us knew about until after his death. It stated that if a great-grandchild was born before his death then the oldest great-grandchild would receive the inheritance."

"Cole!" she screamed. "What does that have to do with Jonah and Hope?"

"Think about it. Hope is Caitlyn's daughter. The first and oldest great-grandchild." Cole had to practically spell it out for Val to understand. "That little girl is set to inherit billions of dollars. That's why it's so important for Caitlyn to get custody of Hope. If she does, then she will be in control of all that money."

"It never crossed my mind that Caitlyn was doing all this for money, but it doesn't surprise me. We have to tell Jonah," Val said.

"Great. When will he arrive?"

When Cole asked that question, Val remembered that Jonah wouldn't be coming home. That was when she explained how Caitlyn had gotten Jonah to move in with her.

"It's time for us to ring the alarm." Cole was eager to expose his sister. "If we go and tell him everything, everyone will win. Jonah can have Hope, and my sister will get nothing."

"I don't think your sister is just going to hand Hope over that easily. She has the courts on her side. It makes no difference if she has an ulterior motive for wanting Hope back. The courts only look at if she's the child's biological mother. It's only a matter of time before she's granted full custody," Val replied.

Cole slammed his hand into his fist. "She can't get away with this. There has got to be something we can do to stop her."

"Why are you doing this?" Just because Cole was helping her didn't mean she had to trust him. "Are you doing this for Hope's sake? Because she deserves to be in a good home with a family who loves her. Or is it because, if Caitlyn returns to Seattle with Hope, then you lose your inheritance?"

He turned his eyes away in guilt.

"You're going to have a hell of a time getting into heaven. Your love of money is greater than your love of God."

"God has nothing to do with my money," he brazenly replied. "Listen, I will gladly set aside a trust that will take care of the baby for the rest of her life, but I need that money. I've been planning for this my entire life."

Val was disgusted with him.

He pulled a business card from out his pocket along with a pen. He scribbled his hotel number on the back.

"Listen, I have a plan that I think would get us each what we want. Me, the money. You, Jonah and the kid." He placed the card in her hand and walked away.

"Good morning," Cole mumbled into the phone. One eye opened wide enough to peek at the alarm clock on his nightstand.

"Good afternoon," Val replied. "By the sound of your voice it sounds like you had a very good night."

"Better than you think." He turned over and jumped when he saw a bush of red hair lying on his pillow. Thinking it was a wig, he grabbed the hair to throw it across the room.

"Ouch!" A woman screamed and shoved him away from her. Then she pulled the covers back over her head.

"Sorry about that." Cole flung his legs over the side of the bed and rubbed his head.

"I hope that's a woman lying next to you and not a man." Val giggled.

Cole looked behind him and lifted the covers to make sure it was a woman. "Yes. It's definitely a woman." He strained his eyes to get a good look at his houseguest's naked body. She had to be the stripper he gave most of his money to last night at the gentlemen's club. He couldn't remember much, but he was sure he had one drink too many. "Val, I'm surprised you put my number to use."

All night long Val weighed the pros and cons of getting involved with Caitlyn's brother. A bad omen hovered over her back, telling her it wasn't good to get into bed with any member of the Haas family. She wanted to trust her conscience, but Cole's offer to remove Caitlyn from their lives forever kept drawing her back in.

By the time sunlight cut through the darkness, Val was still undecided.

She convinced herself that it wouldn't hurt to call Cole and hear what he had to say. She twisted the telephone cord around her finger, something she only did when she was nervous.

"Meet me in the lobby of your hotel in twenty minutes."

"For what? What's wrong with us talking on the phone?" he protested, but she had already hung up the phone. He was talking to a dial tone.

Twenty minutes later Val impatiently waited in the lounge area. She lifted a bottle of mineral water to quench her thirst and impatiently drummed her perfectly manicured fingernails against her chair. "What's taking him so long?"

She watched another busload of tourists crowd around the check-in counter, before Cole finally joined her. He showed up wearing gray sweatpants, slippers and a hotel robe.

"Sorry it took me so long. I had some unfinished business to take care of."

The elevator doors opened, and out stepped Cole's overnight guest. She frantically waved her hands good-bye and flashed the money he paid for her services.

"I don't understand why we couldn't talk over the phone," he dryly replied.

"I didn't want you to say anything incriminating over the phone."

"Oh! So you think I'm planning on breaking the law?" He pulled out a pack of Marlboro cigarettes from his pocket. "Do you mind if I smoke?" He tapped the pack a few times to pull a cigarette out.

"As a matter of fact, I do." Val immediately snatched it out his hands. "I don't know how they do it in Seattle, but you can't smoke in public places here."

"Darling, I didn't come all the way to go to jail. If I did that, I'd never get my money. I'm smarter than that."

Cole raised his hand to get the attention of one of the waitresses from the hotel's bar. He ordered a gin and tonic.

It didn't take her long to return with his drink. She gently set it on the table, and he tossed her a twenty-dollar bill, which accidentally fell to the floor. Instead of him picking it up for her, he arrogantly turned his back to her and faced Val.

The bar maid stooped to the ground, picked it up and threw him a dirty look before switching away.

"Why are we here?" Cole stirred the drink in his hand.

"I slept on what you said, and it's no secret I don't like your sister. And even though Jonah and I aren't speaking, I still can't stand by and watch Caitlyn take Hope away from him."

"I'm glad to hear you say that. But once I tell you my plans, you can't back out on me. There's no turning back from this point forward."

Val fully understood.

"We need to get started as soon as possible. I'm going to run upstairs and change my clothes. When I get back we'll take a short ride and I'll fill you in on what I have planned for my sister."

A half hour later they drove out the city limits and into the suburbs. As they rode, Cole did everything, except reveal his master plan. He called his accountant, his lawyer and a number of other people.

After his last call, Val spoke up, "Do any of those people you spoke with have anything to do with your plans?"

He shook his head no.

"Then why am I here?" She threw up her hands toward the high school they sat in front of.

"Be patient."

Val wished she had gone with her first instinct and stayed home.

Minutes later they heard the final school bell ring, dismissing classes for the day. Teenagers came rushing out the doors. Dozens of kids boarded school buses, while others walked home in hordes.

One kid walked past the car with arms the size of boulders. His muscles bulged under the T-shirt that represented his school's colors.

"What are they feeding these kids that they look like that?" Val pointed.

At that point Cole jumped out the car. "Hey, kid! Wait up."

The kid stopped and turned around just as Val followed Cole out the car.

"Aren't you Max Ferretti?"

The kid moved his book bag from off his right shoulder to his left then nodded his head yes.

"You're the captain of the wrestling team, right?"

The kid smiled a little at the recognition. He figured Cole was a fan who saw his picture in the paper.

"Great! I've been wanting to meet you." Cole held out his hand, and the two shook hands. "You know, I think we have a mutual friend."

"Who?" Max's smile was so wide that Cole could see his tonsils.

"My sister. Caitlyn. Caitlyn Haas."

Max's smiled faded, and his eyes dropped. "Don't worry, I'm not here to get you in any trouble, I just want to talk with you."

Max nervously took a step backwards.

"When's the last time you heard from my sister?"

Hesitant to reply, Max kicked around some pebbles on the ground. He glanced at Val suspiciously.

"Man, that's my . . . my wife."

Val gave Cole a strange look.

"It's okay to talk in front of her. She won't say anything," Cole reassured him.

"It's been a while." Max's face turned red.

"Don't lie. I believe the last time she was here was last week, and I also know what it was she supplied you with. You are one of her favorite customers. She talks about you all the time."

Max gave an uncomfortable grin.

"I'm sure it's almost time for you to replenish your prescription."

Max shrugged his shoulders. "I guess."

"Listen, kid, Caitlyn tells me everything. I know how she's been hooking you up with steroids and how you've been giving them to the entire wrestling team."

When he said *steroids*, Val swung her head around. She couldn't believe what she was witnessing.

"I've read how your team is now ranked number one in the state."

"Mister, what do you want?"

"I need you to do me a favor," Cole said.

Max shook his head no. "I don't know. I think I'd rather just be left alone."

When Max tried to turn and leave, Cole put his arm around Max in a friendly way. "Kid, I would hate to have to go to the principal and suggest he give you and your teammates a piss test, because we both know what the outcome would be."

Val couldn't believe Cole would go as far as to threaten a high school kid to get to Caitlyn. "Cole!" Val was going to put a stop to this and demand he take her home.

"What do you need me to do?" Max looked like he had been blocked into a corner and had no choice but to cooperate.

Max called Caitlyn, after Cole had already coached him on exactly what he needed him to say.

"Hey, Caitlyn! It's Max"—He paused—"I was wondering if you could hook me up. I'm really in desperate need of some juice." He listened to Caitlyn and watched Cole. "Listen, I have practice tomorrow, so I can't meet you at our usual place. Can you meet me inside the coach's office on the second floor of the school?" He wiped sweat off his forehead. "No. The coach will be with us. During practice I'll tell my coach I need to run to my locker. That way, I won't raise no questions by running outside to meet you. Okay, I'll see you tomorrow at four o'clock." Max disconnected the call.

"Good job." Cole patted Max on the back and gave him a hundred-dollar bill for his trouble. "Remember, this is between you and me."

Cole opened the passenger side door for Val to get in.

"I can't believe Caitlyn is selling steroids to high school kids."

"That's the only way she can make any money. I told you she was flat broke." Cole walked around to his side of the car and got in.

"Why did you arrange for them to meet in the coach's office? Aren't you scared they'll get caught?"

"He won't be the one meeting her—I will. When I confront my sister I want to make sure she has no way of escaping. That's why we had to make sure the meeting place was inside the school. That was the only place the kid could guarantee we could be alone with her. He knows the layout of the school a whole lot better than I do."

Cole stopped in front of Val's house to drop her off.

She placed her hand on the handle, but before she got out she had to ask him something that had been bugging her since they left the school. "Do you think Caitlyn had something to do with Julian taking those steroids?"

Cole looked at her. "I really can't say for sure, but it's a good possibility."

Chapter 32

"Dean, are you sure you feel up to this? I told you I don't mind doing this alone." Colin turned off the car's engine. Today was the day he would expose Baxter for who he really was.

For days Colin had been dodging Baxter, still unsure of what to do. He prayed and fasted, but he was running out of time. Sooner or later he would either have to accept Baxter's offer and work side by side with a racist, or resign and start his career all over again at another university.

"What? And have you meet with one of Satan's helpers alone? Naw, I couldn't do that." He opened the passenger side door. "You know you my man. I always got your back."

They gave one another a pound.

"Make sure you stay out the way, just in case I have to start knocking somebody out. I can't allow you to get a scratch, or Olivia will kill me," he joked.

Both men, dressed in black tuxedos, walked up the front steps that led to the prestigious Claymont Country Club.

This club had a reputation of catering exclusively to rich white men. The structure was built several hundred feet above sea level on top of one the steepest mountains in Pennsylvania. Tourists would come from miles away to get a look at the white porcelain and gold palace that towered over the city.

When they entered the lobby entrance, the light buzz from several conversations being held among its members ceased. It was hard for Colin and Dean not to notice that the focus in the room had turned to them.

Dean turned and whispered in Colin's ear, "Why do I feel like I just walked into a Klan meeting?"

"Maybe because we did," Colin shot back.

"Gentlemen." A tall, uptight man with perfect posture and a thick British accent snuck up on them from behind. "Can I help you?"

Although the man was so tall that he towered over Colin and Dean, he still managed to keep his nose in the air, to plainly show they weren't welcome.

"Yes." Colin forced a cheery smile on his face and greeted the man with just as much enthusiasm. "Yes, I'm Reverend Colin Montgomery, and this is a friend of mine, Mr. West. Could you direct us to the awards banquet? We were invited by Reverend Baxter."

A look of confusion filled the man's face. "Reverend Doctor Baxter?" the man stuttered.

"Yes, that's right. Is there a problem?" Colin spoke with confidence. He refused to allow the man to think he was lying.

"Do you have your tickets?"

Dean stared in disbelief. He had never seen a man act so pompous before.

"He told me I wouldn't need a ticket and for me to just walk in."

The man looked uncertain of Colin's story. Reverend Baxter explicitly instructed him to not allow anyone in without tickets.

"Wait here."

They watched as the man called a waiter over and whispered in his ear. They glanced back over their shoulders at Colin and Dean before disappearing behind a pair of closed doors.

As expected, Colin and Dean were ignored by all the guests mulling around in the lobby area. People turned their heads and acted as if they didn't even exist.

"I never thought I would experience the same blatant racism that went on in the sixties," Dean said as they watched two janitors wipe down the glass door handles they entered through.

Seconds later Reverend Baxter charged through the doors. His eyes scanned the room. When he saw Colin and Dean, his face turned white with horror. He took quick long strides until he reached them. "Montgomery, what are you doing here?" Baxter seemed confused.

"Sir, I heard about your banquet, and since we've been missing one another at the school, I figured I would come here to speak with you in person."

"Reverend." Baxter stopped a moment to acknowledge Dean. "Now is not a good time." He placed his arms around Colin and Dean and pushed them toward the exit. "How about we meet first thing Monday morning in my office?"

Colin laughed. "Professor, I feel like you're embarrassed of me."

"No, that can't be true. Why would Reverend Baxter be ashamed of his new assistant dean?" Dean's words were dripping with sarcasm.

"You're going to accept the position?" Baxter was delighted at the news before he remembered something. "How did you know I was going to offer you the position?"

"Remember when you left that note for me to stop by your office? I overheard you talking with your friend."

Baxter looked confused. He wasn't exactly sure what Colin was referring to.

"Now that I've accepted the position, I just want to know, am I going to get a piece of that hefty finder's fee from the affirmative action dollars that will be pouring into the school?"

Clarity unveiled itself on Baxter's face. "Colin, I think you misunderstood my conversation," Baxter tried to explain.

"No, I don't think I did. You're part of an extreme racist group that has terrorized minorities for years." Colin's voice was steadily rising. He was so angry that Dean thought Colin was going to hit him.

"Let me show you something." Baxter led them through a pair of double doors.

Colin and Dean looked bewildered when they looked out at the tables full of people of various nationalities. There were blacks, Orientals, and Mexicans in the room. Everyone was dressed in beautiful ball gowns and talking and drinking amongst themselves as if they were a huge family.

"Excuse me," a black man spoke into the microphone at the podium. "This is a part of the program where we present our financial contributions to our young people."

The crowd applauded and cheered.

"I would like to begin by extending well-wishes to our recent high school graduates, and I want to be the first to contribute to our children's future."

The man pulled out five white envelopes from out his tuxedo pocket and handed one to each one of the children sitting at the head table. There were three white boys, a white girl and one black male boy. Then one by one everyone got up from their tables to give the graduates gifts.

Baxter leaned over toward Colin. "Each one of those envelopes contains at least five thousand each. We take care of our own, and it has nothing to do with color, and guess what? The largest contribution we have is coming from your church."

Colin looked at him strangely.

"What does First Nazareth have to do with this?"

"Remember all that money we collected for Judge West's defense fund? Unfortunately, it never made it to the lawyer's hands. I helped Simms in choosing a lawyer, and I made sure I found the cheapest, most inadequate lawyer in the city. We paid him a small fee, and the rest went in my pocket and toward our children's future."

Then Baxter gestured for them to follow him into an adjacent room. This time Colin was the one with a confused look on his face.

"What's the matter, Montgomery? I told you that you misunderstood my conversation. I'm not a racist, but I do actively support the uplifting of my race, the superior race, in controlling this county."

"So what lies have you told the minorities in that room? Because I can't believe they support the uplifting of the superior race!" Dean shouted.

"Every person out there is a living example of the theory 'a person should not be judged by the color of their skin.' Mexicans shouldn't be allowed any special privileges because they're immigrants. America is a country that does not discriminate. Every citizen of this country is given the chance to get a good quality education and the opportunity to work hard." He pointed at Colin. "Just like you did. You told me that you put yourself through college with no grants and no help from the government. You're successful and smart. The perfect example for your people. That's why I want you to not only to accept my invitation, but to also accept membership into our organization."

"You can't be for real. You really expect for him to join a racist extremist group?" Dean was in shock.

"We are no different than the NAACP. They support the education and the rights of their own. We accept all nationalities, but we actively oppose affirmative action. We want the Blacks and Hispanics to have their own companies and own neighborhoods. I don't believe in blood mixing; it messes with the purity of our race."

Dean rolled his eyes at him.

"You can hate us, but without people like us your grand-father would never had gotten to where he is today. We paid for his law degree. The millions of dollars that are donated each year allow us to strengthen our bond, expand our net-work and help kids like the ones being celebrated outside this room."

"This is insane," Dean cursed. "Why would he join a group of people whose primary goal is to destroy every-thing he's worked so hard for? Like the community centers, free healthcare, and most importantly a better quality edu-cation taught in the ghettos."

"If you join us, you'll have a slew of banks ready and will-ing to give you money for any business venture, community project, idea or proposal you desire. And don't forget about the amount of money you'll be making. Colin, we wouldn't simply look at you as a black member, but someone who chose a better quality of life."

"A better quality of life?" Colin repeated.

"Yes. This is to your benefit. I'm giving you the opportu-nity to live a whole lot better than your ancestors."

Baxter walked closer to the window and pulled back the curtains to display the country club's breathtaking moun-tain view.

The scene reminded Colin of the Biblical story when Satan offered Jesus the kingdoms of the world if he would only bow down and worship him.

"Think about it. The amount of money you'll be making as Assistant Dean will afford you any luxury you desire."

"How much money do you think will be collected at this banquet to support your organization?" Colin asked.

"I can guarantee we'll collect close to a million dollars," Baxter said.

"Colin, you can't seriously be considering this guy's proposal." Dean never thought Colin would betray his own people for a couple dollars.

Colin considered Baxter's offer a moment before speaking up. "What about Ernie West? If you can guarantee the release of Judge West, then I'll join you."

Dean pulled at his friend's arm. "Man, you don't have to do this."

Baxter smiled to himself. He had already been informed that Ernie had agreed to reactivate his membership and was set to be released. "I don't think that'll be a problem. Shall I introduce you to the group?" Baxter extended his open arms toward the banquet hall.

The three walked out together and toward the front of the stage.

The emcee for the evening was just about to wrap things up and wish everyone a safe drive home when Baxter walked up behind him and took over the mic. "Ladies and gentlemen, I know you in a hurry to get out of here, but I had to take this moment to introduce a good friend of mine." He beckoned for Colin to come closer.

Colin went to step on stage when Dean stopped him one last time. "Man, you don't have to do this. My grandfather's not worth it."

"It'll be all right," Colin said before joining Baxter on stage.

"This man not only works with me, but he's also a pastor. Please welcome Reverend Colin Montgomery."

The crowd gave a round of applause.

"And today he's decided to become a part of our organization."

The crowd gave another round of applause, and Colin humbly waved back to the crowd.

Then suddenly the applause was cut short by the raid of dozens of FBI agents storming into the room. They surrounded the place with their guns drawn and told everyone to put their hands up.

Several agents ran onto the stage and pushed Baxter against the wall. Then they searched his body.

"Officer, I'm not sure if you know who I am, but if you get in touch with Federal Agent Charlie Watkins, I'm sure this misunderstanding can be cleared up."

"Sorry, Baxter. Watkins was arrested earlier today. We've known for a while that he's been a part of your organization, and he now has a long list of corruption charges to face." The officer turned Baxter around to face him.

"Dean." Judge West climbed through the chaos in the room.

"Grandpa, what are you doing here?" He was surprised to see him.

"Your grandfather has been working with us from the beginning," a female agent explained to Dean. "The only reason we took him into custody was for his safety. We've been watching this sector of the brotherhood for quite some time. We had no idea one of our own agents was working with them until a few months ago. That agent tipped them off that we were bugging their offices. That's when they fed us bogus information and tried to pin that thirty-year-old murder of that kid on Judge West. We decided to go ahead and arrest Judge West and make it as public as possible. That allowed us more time to further gather enough evidence to convict them."

"I should have never doubted you." Dean felt like a fool for the nasty way he'd treated his grandpa.

"It's all right, son. I understand how you must have felt, but that's why I couldn't tell you the truth. It was all confidential."

"We could have never wrapped this case up without your grandfather's help," the female agent added. "We've worked with him in the past as an informant, so we knew he wasn't responsible."

"Ernie West. You're a traitor!" Baxter screamed. "When

I get out of jail, watch out, because your family will pay for your sins."

Baxter struggled with the two agents who were trying to lead him out of the building. Baxter fought to get at Judge West. He finally got one hand loose and grabbed one agent's gun from out the holster.

Baxter fired shots into the crowd. Everyone ran for cover. Judge West ducked and narrowly escaped the first shot, but the second shot hit Dean straight in the neck. Dean's body fell to the ground hard.

Judge West hollered, "Dean!" He put his hand over the gaping hole as blood poured out. "Hold on!" As the blood stained the carpet and Judge West's clothes, a faint smile formed on Dean's lips.

An eager and hunger rookie agent, looking to prove himself, pulled out his gun and fired at Baxter. He was shot twice in the torso. He also fell to the ground bleeding.

"Somebody call the ambulance," Judge West hollered. Dean's eyes fluttered as if they were going to close. "Don't you do it! Don't you dare die on me!" the judge screamed.

Within minutes the paramedics arrived, and as they lifted Dean onto a stretcher, another ambulance arrived for Baxter. They were both rushed off to the hospital.

Colin had this feeling of déjà vu. Once again Dean was being rushed to the hospital, and again he had the responsibility of calling Olivia. He had to tell her to meet them at the hospital.

By the time Colin and Judge West arrived, Olivia was already there. She told them that Dean had been taken straight into surgery. When she saw Judge West had been released, a fury of uncontrollable tears fell from her eyes. He wrapped his arms around her with enough faith for the both of them that everything would turn out okay.

Thirty minutes later they sat in the waiting room still waiting for an update from the doctors.

"What happened?" Olivia asked Colin.

Colin brought Olivia up to speed on everything that had happened up to the shooting, and just as he finished, Baxter's wife walked into the waiting room.

Her eyes met the attention of Colin, Olivia and the judge, but she didn't want to cause any trouble, so she stayed on the opposite side of the room. In silence she tried to focus on the sitcom that played on the television.

A nurse came in shortly after to inform her that Baxter was in surgery.

When the nurse left, Mrs. Baxter couldn't contain her grief any longer. She had no friends or family around to console her. She cried to herself and tried to stifle her cries by pushing tissues up to her mouth.

Olivia heard her cries, and with compassion in her heart she got up and walked over to Mrs. Baxter. She sat down wrapped her arms around Mrs. Baxter's shoulder. The two women cried together for all the hurt that had been generated between them.

The ladies sat holding hands in silence for over two hours before two surgeons came out.

The one surgeon spoke to Mrs. Baxter. "Your husband is in stable condition."

She breathed a sigh of relief.

"He is a very sick man. The bullets damaged his lungs. He needs an organ transplant."

"Okay. Well, how long will that take?" she asked.

"Mrs. Baxter, we don't have a set of lungs available for him at the time. We'll have to put him on a waiting list, and if a set of lungs become available that have the same blood compatibility as your husband then we can do the exchange. We're going to transfer him to the intensive care unit, and we'll pray that he won't have to wait long for a donor, because the longer we wait, the less his chances are of making it through this successfully."

Mrs. Baxter nodded her head in understanding.

The other doctor turned to Olivia. "A lot of your husband's major arteries were hit, but he is in critical condition. He could still make it."

Olivia immediately held out her hands for everyone around her to join hands. Judge West, Colin, Olivia and Mrs. Baxter prayed together for the Lord to save their loved ones.

"Excuse me." A nurse interrupted them. "If you would like, the doctors said you could visit with your husbands, but please not for long, because they both need their rest."

The two women followed the nurse to the intensive care unit.

Olivia entered Dean's room. She couldn't help but cry. A teardrop fell from her eye and landed on his cheek. He looked so peaceful. She wished he would wake up so she could look in his eyes. Olivia leaned over and kissed Dean, hoping her kiss would waken her prince, but he remained asleep.

When the nurse came in to tell her that visiting time was almost over, Olivia whispered in Dean's ear, "I love you."

Olivia left out the intensive care unit, and behind her she could hear the nurse in the next room over say that her visit was over.

Mrs. Baxter stood next to her husband with tears in her eyes. As she stood over him he opened his eyes and whispered, "Don't let me die."

Mrs. Baxter broke down in tears. She couldn't allow her husband to leave her. She needed him. He was her provider and her mate. What would she and the children do without him in their lives? Mrs. Baxter left out the room and went to speak with a nurse about his condition.

"Nurse, do you think my husband is going to make it?" she asked.

"Ma'am, I really can't answer that question, but it's still early. The sooner we get an organ donor, the better his chances are." The nurse went back to checking patient charts.

"Thank you." Mrs. Baxter moved toward the exit doors

when she saw Dean lying in his room. "Excuse me, nurse. Can I visit with him? I'll only be a minute."

Earlier, that evening the nurse saw Mrs. Baxter with Olivia together praying and holding hands, so she thought it would be okay. "Sure, but don't stay too long."

"I won't." Mrs. Baxter walked into the room and stared at Dean's chest as it heaved up and down from the breathing apparatus. Being in the hospital she realized she was surrounded by death. Her husband could die, Dean could die. She couldn't take it much longer.

She turned around to rush out and ran into Dean's nurse. A bunch of papers went falling to the floor, and so did Dean's chart. Mrs. Baxter tried to help her pick up her things, but in the process she got a good look at Dean's chart and noticed that Dean's blood type was O Negative, the same as her husband's.

The following morning Mrs. Baxter sent her young children off to school and sat at her computer. She typed in the word *euthanasia*.

The Internet listed thousands of pages of information about euthanasia. Mrs. Baxter wrote down all the information she was looking for and headed back to the hospital.

Once visiting hours began Mrs. Baxter sat with her husband, who was still drifting in and out of consciousness, until it was time for her to go.

Before she left out she noticed that Olivia hadn't made it to the hospital yet to see Dean, so she slipped into his room. Mrs. Baxter set her pocketbook down and walked up to Dean's bed. When she did, his eyes unexpectedly opened, startling her. She jumped back when she realized he was watching her. That is when she pulled out the hypodermic needle she stole from her drug-addicted brother and injected a lethal amount of barbiturates into Dean's IV bag. His eyes grew big, but he was unable to speak. He grunted a bit but not enough to alert anyone to what she was doing.

"Sorry, Dean, but if I had to choose between you and my husband, then I will always choose my husband."

She quickly exited because she knew that he would be dead within fifteen minutes. On her way out the door she ran into Olivia, Colin and Judge West.

"Hello, Mrs. Baxter, how is your husband?"

Mrs. Baxter seemed jittery and nervous.

"Are you all right? Is it your husband?"

"I'm fine." Mrs. Baxter was in a rush to get as far away as she could from Olivia and the scene of the crime. "I need to go pray. I'm going to the hospital chapel." Mrs. Baxter raced toward the elevator doors.

Olivia worried about her. She wasn't too fond of Mr. Baxter, but she liked his wife. As they marched toward Dean's room they heard the monitors start sounding off. A bunch of nurses pushed past them and raced into his room. Another nurse escorted Olivia, Colin and the judge out the intensive care unit.

Olivia was hysterical. "What's happening?"

Colin held her for a while, before a doctor came out to give them an update on Dean's condition.

"Mrs. West, your husband has suffered a setback. At the present moment the only thing keeping him alive is a life support machine."

Olivia closed her eye to block out the reality of what the doctor was telling her. Colin pulled her closer to him and she laid her head on his shoulder.

"Medically, there is nothing more we can do for your husband."

"So what?" Olivia screamed. "You're just going to give up and let my husband die?"

Colin walked up beside Olivia and pulled her toward him. "Livie, what the doctor is trying to tell you is that Dean is already braindead. The machine is pumping life into him. It's up to you to decide when we should discon-nect the machines."

Olivia couldn't believe they were leaving the decision up to her of whether or not to kill she could kill her husband.

"This is too much. I need to go pray." Olivia moved toward the elevator doors.

Colin and the judge followed her. 'No." She held out her hand to stop them. "I need to go alone."

Colin looked at the judge, unsure if he should honor her request. Judge West nodded his head to allow her to go by herself.

Mrs. Baxter knelt at the small altar with her head bowed and anguish in her heart. She couldn't believe she was so desperate to save her husband that she tried to kill somebody. That morning when she thought of the plan, it seemed so easy and so right, but after she did it she knew she had done the wrong thing. For the past thirty minutes she prayed that the poison she'd used wasn't enough to do any damage. That's when she heard someone come in and kneel next to her. When she looked to her left, Olivia was next to her.

"He's gone," Olivia cried. "The only thing keeping Dean alive is a life support machine."

"Don't cry." Mrs. Baxter tried to make her feel better, even though she was the cause of her pain.

"Mrs. Baxter, they want me to tell them it's okay to pull the plug. I'm not so sure I can do that. I hate to sound selfish, but I don't want him to go. If I have to spend the rest of my life visiting him in the hospital, then that's what I'll do."

"Olivia, I hate to tell you this, but what you see upstairs lying in that bed isn't Dean. It's just a shell of the man you married. If you keep him alive on that machine, you'll never hear him say the words *I love you* again. You'll never see him open his eyes. You'll never be able to do the things that young couples like you do."

Olivia cried harder. "I don't want to let go."

"I know, honey, but sometimes we have to do things that we don't want to do," Mrs. Baxter said.

Olivia got up from off the altar. "I guess it's time for me to say my last good-byes to Dean."

Before Olivia could walk out the door, Mrs. Baxter stopped her. "Olivia, I hate to ask you this, but I need to ask you for the biggest favor."

Olivia waited for Mrs. Baxter to continue.

"Since you decided to take Dean off of life support, could you wait and tell the doctors that you want to harvest Dean's organs? My husband could use Dean's lungs."

Olivia was stunned by her request. She couldn't believe Mrs. Baxter would ask such a thing. Her husband was the reason Olivia had to make such a decision, and now Mrs. Baxter wanted her to save her husband's life.

"You want me to save the man who killed my husband?" Olivia asked in disbelief. She stormed towards the door, but Mrs. Baxter stepped in her path.

"I know you're upset, but I wouldn't ask this if it weren't a matter of life and death. My husband could die if he doesn't receive a lung soon."

"How do you know Dean and your husband are even compatible?" Olivia was furious.

"I don't," Mrs. Baxter lied, "but we could ask the nurses to check, and if they are I would forever be indebted to you."

Although Olivia was upset, she couldn't deny Mrs. Baxter's request. "I can't promise anything. I'll think about it and let you know."

When Olivia walked out the chapel, Mrs. Baxter prayed that Olivia would have mercy on her and her husband.

By the time Mrs. Baxter returned to the intensive care unit she saw a group doctors and nurses surrounding Dean, and Olivia stood at the nurses station crying.

"Olivia." She gently touched her shoulder. "Are you okay?"

"Yes." She wiped a few tears away from her cheeks. "I told

the nurses what I wanted to do. They're getting the paperwork for me to sign."

"Thank you, Olivia. What you're doing is so brave."

"It's more than brave."

Mrs. Baxter and Olivia looked up at the same time to find
Judge West and Colin standing behind them.

"Yes, it is more than brave," Mrs. Baxter agreed.

"Olivia, I hate to intrude on the promise that you made
to Mrs. Baxter, but I must insist that she compensate you
for your loss."

"Compensate?" Mrs. Baxter shouted.

"Yes," the judge said. "Listen, I used to be a part of the
brotherhood and I'm fully aware that they take care of their
own. You and your husband are sitting on a lot of money,
while my granddaughter has just lost her husband and has a
little boy to take care of."

"So, this is about money?" Mrs. Baxter assumed.

"Judge West, you don't have to do this." Olivia tried to
keep the peace. "I really don't want any money from them."

"It's not about you wanting it. It's about you needing it.
You have a husband to bury and a little boy to take care of."

"All right." Mrs. Baxter pulled out her checkbook. "What
do you want? A couple thousand dollars? Enough to pay for
funeral arrangements?"

"We want half a million dollars," Colin blurted out.

Mrs. Baxter slowly looked up from her checkbook and
turned her head in amazement.

"Lady, don't act like you don't have it. We just left a banquet where the brotherhood received millions of dollars."

"Yes, but that money isn't ours." Mrs. Baxter cried.

"And I know for a fact that your husband stole thousand
of dollars from the church in contributions for the judge's
defense fund. You have the money, and if you don't, then call
your friends and borrow it."

"It's not that easy."

"But it was easy and brave for Olivia to give up her husband's organs to save your husband's life."

Mrs. Baxter swung her eyes from Colin to Judge West. "Fine. I'll get you the money, but it's gonna take me a while."

"The longer you wait, the longer it will be before my granddaughter signs any papers to save the good Reverend Baxter."

"Excuse me." The nurse came in with a clipboard. "Mrs. West, if I can get your signature, then we can go ahead and harvest your husband's organs."

Judge West took the clipboard out of the nurse's hands. "We need to make sure she reads these over thoroughly before she signs anything."

"Of course," the nurse replied before walking away.

Mrs. Baxter realized the longer she procrastinated, the greater her chances of losing her husband. "I'll make a few phone calls." Mrs. Baxter left the intensive care unit to gather the money she needed.

Within thirty minutes she returned. "I'll have the money to you by the end of business today, but you have to promise me that you will never tell my husband where he received the organs from."

"Why?" Judge West questioned. "Because Dean is a black man?"

The judge already knew the answer. He handed Olivia the clipboard. "Now you can sign."

Olivia signed the forms and went to go search for the nurse.

Chapter 33

The whistle blew and the coach yelled, "Max, what's wrong with you? You never allow your opponent to lock your leg. That's why he pinned you. That's a basic move. What's wrong with you today?"

The guy released Max from off the mat and they both got up. "Sorry, Coach." He glanced up at the clock through the corner of his eye. "Can I go to my locker?"

The coach thought his request was odd. "You have to go now?"

Max nodded his head yes.

Frustrated, the coach exhaled before letting him go. "Don't be all day, or I'll have you running laps for the remainder of practice."

Max jogged out the gymnasium and around to the side entrance to let Val and Cole in.

"Your sister is already up there," he said to Cole. "I told her I had to go collect the money from the guys."

They took long strides through the corridor. Val and Cole did a slow jog trying to keep up with him.

"Listen, you can't be long. If you get caught inside the

school, there are going to be a lot of questions." He stopped at the end of the hallway and pointed to the last classroom on the right. "I left her in there."

Again, Cole gave him another hundred-dollar bill. "Thanks, and I promise after today, you will never hear from us again."

Max took the bill. "I got to get back to practice before my coach comes looking for me." Max took off back down the hall and down the stairs.

"Are you sure you're going to be all right?" Cole wanted to be sure Val was okay with the change he made to the original plan. On the way over to the school he thought it would be better if she confronted Caitlyn. Their volatile relationship could be essential in provoking Caitlyn into confessing. "If you need any help I'll be right outside the door listening. You have the tape recorder on you, right?"

Val pulled it out.

"Instigate. Start something. Push her buttons. She'll get so mad, she'll end up telling on herself. My sister doesn't handle pressure well. Get her to confess about the steroids. Once we have her on tape, we'll threaten her to either leave Hope or go to jail." Cole pushed the button to record and slipped it in Val's pocket.

Val took a deep breath before taking the short journey down the hall toward the coach's office. When she stepped inside, Caitlyn spun around.

"What are you doing here?" Caitlyn stuttered. Her eyes blinked rapidly. She couldn't believe Val had found her. "Did you follow me?"

"I'm the one who requested this meeting," Val said.

"I don't know what this is about"—She gave Val a high and mighty look as if she didn't belong—"but I'm leaving." She tried to walk away, but Val wouldn't allow her to pass.

"Sorry." Val folded her arms. "I can't let you do that."

Caitlyn laughed. "What?" She took a step back. "Do you

want your man back?" She swung her blonde hair over her shoulder. "Well, you can't have him."

"How do you think he'll react once he finds out you're a drug dealer?"

Caitlyn acted as if she didn't know what Val was talking about.

"I know all about the steroids you've been selling to those kids, and I would bet my life that you had something to do with Julian and the scandal surrounding his steroid use."

"You have no proof."

"No, I don't, but those same kids who bought the drugs from you are the same ones who told me everything. They would give you up before they sacrifice themselves." Val was trying her hardest to goad her into a confession. "Caitlyn, it's over. Let's go down to the authorities and you can turn yourself in."

Desperation filled Caitlyn's eyes. She felt trapped. A letter opener lying on the desk called out to her. She wrapped her bony fingers tightly around the handle and held it like a weapon. "Move!" she demanded.

Val was careful not to make any sudden moves. She wasn't scared, but she knew Caitlyn wouldn't hesitate to stab her and say it was in self-defense. After all, Caitlyn was the one with the restraining order.

"Now!" Caitlyn screamed.

Val couldn't figure out a way to get that letter opener away from her without getting stabbed, so she slowly slid away from the door.

The first chance Caitlyn got she attempted to dash past Val, but Val rammed her tiny body into the blackboard. The two struggled over the letter opener and they fell back against the desk. Papers, books and pens fell to the floor. Caitlyn landed on top of Val. Caitlyn had the upper hand and used all her strength to push the sharp object into Val's heart, but Val wouldn't let her win. She fought back.

"Cole!" Val screamed.

Seconds later, he rushed into the office and lifted Caitlyn up off of Val. Caitlyn didn't hesitate to go after her brother. She jabbed toward his gut, and he easily took the weapon right out of her hands. Caitlyn was no match for her brother.

Realizing she was outnumbered and without protection, she ran out the room and down the back stairwell.

Val and Cole rushed after her.

"What do we do now?" Val tried to catch her breath.

He pointed in the opposite direction using the letter opener. "You go that way and get the car." He gave her his car keys. "She won't try anything, but we have to keep a close eye on her. I'm going to make sure Max is all right."

They went their separate ways. Val took off one way, and Cole raced off in the opposite direction.

Cole pushed open the heavy steel door that led to the stairwell and sped through. As he crossed over the threshold he wasn't aware that his sister was standing on the other side.

Once he passed through, Caitlyn stuck out her foot. Cole stumbled and flipped head first down the stairs. His body tumbled over itself until he stopped on the landing in-between floors. The letter opener she tried to stab him with was now lodged in his side. Blood poured out of the wound. Caitlyn glared down on her brother from the floor above.

"Help me." Blood spilled from the corner of Cole's mouth.

Caitlyn stepped down the stairs one at a time. "Help you? What would you like me to do?" She pulled out her cell phone. "Do you want me to call 9-1-1?" She pushed the number nine on her phone. Her brother watched with wide eyes wondering why she was being so slow.

Then she hit the one. She looked at her brother, gave a wicked grin and slammed her cell phone shut.

"What are you doing?" he whispered in agony.

"I'm helping you. The same way you helped me." She

stooped down next to him and gazed into his eyes. "How could you team up with Val? You know she's the enemy." Caitlyn took off one of her high-heeled shoes and hammered the letter opener deeper into his side. He cried out in pain. His breathing became labored and more blood gushed out his mouth, then his head dropped down front of him.

"Big brother, you always said I would be nothing. Watch how I capitalize off your demise. You have no idea how many times I've prayed to be the oldest grandchild." She kissed Cole lightly on the side of his cheek. "Who says that prayer doesn't work?" She stood straight up and brushed herself off. Then she sang, "I'm rich!" as she descended the stairwell.

Val sat in the car waiting for either Cole or Caitlyn to emerge from the school. Ten minutes passed. Then another five. Suddenly, a shiver crept through her body, leaving her with a gut-wrenching feeling that something was wrong. She got out the car and ran back into the building. Careful not to get caught aimlessly wandering the halls, Val ducked into the same stairwell she last saw Cole enter. She climbed a few stairs that led her straight to Cole. His body sprawled out across the landing. She ran to his side. "Cole!" She shook him and lifted his hand, but it went limp. Pressing her fingers to his neck she couldn't find a pulse.

Unsure of what to do Val got up and tried to drag his body, but he was too heavy. She didn't want to leave him, but then she heard voices coming their way and she had no choice. She dashed up the stairs and exited the school through a different exit and drove away as fast as she could.

Val slammed the back door behind her. She charged into her kitchen and pulled down the expensive bottle of vintage cognac from the top shelf. Her hands shook as she twisted the cap and broke open the seal. Skipping ice, she poured herself a drink and swallowed the brown liquor whole. The burning sensation hurt her throat and made her yell. After she inhaled deeply to cool her throat she took another drink.

"I know Caitlyn had something to do with her brother's accident." Val paced her kitchen floor. Different scenarios charged through her mind. The most logical explanation was that his sister pushed him down the stairs. Now Val regretted not going with him.

She thought about Jonah. He needed to know about what Caitlyn did. She picked up the phone and placed it back down, realizing he didn't have a cell phone. She had no way of getting in touch with him. It was too late for her to call him at work.

Double vision took over. Two identical cognac bottles moved around her kitchen table. She rubbed her eyes and held out her hand to steady herself. Her head felt woozy. The alcohol was taking control. Val became paranoid and started hearing strange noises in the house. She stumbled around the house, checking to make sure all her doors and windows were locked. *Caitlyn is a lunatic. She could be on her way over here to finish me off.*

Val poured herself another drink. The aroma drifted past her nose. "Oh! This stuff is strong." Drunk, she staggered into the living room before passing out.

The following morning, Val was jolted out of a sound sleep by the telephone ringing loudly in her ear. She clutched her head to try and stop the pain, but every time the phone rang, the throbbing beat a little it harder. She had to stop the pain. The cordless phone sat on her coffee table. She answered.

"Val, it's Mr. Lawson."

"Uh-huh." Her mouth wasn't fully functioning yet.

"Where's Jonah? The judge has called us into court for late this afternoon."

"This afternoon?" Val sat straight up.

"Yes, the courts just alerted my office. The judge has called an emergency meeting. I need you and Jonah down at the courthouse at three o'clock. Don't be late."

Val looked at the clock. It wasn't even ten o'clock yet. "Mr. Lawson, Jonah's not here. Maybe you can catch him at work."

"All right. I'll give him a call and I'll you see at the courthouse."

Chapter 34

Jonah mopped the corridor floor just off the main hospital entrance. This was one part of the hospital that didn't get a lot of traffic. It was times like this, when he was all alone at work, that he talked with God. "Father, I know a lot of times I stray so far away from You that it may seem like I don't even know who You are, but here I am again. Like the prodigal son, I've come home and I'm begging for Your help."

"Fortunately, God doesn't condemn us for our transgressions."

Jonah turned around and found Mrs. McCormick standing a few feet away.

"Isn't it a blessing to have a Father who doesn't hold a grudge?"

She walked up closer. "I hope I'm not intruding, but I remember meeting you and your daughter with Val in front of the museum. I was on my way to visit with a few members from my church and I thought you looked familiar."

He quickly remembered her face.

"I didn't know you worked at the hospital."

"I haven't been working here for long," Jonah replied.

"Well, can you tell me how Val is doing? I haven't heard from her since I saw the two of you together."

"I really haven't seen too much of her lately."

"Oh!" Mrs. McCormick sounded disappointed. "I hope everything is all right between the two of you."

Jonah rubbed his face, unsure of what to say.

"When I saw the three of you at the museum together, that was the first in a long time I saw Val with a genuine smile on her face. I could tell she was happy. I don't know if she told you, but at one point Val was engaged to my son."

"Yes, she told me." He dipped the mop he was holding back in the bucket. "I'm sorry about your loss."

"Don't be. My son did more in his lifetime than most people who live to be sixty years old. He went to college, played in the NBA, and most importantly he knew what it felt like to be loved."

She noticed Jonah's eyes fall to the floor. She placed her hand on his shoulder. "Val is such a remarkable woman. She reminds me of myself. That girl will do whatever necessary to protect those she loves. She's a good person to have in your corner. You know, when I saw you with her I was surprised, but I'm glad to see she found such a nice young man to hang out with. I'm not going to say it doesn't feel a little odd to see her with someone besides my son, but you look like you have a good head on your shoulders and you have that beautiful little girl. Val is like a daughter to me, and I want to see her happy, and it looks like you make her happy."

Jonah smiled a bit.

"See, I knew I could get you to smile."

Mrs. McCormick waved good-bye, and Jonah thought about what she said about Val. He had to admit that since Val walked into his life, she had been a steady rock, always there when he needed her most. She saved him from the beating, gave him clothes, food, a roof over his head, not to mention the lawyer she hired on his behalf.

He slammed the mop down on the floor and it broke. "How could I be so stupid?"

"Reynolds." He turned around to face his supervisor. "A Mr. Lawson called and left this number for you to call him back. He said it was important." He handed Jonah the slip and walked away.

Val arrived at the courthouse early. Instead of going straight inside, she chose to sit on the benches outside the courthouse. She didn't want to miss either Jonah or Mr. Lawson when they arrived. She was still unsure of how Jonah would react when he saw her, but she had to speak with him.

Val pulled her sunglasses down over her eyes. The excruciating headache from her hangover prompted her to pull out a bottle of aspirin.

"Do you have a headache?" Caitlyn stood over Val. "Does your head hurt because you feel responsible for my brother's death, or is it because you in some way feel responsible for Jonah losing Hope?"

"What happened to Cole?" Val pushed the aspirin bottle back down into her purse.

"How would I know?" Caitlyn acted innocent. She pulled a cigarette out her purse and lit it up. She blew cigarette smoke out her mouth and walked closer to Val. "Stay out of my way. Hooking up with my brother was the biggest mistake you could have ever made. If you're not careful, you could take an accidental fall." She chuckled.

Val pointed her finger in Caitlyn's face and squared her lips to rattle off a list of four-letter words when Jonah walked up.

"Caitlyn?" He was happy to see Val, but he didn't want to talk with her in front of Caitlyn. "I got a call from my lawyer that you requested this hearing. What is this about?" He took her by the elbow and guided her away from Val so they could talk in private. "You were gone all day yesterday. When I got up this morning you were already gone. We need to talk."

"Jonah," Mr. Lawson interrupted, "the hearing is about to begin, and I need to speak with you and Val."

Jonah looked torn. It was important for him to speak with Caitlyn. He was having second thoughts about them getting married. He prayed that wasn't the reason she initiated this meeting.

Mr. Lawson gestured for Jonah and Val to follow him. Caitlyn and her lawyers followed behind them.

"Do either of you have any idea what this is about?" Mr. Lawson asked. "It must be important for the judge to grant an emergency hearing."

Jonah mulled over telling them about him and Caitlyn getting married.

"Well, it doesn't matter now because we're about to find out." He nodded toward the judge entering the courtroom.

Everyone stood to their feet, and the judge didn't procrastinate on starting the proceedings. "Ms. Haas, I would like for us to get straight to the point, since you insisted I cut my lunch short in order to get you on my calendar this afternoon."

Caitlyn stood to her feet,

"Your Honor, I know that you were about to rule on the custody case for my daughter, but after much consideration I have decided to withdraw my request."

Judge Cohen was surprised. "What made you change your mind?"

"Jonah is an awesome father. He is so good to my daughter. He is both a mother and father to Hope, and right now I'm not ready to be the kind of mother she needs. Plus, with the news that I received this morning concerning my brother, I feel like now is not the time."

"Ms. Haas, I heard about your brother's accident, and I'm sorry to hear about his passing."

She nodded her head thank you.

"So, if it pleases the court and Jonah agrees, I would like to sign away my parental rights, and I will not stand in the way of him officially adopting Hope."

"Is this arrangement all right with you?"

Jonah was in a daze and didn't realize the judge was talking to him.

"Mr. Reynolds, is this a good deal for you?"

Jonah stood to his feet. "Yes, Your Honor."

"Good. I will have Mrs. Chambers contact you about getting the adoption process started. Just to inform everyone, the blood test results came back. Hope is undeniably Ms. Haas's daughter, and I would have ruled in her favor."

Caitlyn acknowledged his remarks by a nod of her head. Judge Cohen adjourned court and slammed his gavel down.

"Well, this is definitely a miracle." Mr. Lawson patted Jonah on his back. "Somebody must have been praying for you."

Jonah looked over at Val. "I've been meaning to call you. I really need to—"

Caitlyn interrupted them by calling out to him.

He got up from his seat. "Stay right here. I'll be right back." He went to her with open arms. "Caitlyn, I really appreciate this. You won't regret this decision."

"I know I won't." She gave him another hug, and from over his shoulder she winked her eye at Val.

Then Mr. Lawson called Jonah. While Jonah finished up his business with Mr. Lawson, Caitlyn sashayed over to the table where Val was sitting.

"I can tell by the confused look on your face that you're surprised at what happened here today."

"I guess I am."

"Let me take you out of your suspense. Now that my

brother is dead, I'm rich. The inheritance that was entitled for my brother is now mine."

"So you no longer need Hope." Val was repulsed by the mere sight of Caitlyn.

"Exactly." She pulled her coat tightly around herself and left.

Anger boiled through Val's veins. She was furious that Caitlyn would again get away with the wrong she had done. Val was ready to tell the whole world how Caitlyn was responsible for her brother's death. She would love nothing more than to see her rot behind bars, but then her eyes rested on Jonah. He was finally happy. He and Hope would finally be reunited forever, and if she told what she knew that could jeopardize his happiness.

For now she would have to swallow her pride and allow Caitlyn to bask in her triumph. Val prayed that today would be the last time she ever laid eyes on Caitlyn. Hopefully, she would be walking out of their lives forever.

Jonah shook hands with Mr. Lawson before returning back to Val. "Mr. Lawson said if I wait here they'll bring Hope to me."

"Are you still upset with me?" Val asked.

"No. I apologize for acting a like a fool." He took her hand in his. "I overreacted, and I wouldn't blame you if you didn't accept my apology." Then he bent down and kissed her lightly on the lips.

"I think I can accept your apology." She smiled.

Later that evening Hope, Jonah and Val stood on Mrs. McCormick's doorstep.

"Are you sure you're ready to do this?" She held her finger inches away from Mrs. McCormick's doorbell.

"Yes, I think it's time for Mrs. McCormick to meet her granddaughter." Jonah kissed Hope on the cheek, then turned and also gave Val a kiss.

She nervously pushed the doorbell. This reminded her of the first time Julian brought her home to meet his parents.

When Mrs. McCormick answered the door, she was so happy to see Val, Jonah and Hope together that she insisted they stay for dinner. Mrs. McCormick loved to cook and she made enough to feed the entire neighborhood.

After she served dessert and everyone was chatting around the table, Jonah gave a subtle nod to Val that he was ready to tell them.

"Mr. and Mrs. McCormick, we have some startling news to tell you and we don't want you to get alarmed."

Mrs. McCormick braced herself for the worst.

"Hope." She nodded toward the little girl who was licking the vanilla ice cream from her fingers. "She's adopted."

Mrs. McCormick laughed. "Oh! Is that all? Val, that isn't startling news." Relief showed over her face.

"Yes, but"—Val suddenly wished she didn't have to tell her this—"what you don't know is that Hope is your grandchild."

Mrs. McCormick looked at her strangely.

"I know this may be hard for you to understand, but Julian might have fathered a child before he died."

Speechless, Mrs. McCormick dropped the butter knife she was holding on her plate. She looked toward her husband then she looked at Hope. The little girl was so absorbed in eating her ice cream, she had no idea what was going on around her. Mrs. McCormick got up and walked around to Hope's chair. When Hope saw her, she smiled at her grandmother before pushing another spoonful of ice cream in her mouth.

"This is my grandbaby?" Mrs. McCormick ran her fingers over Hope's hair. "She's really Julian's daughter? How could this be?"

After Val explained Caitlyn's pregnancy and the DNA

tests that were performed by the courts, Mrs. McCormick cried tears of joy and hugged her grandchild close to her.

"You don't know how badly I've wanted a granddaughter. I loved Julian and I always will, but to have a second chance with his daughter is a blessing. The Lord took my son, but He kept his promise to give me a grandchild." Then she got up and hugged Jonah. "Thank you! Thank you so much for taking care of this child and enduring everything you had to go through. You had to risk your life, and I love you for that." Tears fell from her eyes. "And I want you to know that I would never try to take her away from you. Since Val recommended we do a DNA test I will contact my lawyer sometime this week, but I would never try to disrupt Hope's life with you."

Hope's new grandparents wasted no time in spoiling Hope. They started making plans for Disney World and private school.

With so much movement in the house and everyone making such a big fuss over Hope, Val slipped away into the living room for a moment by herself.

It was hard being back in Julian's parents' house. Memories filled the room. Mrs. McCormick still had the room full of his pictures. She remembered the day they got engaged. Julian asked her to marry him in the same spot she was standing in.

"Are you happy?" Jonah scared her.

"Very. No more secrets and no more lies."

"You how know important it is for me to give Hope a family," Jonah said, "and with her grandparents being a part of her life, the only thing missing is a mother."

Val closed her eyes a moment, and when she opened them again he was down on one knee.

"Marry me?" Jonah popped the question.

Val was unsure how to react. They were in her ex-fiancé's parents' house.

"Valencia."

The sound of her name brought back memories of Julian. He was the only one who called her Valencia. She looked around the room, and it was Hope calling out for her.

Hope walked over to Val and opened up her arms for a hug.

"I told you she would warm up to you," Jonah reminded her.

Val picked her up and hugged her so tight that she cried.

Chapter 35

Five days following Baxter's successful lung transplant, Colin returned to the hospital to visit with his former boss. When Colin walked in, Baxter was asleep. Colin stood for a moment and watched as the breathing apparatus pumped life into his lungs. Baxter's chest rose up and down. Colin couldn't believe a part of his friend now lived inside Baxter. He reached out his hand to touch Baxter's chest. He just wanted to feel a small piece of his friend again, but before his hand settled, Baxter's eyes flung open.

Baxter looked petrified. Colin pulled his hand back and waited to see what Baxter would do.

Baxter moved the mask from his face. He had a little trouble breathing, but he talked rather well. "How is West's grandson?"

"He's dead," Colin told him.

"Good. At least something positive came out of this." Baxter seemed to relax better at the sound of that news.

Colin chuckled. He didn't question God when He took Dean home to be with Him, but he often wondered why God would leave Baxter on earth with them. "It's good to know you're pleased with the outcome, but just because Dean is dead doesn't mean parts of him won't live on."

Baxter looked at him strangely. "What do you mean by that?"

Colin gave him a sly grin and walked out the room.

O livia spread every outstanding bill she had over the kitchen counter. She studied the balance of each credit card statement, her car payment and her monthly utility bills. She gathered everything into one pile and prayed over it.

She refused to worry because she knew God would make a way when she had none. Her daily prayers went up and God knew the petitions of her heart. Dean was a great provider when he was alive, and she thanked the Lord every day for their union, but she knew God wouldn't leave her wavering in the wind. It wasn't easy to let go and let God, but ultimately she had no choice. Olivia was sure she was living in the center of God's will.

One worry she didn't have to burden herself with was a mortgage or rent payment. Judge West opened his home to Bryce and Olivia for as long as they needed. Living rent-free would help her in paying off her bills. But, as soon as she was financially able, Olivia wanted to look for a house of her own. This place held too many memories of Dean.

Olivia took a sip from her coffee mug before realizing how late it was getting. Dean's lawyer had set up a meeting for her to finalize his estate. She finished off her cup and did a little cleaning before leaving.

T he huge gold-plated revolving doors were much heavier than they looked. Olivia pushed her way into the office building and stopped in the middle of the floor.

"You look lost. Can I be of any assistance to you this afternoon?" A friendly overweight security guard grinned at her.

"Yes, I'm looking for Mr. Sexton's office."

"He's located on the seventh floor. Walk around to the elevators on the far right side of the building, and the doors will open right in front of his office."

"Thank you."

Olivia maneuvered around the maze of office workers and mail carriers as they raced to and from their destination. She found the elevators with ease and boarded along with a crowd of people. The elevator stopped at every floor, making the duration of the ride longer than expected.

Finally it reached Mr. Sexton's floor. She got off the elevator and walked straight into the law office of Marcus Sexton. Marcus was a close college buddy of Dean's, and after Dean passed she'd learned that he was handling most of Dean's business matters.

She introduced herself to the receptionist, and within seconds Marcus came out into the lobby to greet her. "Olivia, I'm so glad you could make it."

They shook hands, and he escorted her down a narrow hallway. They entered his plush office, and he offered her a seat.

"How are you making out?" He sat down behind his desk.

She sighed deeply. "Every day I think it gets a little easier, but it's still hard to believe that my husband is gone. I still don't think my son understands that Dean isn't coming back."

"I understand. I miss him myself. A few times I had to catch myself from picking up the phone and dialing his office." He grabbed a huge manila envelope and pulled out a copy of Dean's will. "I guess we should get started. It's not really that difficult. He left you everything. You are the sole beneficiary of Dean's estate. Today, I'm going to take the time and go over everything with you. If you have any questions, don't hesitate to ask. I'm here to assist you." He laughed to himself. "Dean gave me strict instructions to treat you special."

Olivia smiled.

"He also told me not to hit on you."

Olivia gave him an amused look.

"Don't worry, I'm not going to hit on you. You're pretty, but I'm married." He flashed his wedding ring.

He pulled out some forms and placed them down in front of Olivia. "Before I give you any checks, you must sign for them." He pointed to a few lines on the paper.

Olivia squinted. "These are a lot of forms."

"Well, this one is from Dean's pension plan." He pointed to the first form. "I took the liberty of rolling his pension into an IRA in your name so that you wouldn't be penalized."

Olivia picked up a check that was written out for over seventy-five thousand dollars and set it back down. "At least I don't have to worry about retirement," she commented.

"This is also a pension fund that he had from his second job." Marcus pulled out a second packet and had her sign in various spaces. The check for that pension was close to eighteen thousand dollars. "I'll also roll that over into an IRA account for you if you want."

"I had no idea Dean had so much money put away for retirement."

"Yeah, he often called me for legal advice. Fortunately, we both learned how to save a dollar when we were in college." Marcus chuckled. "These next four documents are from different stocks and investment clubs Dean was involved in. He was sure you would need the money, so he asked me to cash these out for you."

Olivia signed for all four checks, and he handed her checks that totaled close to a million dollars.

"This is all mine?" Olivia stared at the dollar amounts. She never saw a check with so many zeros. Each check was written out for no less than two hundred thousand dollars. Her eyes began to get blurry, so she rubbed them and sat back in her chair.

"Let me get you some water." Marcus ran out his office and returned with a cold bottle of spring water.

"Dean never mentioned he was into the stock market," Olivia said.

Marcus opened the water bottle before handing it to her. "He didn't participate that much. I encouraged him to invest, and fortunately he invested at the right time. His stocks doubled in a few short years."

Marcus could tell Olivia was not expecting to receive this kind of money. "The last check is from his life insurance policy. He had three policies that equaled over two hundred thousand dollars each. Two of the checks are made out to you, and the third he wanted put into a trust fund for your son."

Olivia cried. She couldn't believe Dean was providing for her even after his death. Marcus handed Olivia a few tissues to wipe her face.

"I'm sorry, I wasn't expecting all this," she cried.

Olivia knew that Dean was gone, but she never felt more alone than she did at that moment. More than anything in the world she wished her husband was still alive. Having all this money and not being able to share it with the one she loved broke her heart. She wished she could tell him one more time how much she loved him.

"Thank you, Marcus." Olivia put her signature on the last of the forms.

"There were a few more checks, but that went toward

Dean's medical expenses and the funeral. Believe me when I say you and your son were Dean's first priority. He said his soul would be at ease knowing you were well taken care of." Marcus sounded so sincere.

Olivia held out her hand. "I appreciate all your help." They shook hands.

When she stood to her knees she felt a little weak. The room spun, and he quickly held on to the chair until she was able to regain her balance.

"Are you all right?" Marcus asked.

"I'm fine," she reassured him.

"Olivia, spend your money wisely, and if you need any legal or financial advice you can call me day or night."

She smiled warmly before closing the door behind her.

"Thank you, Dean," Olivia whispered in the elevator. "You always did have my best interests at heart."

Chapter 36

Four months later

Today was opening day for the Dean West Elementary School. Olivia gave a generous donation to the school, which helped expedite the opening for next school year. Colin and Judge West worked hard to make sure their dream of opening a good, safe school for their children was a reality. Standing in front of the school steps were the mayor, along with numerous other government officials. Even the governor of Pennsylvania had made it to the ceremony. Lots of people stood out in the audience anxious for them to open a school that cares about their children getting a good education.

Val held Hope's hand as they listened to the different speeches being given by several city dignitaries when Jonah approached her with a copy of the *USA Today* newspaper.

"Look at this," he said.

Val took the paper in her hand. The front page displayed a picture of Caitlyn being hauled into the Seattle police headquarters. Val quickly skimmed through the article to discover Caitlyn had been arrested for her third drunk driving offense. Currently her lawyers were working overtime to avoid her from doing any jail time.

"I guess money can't buy everything," Val whispered.

"I guess not," Jonah replied. "It's a blessing she did what she did and gave full custody of Hope over to me."

"Yes, I have to agree, Caitlyn made the right decision."

Jonah hugged Val tightly around her waist and planted a wet kiss on her cheek.

After Caitlyn left town, Val had told Jonah everything about Cole and the inheritance. The couple cleared up any misunderstandings they had and made a vow to never keep any secrets from one another again.

Right beneath the article about Caitlyn there was a small article that reported Reverend Baxter was sentenced to fifteen years in jail for the murder of Judge West's grandson.

Val tossed the paper in the trash.

"Parents," Judge West announced, "I promise you that this will be a school that will reach high. We will strive high in expectations, and we will not let your children down."

Everyone cheered. Judge West and the mayor cut the ribbon strings together, and everyone was welcomed into the school to get a grand tour.

Olivia, Bryce and Danyelle stood on the far end of the stage together.

"Dean would have been so proud." Tears poured out of Olivia's eyes.

"Yes, he would have," Danyelle replied.

Chapter 37

The wedding

It was a splendid fall day for a wedding. First Nazareth looked more like heaven than a church. The entire interior of the church had been covered in white. The pews were decorated with white sheets. Huge long white centerpieces sat in each windowsill adorned with red long-stemmed roses.

Tressie looked around. She had never seen the church look lovelier. She was a bit jealous, but at the same time happy for her friend. She wished that she was the one getting married, but she knew her turn would come one day.

Val took Jonah's hand in hers. The couple snapped pictures of Hope as she stood at the front of the church dressed in a simple yellow-and-white flower girl's dress. Hope saw them, smiled and waved back. She and Val were quickly becoming close friends. They did things a mother and daughter would do together.

After Jonah had proposed, Val took her time giving him an answer. As a matter of fact, he was still waiting. Once he realized she was stalling for time, he told her it was no rush. He would wait until she was ready to say yes.

Grateful for his patience, Val took that extra time to go back to school, get to know Hope better and make sure they had God situated right in the center of their relationship.

The bride looked radiant in her gown. After searching endlessly for the perfect dress, she had decided to wear her mother's gown.

"Do you, Danyelle Benson," Reverend Simms began, "take Colin Montgomery to be your lawfully wedded husband?"

The look of love in their eyes was obvious.

"Yes," she replied.

It came as a complete surprise to everyone when Danyelle announced that she was getting married. No one even knew they were dating.

Colin repeated his wedding vows, and before they knew it, Reverend Simms was pronouncing them husband and wife.

"You may now kiss the bride."

Colin lifted her veil and sealed a kiss on her lips that would last a lifetime.

About the Author

Jersey girl Dynah Zale was born and raised in Deptford, New Jersey. She graduated with an Associate's Degree from Camden County College and then moved to Atlanta, Georgia to complete her studies at Spellman College. Her move to the Atlanta was short-lived, and she soon returned back to her home state, where she currently resides.

Dynah's love for books and the admiration she holds for the writings of Terry McMillan, Connie Briscoe, and Victoria Christopher Murray are what encouraged her to embark on her own professional writing career.

She hopes her unique writing style combined with an inspirational flair will not only tell a story, but deliver a message; a message of hope to the hopeless and tranquility to all troubled hearts.

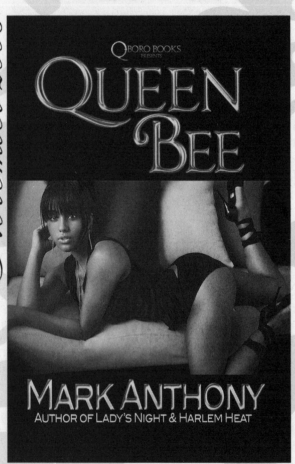